SABOTAGE AT SOMERSET

An Oxford Key Mystery

LYNN MORRISON

The Marketing Chair

Cover design by Emilie Yane Lopes

Published by:

The Marketing Chair Press, Oxford, England

LynnMorrisonWriter.com

Paperback ISBN: 978-1-8380391-3-4

Per le mie bimbe - siete stupende!

Contents

Chapter One

I pull open one drawer after another, but none of them holds the item I'm desperately hoping to find. Instead, a cluttered jumble of items is all I see.

"Has anyone seen my mobile?" I shout, but the only answer I get is the sound of the shower running upstairs. I mutter under my breath, "This is the problem with living in a remodel project. Nothing is where it should be."

That sentence sums up my life right now. Ever since I found out I, Nat Payne, inherited my grandfather Alfred's house here in Oxford, my life has been a mess of moving boxes, sawdust and missing items. Moving out of my flat at St Margaret College and trying to oversee a monstrous remodel project while doing my day job would be crazy enough. Organising a plan to catch a master thief on top of that... it is possible I took on a bit too much at one time.

The chaos cluttering my kitchen agrees. I scan the room, struggling to look past the half-emptied boxes of dishes and pans and the sink full of dirty breakfast dishes. Underneath the mess, there is a new oak table and chairs sitting near the back window. The smattering of breadcrumbs can't hide the warm blue and grey tones of the upgraded kitchen countertops. The bright white paint lightens the room, giving me hope that the rest will come together as soon as I finish putting things away.

But unpacking boxes will have to wait for now. As the Head of Ceremonies at Oxford, I'm the assigned liaison between the university and a TV period drama which is coming here to film scenes for their programme. For the next two weeks, I'll be spending my days acting as an advisor to the show. Since my Uncle Harold happens to be the producer, I'm not viewing the assignment as a hardship.

The truth is, my assignment is no accident. It is one part of the plan my friends and I put together, aiming to stop Oswald Beadle and Thomas Hobbes from stealing the magic of Oxford. And that is why I am in such a rush to get out the door.

I check the clock on the nearby stove, distraught to see another five minutes have gone by. I do not want to be late for the first day of filming, but if I don't find my phone in the next two minutes, I may not have a choice. Thankfully, my best mate and cheeky wyvern H pushes his head through the cat flap, offering a hand before I completely lose the plot.

"Oi, Nat! What's with all the shouting? I can 'ear you all the way out in my garden 'ouse."

"I can't find my mobile anywhere and I really need to get out of here if I want to make it to the set before my uncle and his film crew show up," I explain, still searching through the cupboards.

"Did you check your 'andbag?" H asks as he crosses the room. He passes behind me, pausing mid-step. "Wait, did you say you're looking for your mobile? The one with the bright red ladybirds dotted all over the case?"

I stop and spin around, a hopeful expression on my face. "Yes, that's the one! Do you see it?"

H snorts out a fiery laugh, setting a nearby box of crumbled wrapping paper alight. "It's in your back pocket, Nat."

A flush rushes up my neck and onto my face as I reach around to my trouser pocket and find the item in question half sticking out of it. After stamping out the fire, H takes pity on me and uses his wings to blow some cool air across my flaming cheeks.

I slump against the kitchen counter. "Thanks, H. You're a lifesaver. Are you ready to go? And where is Edward? What's taking him so long?" I push off to dash upstairs, but H loops a talon through my waistband, pulling me to a stop.

"Lor luv a duck, Nat. Look at yourself." H arches an eyebrow, taking my measure. "Why don't I stay 'ere and keep Edward on track? We shouldn't be long behind you."

I take a deep breath, exhale, and then reward H with a smile. "Good idea, mate. I'm working myself into a flurry this morning, and it isn't doing me any favours."

H looks at me in surprise. "Are you that excited to meet the famous actors in your uncle's show? I wouldn't 'ave put you down as someone who'd get star-struck."

"The actors? Definitely not." I shake my head. "I met plenty of famous people when I worked on Disney events. Without the fancy costumes, hairdressers, and make-up, they are just like any other bloke on the street. No, I'm nervous about Oswald Beadle and Thomas Hobbes. This is our best chance to catch them in the act of committing a crime, and I don't want to risk missing a minute."

H nods, his expression serious. "I get that, but I don't think they'll show up at eight in the morning, Nat. 'Owever, I can see you're convinced, so maybe you'd better go on ahead. You can look around, reassure yourself everything is okay."

H flutters off to check on Edward, waving me on my way. I grab my handbag and bicycle keys off the kitchen table and rush out the door.

Just as H predicted, the fresh summer morning air does me a world of good. The sun beams above, balancing the cool edge to the breeze. I can feel the nervous energy flowing off me, replaced with my normal sense of calm and levelheadedness. I cut through quiet side streets and alleyways, moving quickly enough to feel confident I'll have plenty of time to check my To Do list before the crew shows up.

Setting my worries aside, I take a moment to reflect on the last six weeks. The exhibition grand opening event at the Ashmolean was barely finished before we began working on our plans for luring Oswald Beadle and Thomas Hobbes — the two men responsible for the problems with the magic of Oxford — back to town where they can be stopped, once and for all.

Our plan seems simple. My Uncle Harold, a film director, is working on a historical period drama, with none other than Sir Christopher Wren as its main character. With the help of the Eternals, we convinced my uncle to bring his crew to Oxford for two weeks of filming in the very halls where Sir Christopher used to walk. In her role as the Director of the Ashmolean, Kate arranged for them to borrow priceless antiques, portraits, and artefacts, to make the film set as historically accurate as possible. We hope that Beadle and Hobbes will take the bait, turning up in Oxford and trying to make off with these priceless treasures.

If catching a pair of dangerous criminals wasn't task enough, I also had a tonne of work to do to help the scriptwriters and set designers depict Oxford's ceremonies exactly as they would have been in the 1660s. If I hadn't had the aid of Mathilde and the Bodleian's Eternals, I'd probably still be buried under a pile of books.

Finally, in my spare moments, I've had a house to remodel.

Edward had suggested holding off on starting the renovations until after we caught our criminals. While I knew that logically such a decision made sense, my heart was shouting to get a move on it. After my whirlwind first year in Oxford, I want nothing more than to settle down with Edward in our new home. Given how great I am at juggling complex tasks and organising a variety of moving parts, surely a home remodel would be a piece of cake. Right?

Wrong!

First, we found mould under the wooden floors, then a pipe burst in the kitchen. One thing after another threw my construction timeline straight out of the window. But we're halfway through now, and the downstairs, with its new kitchen and polished hardwood floors, gives me hope that we'll make it to the other side.

As the signs for the University Botanic Gardens come into view, my thoughts shift from my moving boxes over to the movie set. The filming schedule spans the next two weeks, with the first few days here in the gardens and the rest of the time at Somerset College.

I've got a pretty good idea of what to expect. After all, staging a scene and organising an event aren't that far removed from one another. You need a clear vision, the right backdrop and capable people filling all the key roles. The only difference is that filming runs for days and uses a lot more cameras.

After I lock my bicycle to the rack nearest the garden entrance, I turn around to find Harry waving at me from inside the gates. I am not at all surprised to see she has beaten me here. No one, and I do mean *no one*, is more excited about the film crew coming to town than Harry is.

"Morning, Nat. Today's the big day!" she squeals as I make my way over. "What time do you think Caleb Farrow will get here?" She pats her hair, her brow wrinkling in concern. "Do I look okay?"

I struggle to hide the grin stretching across my face. On any other day, Harry is an extraordinarily capable executive assistant who doesn't take nonsense from anyone, regardless of how lofty their title might be. But apparently handsome male television stars are her weakness. Caleb Farrow, with his windswept dark locks and muscled form, is practically kryptonite.

Harry's husband Rob, completely comfortable in their relationship, volunteered to drop Harry off at the gardens this morning. I guess he figures it is easier to let her get the excitement out of her system than to convince her that the man she sees on screen might not be the same in person. Having met my fair share of stars, I suspect he is right.

I link arms with Harry, directing us towards the back of the gardens where the film crew is due to set up the morning shots. "You look absolutely fabulous, darling," I drawl and give her a wink. My outrageous tone does the trick, jostling a laugh out of her and easing her nerves. "And no, I don't imagine Mr Farrow will turn up anytime soon. The actors are typically the last to arrive on set, having little interest in standing around while the lighting and camera crews do their work."

"I don't know how you can be so cool and collected, Nat," Harry murmurs.

Now it is my turn to laugh. "If you'd seen me turning my kitchen upside down this morning searching for my mobile, you wouldn't say that. But my nerves have less to do with Hollywood and everything to do with Hobbes and Beadle. I'll leave it to you to ask for autographs. I want to keep my eyes peeled for any signs of trouble."

Harry's enthusiasm diminishes at the reminder of why we are really here. "We'll catch them, hun. Now that we know who is responsible, it will be impossible for them to slip past us again."

I straighten my shoulders and lift my head, looking determined. "You're right, Harry. Now let's go find our friends."

Edward and H turn up soon enough, both relieved to find me

in a more placid mental state. They are quickly followed by the first of the film crew lorries. As the set team descends, pulling metal fixtures and oversized lights from their vehicles, we decide to get out of their way.

"Why don't we have a walk around and familiarise ourselves with the layout of the gardens?" I propose. "We can identify the best places to station ourselves and the Eternals to keep a watch out for Hobbes and Beadle."

Edward, Harry and H voice their agreement, falling into step beside me on the dusty yellow pathway.

Fortunately, the garden space is well-contained and offers limited access points. The Cherwell River borders one side, with stone benches dotted along it calling for visitors to rest and watch the punts float by. The back corner of the garden juts up against Christ Church Meadow, blocked by a fence and shrubbery.

The other side of the garden is our area of most concern, where a small access road provides a means of approach to Christ Church Meadow. Despite its small size, the road will be nearly impossible to monitor as it is used by a constant stream of locals and tourists alike, all wanting to take advantage of the scenic shortcut between Christ Church and Magdalen College.

But for the moment, we turn our attention to the rest of the gardens. Under the glow of the warm summer day, the garden is a riot of colours. Everywhere the eye can see, flowers blossom, perfuming the air with their soft scent. A stone fountain tinkles away, providing the perfect soundtrack for this idyllic scene. It is no wonder my uncle decided to film the exterior shots here.

As she flips through a garden guide, Harry comments, "I had no idea the Botanic Garden was so old."

"Oh yes, this part of the garden dates back to the 1600s. Likely, Wilkins and Wren would have come here to gather medicinal herbs for some of their experiments," I reply. "Those trees over there testify to the age of the garden — the oldest was planted in 1645, if you can believe it."

"And the greenhouses?" Edward asks, pointing towards the gleaming glass roof in the distance. "Will they be filming there?"

I shake my head. "Thankfully, no. They are filled with plants and small ponds. It would be nearly impossible to film there without the greenery blocking the shot. I think we can safely leave them off our list."

We stroll ahead, crossing under the leafy shadows of the wooded area and emerging on the riverside path. The greenhouses sprawl along our right, their glass windows providing only brief glimpses into the interior.

"I see what you mean," Edward comments as he rises on his toes to try to peek inside.

My mobile pings with a message. "Kate has arrived. Hold on, let me tell her to wait for us at the events lawn." I dash off a brief message and then pocket my phone again. Hopefully, this time I'll remember where I put it.

Our riverside path curves, leading us toward the lower garden. Here, the flowers run riot, growing in dense, colourful shrubs which line the paths. We spy several nooks which look ideal for picnics. I make a mental note to come back with Edward as soon as our lives calm down. When we can finally put all of this chaos behind us, we'll certainly be due for some quality time together.

Harry makes notes on the map in her guide, indicating the best locations for us to take up our watch for the next few days while the film crew uses this as their location. H volunteers to rotate around amongst the treetops, taking a wyvern's eye view of the surrounding area.

"Iffen that crow from the Torture Museum dares to show its face, I'll be 'ere waiting for it," he declares, shadowboxing around in a circle.

Finally, the main fountain comes into view. The events lawn

isn't far away, sitting near the front with a side street gate at its edge. The film crew have planned to utilise the open space, setting up their trailers for food, hair and makeup, costumes, and the crew.

Kate looks like the picture of relaxation in her wide-leg linen trousers, eyelet top and espadrilles, a far cry from her typical suit and pearls she wears as the Director of the Ashmolean. She pauses her conversation with another woman to wave us over. It isn't until we get close that we figure out who the other individual is.

"Mathilde?" I ask, confusion heavy in my voice. Harry looks as flummoxed as I do when the short-haired woman in the flowing skirt turns around.

"You cut your hair!" I squeal. Mathilde's cheeks flush as she bites her lip, waiting for our judgment.

I look closely, noting it is more than her hair that has changed. Gone are her worn jeans and trainers, tossed out with her ever-present messy hair bun. Instead, she is sporting shoulder-length waves, held back from her face by a pair of turquoise sunglasses, a summery skirt, and a light blue denim jacket. She looks great, but I can't help wonder why the sudden change.

Harry arrives at the same question. "I love it, but why didn't you tell any of us you were planning a makeover?"

"Honestly, I wasn't sure I would go through with it until I sat down in the salon chair," Mathilde responds.

"I cannot believe you cut your hair. Where are you going to store your spare pens now?" I ask, ribbing her for her habit of tucking items into her bun.

"I had been contemplating a change for a while now. The tipping point happened at the Bodleian last week, when three different professors in a row took me for a student instead of a staff member. I can hardly blame them, given how much of my wardrobe dates back to my uni days. I decided it might be time for a refresh." Mathilde twirls around in a small circle, letting us take in the full extent of her new clothing and hair.

"But how will we know it's you?" I ask, gently mocking. With a cheeky grin, Mathilde unbuttons her jacket to reveal one of her classic snarky t-shirts hidden underneath it. I snicker. "Ahh, there's the Mathilde we know and love."

Edward rolls his eyes at our antics and then adds his own compliment to the mix.

"What's our plan for the day, Nat? Do you have a copy of the shoot schedule?" Kate asks.

"Oh, yes!" Harry adds. "What time will Caleb Farrow arrive, do you think?"

Kate, Mathilde and I exchange amused grins. "I looked it over last night. They've blocked out most of the day for set-up. As you can see, they've got quite a lot of lighting, cables and camera mounts to put in place before they can begin." I wave a hand at the piles of metallic rods lying scattered about, waiting to be assembled. "But theoretically, the actors could turn up today. I guess it depends on whether they want to look around before the filming begins tomorrow."

That's all the confirmation Harry needs. She quickly lays claim to one of the wooden benches. She refreshes her lipstick and smooths her dress, shifting until she is certain she is displaying herself to the best of her abilities. H curls up beside her for a quick catnap under the warm sun.

Mathilde and Kate look around, their excitement palpable. They may not be as star-crazy as Harry, but being on the set of a big budget production is still an unusual way to spend their day. From my visits with Uncle Harold in the past, I know better. I try to warn them when I ask Edward to pick up coffees at the garden cafe. "Standing around on set will quickly get boring. Trust me, you'll soon want the extra shot of caffeine."

When Edward heads off, Kate asks the question on her mind. "Have you seen any of the scripts, Nat?"

I shake my head no. "I've only seen the shot locations and the cast list."

"Since the show is already airing, Bartie and I binged through the first few episodes over the weekend," Kate confesses. "They all take place in London, in the months after the Great Fire. Neither of us could guess what would bring the storyline to Oxford."

I give her a bright smile. "That much I do know. The Oxford scenes will be a flashback, to help the viewers learn more about Wren's background. A history lesson, of sorts, but with a love scene thrown into the mix."

By the time Edward returns, juggling trays of steaming cups, the lawn is a hive of activity. Uncle Harold arrives and comes straight over to say hello. He is pleased to meet Kate and Mathilde, making sure to thank them for their help with researching and staging the set.

"And you must be Harry," Uncle Harold exclaims warmly when she rejoins the group. "I've heard we have you to thank for the speed with which our filming permits were granted."

Harry tries to brush off the compliment, but I refuse to let her. "Harry knows the university administration inside and out... There is one thing you could do to thank her..." I let my voice trail off, hoping my uncle will take the bait.

"Of course! What is it?" he asks.

"Can you make sure she has time to meet Caleb Farrow before filming wraps up?"

My uncle lets loose a chuckle. "Done! However, I should warn you. He can be a bit..." he pauses, hunting for the right description. "Er, changeable. But we'll do our best to make the arrangements."

"Oh, thank you," Harry gushes, and she gives my uncle Harold an impromptu hug.

When he extricates himself, he asks whether our group would be interested in a behind-the-scenes tour of the crew trailers. He doesn't need to ask twice. Even Edward agrees to go along. He is less interested in seeing how they bring the 17th century to life in costumes and hairstyles, instead expressing enthusiasm about seeing the editing and sound equipment.

Harold calls one of the assistants over and asks him to escort the group around. I choose to stay behind, more interested in catching up with my uncle. I'll be on set for the entire time the crew is here, so there is no urgency for me to see everything this morning.

When the others walk off, I pepper him with questions. "Where are you staying, Uncle Harold? And Dominic? Did he come up with you? How soon can I see him?"

Uncle Harold and Dominic have been a couple for as long as I can remember. Harold is similar to my dad in looks, the family resemblance being strong on that side of the family. He has the same fair skin and emerald green eyes, but unlike my dad, his blonde hair is usually an overgrown, dishevelled mess. Dominic, on the other hand, is a Spanish beefcake with a handlebar moustache and a bald head. How the two of them met, I don't know. But they somehow work perfectly together.

"Whoa, slow down there," he says, laughing. "Yes, Dominic came up with me. He doesn't normally follow me around to my filming locations, but I found a particularly interesting Airbnb to rent and he couldn't resist."

"I'm intrigued," I reply with a sly grin. "Tell me more."

"Dominic will tell you I'm living out a childhood fantasy, and he might be right. Whenever I'd come to visit your grandparents and dad as a child, we'd go for a walk along the Thames canal. The little houseboats moored to the path fascinated me..."

I interrupt him. "You rented a canal boat? That's so cool! I want to come over and see it!"

Uncle Harold chuckles. "That was exactly how Dominic responded. No wonder you two get along so well. It's not too far from The Perch pub. Do you know where that is?"

"I know exactly where that is!" I exclaim. "As you know, I've inherited grandfather's old house. It's a short walk across Port Meadow from where your canal boat must be."

"Text Dominic and sort out a date," Harold instructs me. A young woman waves in our direction, calling Harold's name. He gives her a nod of acknowledgment and then turns in my direction. "Oh dear, that's Joyce, looking for me. I'm sorry to dash off on you, but I'd better go see what she needs."

I pass the rest of the morning, alternating between walking a circuit of the garden to ensure all is well, and sitting on a wooden bench, replying to my emails. Around noon, H tracks me down, circling above my head before swooping to land on the bench.

"Oi, missie, what's a wyvern got to do to get lunch 'ere?" He groans and rubs his round, scaly belly, emphasising how close he is to wasting away. I barely hold back a laugh.

"What happened to the others?" I ask as I rise to my feet.

"They said to tell you goodbye. When they figured out none of the actors were planning to show up, they all went back to work. Since they finished their tour near the exit, they 'eaded straight out."

"In that case, H, I've got an extra special tour, just for you."

"Where's that?" he asks, his eyes wide with curiosity.

"Craft services."

Chapter Two

Now that H spends most of the evenings in his house in the garden, when we see each other, we have a lot more to catch up on during our walks to work. For example, this morning I have a pressing question.

"H, what was that awful caterwauling in the garden last night?"

H flinches, causing him to tumble sideways in mid-flight. "Eh, you 'eard that, did ya? Sorry iffen we woke you up."

I rush to reassure him. "It's okay, I wasn't asleep yet. I was determined to get the last of the kitchen items put away."

"I thought somethin' was different about the kitchen this morning," he mumbles, avoiding my question.

"The screeching howls, H? Are they going to be a nightly performance?"

"I sure 'ope not," he grumbles, snorting a dissatisfied plume of black smoke from his nostrils. "It's them neighbourhood cats. It's not my fault all the babes like my new digs. But none of the Toms want to 'ear what I'm sayin'. They think I'm trying to lay claim to their territory."

I laugh but catch myself when I see how miserable H looks.

"Oh mate, don't let it get to you. They might think you're a cat, but you know the truth. Crisp their tails or something."

H stares at me, surprised I'm advocating violence.

"Don't set them on fire, H," I clarify. "But a singe or two wouldn't be so bad. It would give them something to consider the next time they think about bringing their cat chorus to sit below my bedroom window."

I leave H to ponder his revenge, turning my attention to the people walking through the centre. The shopping district offers ample people-watching opportunities on a normal day, but summer takes it to a whole new level. Despite the early hour, the streets are crowded with tourists, their bulky cameras and guidebooks immediately giving them away. Locals on their way to work dance from one side of the pavement to another, dodging the families looking at maps and the oblivious teens posing for selfies.

If I thought the summer would provide a break from the ever-present student population, I was wrong. Within a week of term ending, the Oxford students were replaced by hordes of teens from around the world. The colleges convert into language schools and summer programmes, promising teenagers a chance to experience university life. They sprawl across every flat surface — benches, bus stops, traffic bollards and even a row of bins — chatting away, flipping their hair, and posturing for attention.

A flash of light draws my attention, a ray of sun glinting off a bald head. My mind immediately leaps to my uncle's partner, Dominic, and I speed up to catch him.

Further ahead, the crowd parts, giving me a head-to-toe view of the bald man. Definitely not Dominic, unless he has traded in his tight Spanish trousers for a costume. I tap H's snout to get his attention. "Is that bloke wearing a black medieval robe?"

"Eh?" he asks, his gaze darting around, trying to figure out to whom I am referring. I point my finger in the right direction, aiming to help. "Yeah, looks like somethin' an old monk would 'ave worn. Weird."

The bald man turns onto a side street, giving me a quick glance at his profile. "I don't think that's a monk's robe, H. It looks more like one of the hulking executioner characters we saw at the Torture Museum in London."

The words are barely out of my mouth before H and I both stop dead, barely avoiding getting bumped from behind. H shoots out a jet of flames, clearing a space for us to stand without getting jostled.

"Are you thinking what I'm thinking?" I ask, my voice trembling with excitement.

H doesn't reply, instead flapping furiously towards the side street where the man disappeared. "Come on, Nat. We need to 'urry up and follow 'im!"

H's wild flight turns out to be surprisingly effective at creating a path through the crowd. Their brains might be telling them that H is a cat, but some part of their minds senses he is something more. People scatter left and right, leaving space for me to slide between.

As a result, the bald man in the medieval robe doesn't get very far. As soon as we enter the side street, H spots him up ahead. By unspoken agreement, we slow our pace, not wanting to spook the man before we can figure out what he is doing.

H perches on my shoulder, tucking his head close to mine so we can safely whisper.

"What would a Torture Museum Eternal from London be doing in the centre of Oxford?" I whisper.

"Getting the lay of the land?" H replies, squinting his eyes as he stares ahead. "Are we sure that 'e's an Eternal? Maybe 'e is just some bloke in a costume. This is Oxford."

We're both so engrossed in watching the man, neither of us notices the pallet of boxes sitting on the pavement. I tumble over it, sending H flying off my shoulder. My screech slips out before I can stop myself.

There is one upside to me making a scene in the middle of the street. The bald man glances back to see what is causing the ruckus. His eyes land first on me and then on H, growing wide in shock. His expression shifts from surprise to recognition and then to frustration. He spins around and darts into the nearest doorway, which just happens to be the entrance to the Covered Market.

"He's definitely an Eternal, H," I cry. "He walked right through that crowd of people."

Dating back to the 1770s, Oxford's Covered Market is a favourite tourist attraction. Small shopfronts, fresh fruit and vegetable vendors, cheesemongers, butchers and bakers offer their wares along the narrow aisles, enticing visitors to stop and look around. Wooden beams painted a bright white crisscross the ceiling. As a nod to Oxford's literary history, characters from Alice in Wonderland decorate the open spaces.

I sprint forward, shouting at people to move out of the way. If he gets too far ahead, we'll lose him inside the narrow aisles. I dash inside, H hot on my heels.

Normally, I'm happy to spend a morning here window shopping or sitting down with a cup of steaming espresso. But today, the crowd of tourists and colourful shop windows aren't doing me any favours. I dodge right, avoiding a display of bright red apples sitting in front of the fruit and veg stand. I pick up speed when I pass through a crossway, but nearly lose H at the butcher stand. He swipes a talon across a string of sausages, making off with a few. Lucky for him, I'm breathing too hard to chastise him.

I execute a stunning leap, clearing a wooden box planter, and race the last few steps until I emerge on the far side. Windmilling my arms, I barely stop before I step off the kerb in front of a passing bus. H arrives in time to grab the strap of my handbag, sacrificing one of his sausages in order to save me.

A nearby lamppost draws my attention. I rest against its rectangular base, half-draped over, as I catch my breath. H doesn't look much better, with small jets of flame shooting out of his mouth in time with his pants. With no sign of our wayward Eternal, an important fact crosses my mind. I was chasing a ghost. Most likely, he simply blinked himself out of the Covered Market.

Frustrated and annoyed, I rub my heels, quipping to H, "If I'd known we were going to run to work, I'd have chosen more appropriate footwear."

As it is, I'll be lucky to get away with only a blister or two. My blood pressure inches downward as I recover from my frenetic dash, only to skyrocket again when I remember where H and I were headed before we were distracted.

"H, the film set! We'd better hurry over there and make sure the Eternal hasn't made it his next target!"

The crowded pavement and busy street send us scurrying across to another alley, this one leading to a side entrance to the Christ Church meadow. Its paths are still relatively clear, so we make good time as we follow the shortcut to the side street, which leads to the Botanic Garden.

I slow my pace to something closer to normal, not wanting to alarm the security guards standing at the garden gate. After all, it isn't as though they can see any Eternals. The hulking bald man we chased could waltz right past them without anyone having a clue. If I come running towards them, they are more likely to see me as the threat.

The guards are alert, but also somewhat bored with their duty at the gate. I decide that is a good sign. If anything were remiss, surely they'd look more obviously vigilant and attuned to their surroundings. Nonetheless, I send H to survey the grounds while I stop to show my badge.

"Morning," I wheeze, still slightly out of breath. "Lovely day, isn't it? All good inside?"

The guard raises an eyebrow but chooses not to comment on my dishevelled state. I suppose I could just as easily be rushing back from an errand for one of the actors. That seems more logical than chasing an invisible bad guy.

"Everything is fine, Ms Payne," he reassures me. "Your uncle wants you to look for him when you get inside. Something about introducing you to his production assistant." He nods at the other guard, who steps aside and opens the gate, allowing me to slide past.

Between the garden wall, the shade trees and the row of trailers, my view is limited to only a few metres in front of me. I glance back to make sure the guards aren't watching me before I speed walk along the path, my elbows tucked against my side as I rush along.

A loud flapping noise alerts me to H's imminent arrival. "No sign of 'im, Nat!" he shouts.

Before H can glide down from the sky, a booming crash and high-pitched shriek rip through the air, coming from within the gardens, and sending a flock of birds scattering from the treetops.

I abandon all pretence, shifting into a flat-out sprint in the direction of the commotion.

H somersaults in mid-air and skyrockets above the tree line. He quickly spots the scene of the trouble and calls down to me to turn towards the event's lawn.

When I left the garden yesterday evening, it was well on its way to turning into a proper film set. Trailers of various shapes and sizes lined three sides of the grassy lawn, offering temporary housing for the film crew. This morning, the transformation is complete. Cables snakes across the ground, connecting lights and camera rigs with their power sources.

I spot a cluster of people standing near the trailers, concerned looks on their faces. I motion for H to get closer while I stop to chat with the nearest person, a lanky man wearing an apron, standing near the Craft Services trailer.

"I heard the noise as I was coming into the garden. What happened? Is everyone okay?"

The man looks at me, arching an eyebrow in my direction, clearly wondering who I am. I stick out my hand and add, "I'm Nat, Harold's niece... and Head of Ceremonies at the uni. I'm a consultant on the production."

The man's expression relaxes as he gives a firm shake. "I'm Sam. Nice to meet you. And yes, it looks like everyone is okay, although that was a close one."

I rise on my tiptoes, but there are too many people grouped around the scene for me to see what happened. Sam notices my difficulties and offers more information. "I saw it all from the serving window in the trailer. See that giant lighting rig over there?" He points towards a silvery metal ladder with lights and a pale grey filter set on top. "There are supposed to be two of them. The other one fell over and nearly took out Vivian Edgemont and one of the production assistants."

I suck in a breath. "Vivian... as in the lead actress?"

"Yup. The light was heading right for them, but she must have seen it wobbling or something. I've never seen someone move so fast. Vivian shoved Joyce out of the way and probably saved them both from serious injury by doing so."

The larger group breaks up, my uncle Harold signalling for everyone to get back to work while a pair of burly men hoist the lighting stand back into place. Sam tells me to come by later for lunch before heading back into the trailer. Left standing alone, my mind goes into overdrive wondering whether this was nothing more than a freak accident or if Hobbes and Beadle were behind it.

I stifle a small shriek when my grandfather unexpectedly appears beside me. After his death some twenty years ago, he returned to Oxford as an Eternal. He revealed himself to me a few months ago, but I still cannot believe my good fortune in having a second chance to spend time with him.

He gives me a quick squeeze hello before launching into his questions. "H told me about the incident. Have you learned anything yet?"

"No," I admit. "I was hoping either you or Bartie might have been close enough to see the event as it happened."

My grandfather shakes his head. "Sorry, Nat. Bartie was near the main entrance and I was keeping an eye on the riverside pathway."

I update him on my morning adventures, his expression growing grim as I describe the strange Eternal we spotted in the city centre.

"Sounds like a medieval henchman, one of those men who used to chop off heads and burn people at the stake," he mutters. "Knocking a giant light fixture on two unassuming women would be a simple task for such a person."

I weigh the idea in my mind, but for some reason, it doesn't sit quite right. "But why would Beadle and Hobbes want to injure an actress? And why so soon, before they've had a chance to steal the treasures? We're hoping Beadle will follow us to Somerset College and attempt to make off with the priceless artefacts. If something happens to Vivian Edgemont, Uncle Harold would have to stop the production and Kate would put the items back into storage."

My grandfather taps his chin, deep in thought. "That is a very good point, Nat. Perhaps we'd better do some investigating before we leap to any conclusions."

"I agree." I scan the crew, making note of which people were closest to the accident scene. "You and Bartie keep an eye on the garden entrances. I'll chat with the crew and see if anyone saw anything out of the ordinary."

My grandfather gives me a quick pat on the back and then disappears from sight. I turn my attention to the surrounding people. Uncle Harold stands on the far side of the lawn, his forehead pinched with worry as he escorts a woman wearing an old-fashion corseted gown to a chair. Although I can't see her face, it isn't hard to guess that the woman must be Vivian Edgemont. I discard the idea of approaching them, rationalising that now isn't the best time to question either of them.

The camera crew might be my best opportunity. Two men and a woman idle near the cameras, busying themselves with checking the equipment. I sidle over slowly, not wanting to arouse suspicion, but pick up my pace when I hear one of the men mutter, "It's the curse, I tell you. We're cursed."

The other man scoffs at the notion, but the woman seems thoughtful. I take advantage of the pause to interject, introducing myself to the group. The trio back up to make space for me to join them.

"Thank goodness no one got hurt. Did you see what happened?" Turning to the large camera, I add, "Were you filming when the light fell?"

"No, we aren't due to film for another half hour," the woman replies. "Everyone was busy setting up equipment, checking light levels and that sort of thing. I'm not sure why Vivian was even out here yet. None of us were paying attention to her. I figured she was wandering around, trying to get into character."

I nod in understanding. "I heard her scream as I came into the garden. I assumed it must have been an accident, but then I couldn't help overhear you saying something about a curse..."

"Don't get Andy started on that again," the other man grumbles.

"And why not?" Andy replies. "You can call me crazy all you want, but I'm telling you, something weird is going on here."

I raise my eyebrows in confusion. "You think a light falling over is a sign of a curse?"

"If it were just a light falling, that would be one thing," he explains. "But this isn't our first problem during production. We've had problems on our main set in London. It is the latest in a series of pranks and annoyances that are quickly becoming dangerous."

Glancing at the woman, I wonder if she agrees. She meets my gaze and frowns, but doesn't shake her head. "I hate to admit it, but I think Andy is right. Not about a curse, mind you. I think someone is trying to sabotage the show."

I press for information, but the trio of filmmakers clam up, suddenly realising they are airing the production's dirty laundry in front of a virtual stranger. When Andy suggests I ask my uncle for more information, the other two quickly voice their agreement with the suggestion.

Parking that line of questions, I return the conversation to the most recent incident. "Do any of you have a clue who might be behind the accident here? Did you see anyone out of the ordinary milling around before the light fell?"

"No," Andy replies. "I hate to say it, but I think it has to be a crew member. Who else could come onto the set without being noticed? There are always security guards covering the entrances."

The woman interrupts, "But we've all been on the production team since filming started in London. Why would someone start making trouble now?"

Andy coughs, looking pained. "There is one new person — Vivian Edgemont. She was cast as Wren's love interest about a month ago and joined the production shortly after. But why would an actress want to doom her own show? It doesn't make any sense."

We chat for a bit longer, but I don't learn anything more. Eventually, my uncle calls for filming to begin and everyone leaps into action. I take that as my cue to step away and phone Edward.

He picks up after one ring, as he always does when I call. I get him up to speed on the Torture Museum Eternal, H and I giving chase, and finally the accident on set. He is as stumped as I am.

"It might be Beadle," he mutters. "I wouldn't put anything past him at this point. However, I agree that the timing and the actions seem out of character for both him and Hobbes."

"What do you propose we do?" I ask.

He grows silent, weighing the options. "Two things come to mind. First, we need to get more information on the production troubles. Talking to your Uncle Harold is the logical place to start."

"And the second?"

"I still think we should bring Trevor Robinson into the fold. I know you, Kate, and Mathilde are reticent, but we need police support."

"We've been over this, Edward," I groan. "Unlike Harry, Trevor hasn't spent the last twenty years working in the colleges. And unlike you, he doesn't have the magic of Oxford running through his family line. He might not believe us, or worse, he could go public with the information. It's too risky!"

"I know, I know," he grumbles, half-heartedly. "But you did ask what I thought we should do."

Silence again falls on the line, the two of us at an impasse. Then another solution crosses my mind.

I clear my voice and pose a question. "What if there is a halfway point?"

"What do you mean?"

"We need more information from Uncle Harold, and we want

Trevor Robinson's opinion on the matter. What if we got them together in an informal setting and brought up the topic?"

"Hmm, yes... that might work," Edward admits. "Do you have something specific in mind?"

"Well, we finished unpacking the kitchen and dining area yesterday. Why don't we invite Harold, Dominic and Trevor over for dinner? You and Trevor have been talking about getting together soon, anyway." I think through the logistics and then add, "We could invite Mathilde as well, to round out the numbers. We'd better make it tonight. The production isn't in town for long; we can't afford any delays."

"I guess you want me to call Trevor?" Edward asks, although he knows the answer.

"Yes, please. Let's say 8pm. That will give me time to pick up something I can throw in the oven."

❖

Amazingly, everyone agrees to join us for a very last-minute dinner. I make a quick stop at the supermarket on my way home, grabbing strawberries and cucumber before I check out. An icy cold glass of Pimm's is a must have on a warm summery day, and hopefully will loosen my uncle's tongue. I need him to tell us everything he knows about the production's alleged curse.

Edward turns up shortly after I do, freshly showered and ready to lend a hand. He hasn't yet made the full move over from his flat at St Margaret. He says he doesn't want to bring over his belongings until the remodelling work ends, but I think he is holding off until H and I get settled. Either that, or he doesn't like reality television programmes as much as H and I do.

We make quick work of the dinner preparations, splitting up the tasks and working comfortably side by side. H, wisely, is staying out of the way, curled up on the sofa, snoring after a hard day of flying rounds over the Botanic Garden.

Harold and Dominic are the first to arrive, breezing in the front door in a cloud of cologne. Harold looks somewhat haggard, a sure sign that he came straight from the set. Most of us took our leave when filming broke for the day, but not Uncle Harold. As the director, he is expected to stay long afterward, looking over the day's footage and meeting with the writing team to discuss any changes in the script.

Dominic looks exactly the same as the last time I saw him, which must have been two years ago. The man, with his deep golden tanned skin, bald head and muscled frame, shows no sign of ageing. If I didn't know he was in his fifties, the same as my uncle, I'd swear he was forty, at most. Dressed in linen trousers, a loose white shirt and sandals, you could transport him to Ibiza and he would perfectly fit in.

He pulls me into a friendly hug, pressing air kisses near my cheeks in the Spanish style. Once the greetings and introductions are out of the way, he steps back and casts a critical eye over the front hallway.

With his hands on his hips, he announces, "I need a full tour, *chica*. This house has great bones, but we need to discuss what you are planning to do with it." He sashays up the stairs without waiting for a reply.

If it were anyone else, I would try to stop them. The house is in no shape to be shown off, with boxes, tools and construction materials scattered about the upper floor. However, Dominic is an interior designer and a well-known one at that.

I leap at the chance to get some suggestions. Harold waves us on our way, saying he'll wait until the remodel is done to see what changes I've made. Given how many times he came as a child, I imagine he knows the layout of the house all too well. Edward offers to get Harold a drink, leaving Dominic and me free to take our time.

Dominic and I are in the large bedroom, weighing the merits of a window seat versus more closet space, when we hear our next guest arrive. I put a pause on our conversation, the gleam in Dominic's eye reassuring me it won't be forgotten. He's certainly intrigued, not the least because the love of his life made plenty of fond childhood memories within these walls. With any luck, he'll decide to take me on as a special project and remove the bulk of the design decisions off my plate.

I open the front door, fully expecting to see Mathilde, but I find DCI Trevor Robinson instead. Dressed in tailored navy shorts and a polo shirt and holding a bottle of white wine, he looks about as far from his policemen persona as possible. As I stand there, wrestling with whether I should address him as Trevor or DCI Robinson, Dominic loses patience with me and uses his hip to bump me aside.

"*Hola*," he drawls, emphasising his Spanish accent, "and who might you be?"

Trevor doesn't bat an eyelid. He offers out his free hand and says, "I'm Trevor Robinson. Nice to meet you..."

"Dominic. Dominic Garcia." My uncle's partner shakes Trevor's hand and makes no secret of checking him out.

I nudge Dominic out of the doorway and wave Trevor inside. "Hi Trevor, come on in. I'm glad you could make it on such short notice."

Trevor passes me the wine as he comes through the door, and I send him on into the front room. Dominic, however, remains firmly in place, staring out the door. While I was distracted with Trevor's arrival, I failed to notice Mathilde coming up the front path.

"If it weren't for the Smash the Patriarchy t-shirt, I wouldn't have recognised you," I exclaim as I welcome her inside.

Mathilde smirks back at me and flips her now short hair over her shoulder. "I don't know why I held off on buying anything new for so long. Although, watching you and Kate react to my new wardrobe is an unexpected source of entertainment."

"I don't know how you dressed before, but I definitely approve of this version of you," Dominic adds, looking over my shoulder. In her denim mini and strappy sandals, Mathilde is every inch the confident 20-something she is.

I finish up the introductions and we all move to the back garden, settling on my new garden furniture and enjoying the last rays of sunshine. At this time of year, the sunset isn't for at least another hour.

It doesn't take long for the initial awkwardness to wear off, especially when Uncle Harold and Dominic tell stories of my childhood. No one is surprised to hear about the extravagant birthday parties I would organise for myself where even the adults had fun.

I hold my finger to my lips and swear the others to secrecy. "Don't tell anyone else, but Harold's and Dominic's presents were always the best. Exotic stationery, shimmery pens, desk organisers..." my voice trails off as I wistfully remember the past.

Dominic brushes off my compliment. "*Chica*, you and I might not be immediate family, but our spirits are related. I always knew you'd much rather have something you could organise or play party planning with than whatever the toy of the year might be." He leans over and winks at Edward. "If you ever need gift ideas, you know who to ask."

Edward blushes, but I suspect he'll ask for Dominic's email address before the night is over. There are few men in the world who wouldn't like a hand with picking presents for their partner.

The oven timer beeps, calling us to the table. I dish up a plate for H and set it aside for when he wakes up from his nap. That done, I serve family style, putting the oven-warmed dishes in the middle of the table and encouraging everyone to help themselves. Edward pours the wine, and we all settle in to enjoy the meal.

Over dinner, I wait for the right opportunity to ask Uncle Harold about the so-called curse, half-hoping that he will bring it up himself. But it turns out to be difficult to find an appropriate moment to bring up potential criminal activities at your uncle's workplace. The last thing I want to do is put him on the spot. I need him to open up on his own.

Finally, over heaping bowls of Eton Mess, Dominic rides to the rescue.

"Nat, now that you've spent a couple of days on set, what are your thoughts on the movie business? Any interest in making a career change?"

"Nothing could pull me away from the magic of working here in Oxford," I admit, being more truthful than most of my guests realise. "The film set has been both extraordinarily boring and wildly busy, but not in equal parts." I mimic a yawn.

My comments cause Harold to chuckle. "That sounds about right. We rush around getting everything in place for the perfect shot, and then wait for hours for the actors and camera crew to be happy with the footage."

"Speaking of the camera crew..." I hold for a second until I am sure I have everyone's attention. "I met a few of them today, after the big lighting fixture fell over. They mentioned something about a curse?"

Uncle Harold rolls his eyes and looks over at his partner. Dominic shifts uncomfortably, explaining, "The 'curse' is my fault. I was visiting Harold on set the day Vivian's costume went missing. I knew there had been a handful of other problems. I made an offhand joke about the production being cursed, and somehow it stuck." He leans over, looking serious. "But it isn't cursed. Nothing my Harold does could be cursed. He wouldn't stand for it."

Trevor, ever the police investigator, rises to the bait just as I had hoped. "What kind of problems have you been having?"

My uncle brushes off the question, but the rest of us are too curious to allow him to get away with a non-answer. Trevor and Mathilde urge him to explain.

"It all started about a month ago. Before today, I would have classified them all as nothing more than annoyances. For example, one of Vivian's costumes went missing shortly after she joined the cast. It turned up a day later, buried in the back of Gideon's wardrobe."

"Gideon is playing Wilkins, right?" Mathilde asks, jumping in.

"Yes, that's correct," Uncle Harold confirms. "You'd think it would be hard to hide a 17th century dress in the midst of men's clothing, but that costume was dark brown. It was probably there the whole time, blending in with Gideon's trousers and waistcoats."

"What else happened?" I prod him to come out with the rest of it.

He huffs, but drops his shoulders, recognising defeat. "Next, it was the day's footage. Someone deleted the camera memory, and we lost everything we'd shot that morning."

He carries on, recounting more incidents than I expected. For the most part, they are harmless, designed to delay production or force reshoots. I keep a close eye on Trevor, watching his face for a hint of what he is thinking.

He doesn't bother with keeping a poker face. Instead, his eyebrows raise a little higher with each story. When Harold finally gets to today's episode, Trevor's brow is wrinkled with concern.

"What does your security team say?" Trevor asks. "I'm assuming you must have one, given the calibre of actors involved."

"They seem as stumped as the rest of us, and there is a limit to what they can do." Harold shrugs. "The London set is relatively small, and once we have all the crew working in their various roles, there simply isn't much space left for guards to stand around idle. They focus their attention on the entrances and exits or guarding the actors when they leave the set."

"Hmm." Trevor takes a sip of his wine and considers my uncle's answer. "I hate to say it, Harold, but my first guess would be that it is someone on your crew. From what you've described, it would be difficult for a stranger to wander around unnoticed."

Pale, Harold can't do anything other than nod his agreement. "I fear you're right, but for the life of me, I can't imagine who it would be. These are people I've known for years. We're all invested in the film's success."

"Maybe you need someone to come in with a fresh set of eyes, someone who isn't connected with the production and won't be swayed by their history with the crew," I suggest.

"Someone like you?" Dominic asks.

"No, I was thinking of someone with more relevant professional skills."

One by one, all eyes move over to focus on Trevor.

"Me?" He shakes his head. "Don't take this the wrong way, but I'm a major crimes detective. Most of the people I deal with are hardened criminals. I'm sure there is someone else who would be better suited." Trevor glances left and right, but none of us are moved to offer him a way out.

"At least come by the set," Dominic suggests, ever ready to take control of a situation. "You can get a behind-the-scenes tour, meet the actors..."

"And if you wait a day, you could also see the inner sanctum of one of Oxford's oldest colleges," I add. "Tomorrow is our last day in the Botanic Garden. After that, we'll be at Somerset College for the next ten days."

Trevor looks like he is wavering, but we need one more thing to push him into saying yes. I wrack my brain, but Mathilde comes in with the surprising win.

"Err, I could come along... With you, that is. I know quite a lot about Somerset's history." She stops awkwardly, shifting uncomfortably in her seat. "Or I don't have to come, if history isn't your thing..."

"No, I'd like that," Trevor interrupts, smiling at her.

I catch Dominic's attention, wondering whether he is seeing the same thing I am. He gives me a small smile and wink before turning his gaze back to Trevor.

That's all the confirmation I need. *Mathilde* and *Trevor*? Who would have seen that coming?

Chapter Three

On the way to the Botanic Garden the next morning, I mull whether I should tell Kate about Mathilde and Trevor. It might seem like a silly way to pass the time on my cycle to the set. However, it's nice to have a completely innocuous question to ponder for a change.

As I lock my bike to the cycle stand, I land on a decision. I won't say anything to anyone yet, not even Edward. After all, I may have been reading too much into their small exchange last night at dinner. It would be better to wait until tomorrow, when we meet at Somerset, to see if a *tendre* between the two actually exists.

"Natalie? Natalie Payne?" an unfamiliar voice calls from the garden's main entrance.

I spin around, tucking my bike keys into my handbag. "Yes, that's me."

A young woman approaches me, her long stride eating up the ground between us. Dressed in jeans and a short-sleeve top, the clipboard under her arm and headset draped around her neck immediately identifies her as a member of the film crew. Her chestnut brown hair swings in time with her steps, a long fringe covering her eyes. She carelessly brushes it out of her face, revealing a youthful countenance and a friendly grin. She holds out her hand for an introduction. Although she looks vaguely familiar, I can't place her.

"Hiya, I'm Joyce, Harold's production assistant," she says, squeezing my hand in a surprisingly powerful grip. "He asked me to take you to meet everyone today."

"Thanks," I reply. "I had planned to make my way around yesterday, but after the incident with the lighting rig, everyone was scrambling to get back on schedule."

Joyce flinches and the shivers. "Yes, that was a close one. I was lucky."

Lucky? "Wait, were you the other person who was almost hit?"

A flash of anger crosses her face and disappears so quickly that I wonder whether I saw it. "Yes, Vivian shoved me into the flowerbed when she leapt out of the way. I had to go back to my room at Somerset to change clothes afterwards. I had dirt ground into everything."

"Everyone was talking about how quickly she reacted. Good thing she did since I heard that lighting fixture weighs a tonne. You two could have been badly injured, or worse."

"All's fine and today's a new day," she declares, drawing the subject to a close. "The main cast and entire crew are on hand as we have multiple scenes to film and several costume changes are required. Shall we make our way inside?"

Joyce breezes past the gate guards, but they stop me in my tracks.

"We need to see your ID, please." The guard holds out his hand in readiness.

Joyce backs up. "She's with me, Donald. She's Harold's niece."

Donald, the no-neck security guard, refuses to budge. "I don't care who she is," he grunts. "We're checking every ID, and we aren't letting anybody on set if they aren't on the list."

He shifts sideways, using his beefy frame to block the entrance.

I smile at Donald as I pass him my university badge. My name, picture and title are clearly printed on the front. "I don't mind, Joyce. I'm glad the team takes security so seriously."

Donald checks my name against the list and then steps aside, allowing me to enter the gates.

Joyce proposes we get a coffee from Craft Services. Sam, the lanky man I met yesterday, is the barista manning the window. He gives me a friendly welcome and goes to work at the coffee machine, spinning dials and steaming fresh milk. In the meantime, Joyce surveys the scene on the events lawn with an experienced eye, her gaze skipping around as she assesses who might be free.

I expect I'll spend a fair amount of time with Joyce over the coming days, since Harold has seen fit to pair her with me. I might as well strike up a friendship. "How long have you been a production assistant?"

"Four years now, most of them spent working with Harold's team." She turns to look at me. "He's lovely, really. He always has a clear vision for the production and keeps everyone on track."

I search her gaze, but her comments seem authentic. If she is a fair representation of the other crew members, I can see why Harold would have trouble believing one of them could be responsible for the problems.

Sam hands us our drinks and sends us on our way. Joyce does a final scan, landing on the tall male figure standing alone on the garden path. He's dressed in period clothing, so he must be one of the actors, but with his back to us, I'm not sure which one.

Joyce nudges me with her elbow before setting off in his direction. "Follow my lead," she instructs.

I struggle to make sense of her words as I walk behind her. She circles around and stops in front of the man, clearing her throat to get his attention. Now facing him, I can see it is Caleb Farrow, lead actor in both the show and Harry's wildest dreams.

Up close, he is just as handsome as he appears on screen. His hair gleams with chestnut highlights, his blue eyes twinkle with some secret delight. If I look closely, I can see hints of make-up, expertly applied to accentuate his natural good looks without showing up on camera. Harry would swoon with delight if she could stand in my shoes right now.

He strikes a casual pose with his shoulders thrown back and his head held high, reminding me of Gaston in *Beauty and the Beast*. With his lazy smile, he looks every inch the entitled 17th century Lord. That impression solidifies as soon as he opens his mouth.

"Good morn to you, Joyce," he says with a regal nod. His smile slips, replaced with a concerned look. "There was much by the by yesterday. Are you well?"

"I'm fine, Sir Christopher. Thank you for asking," Joyce replies, throwing me for a loop. "Might I beg a moment of your time to make an introduction?"

"By all means, Joyce," he booms.

She angles in my direction and tilts her head, encouraging me to step forward. "This is Lady Natalie. She is Lord Harold's niece. She is a local to Oxford and has kindly offered to share her knowledge of the area and the institutions with us."

"How do you do, Lady Natalie?" Caleb intones, his voice full of respect. He gives a slight bow, and I find myself sinking into a shallow curtsy, my hands holding wide the skirt of my floral summer dress.

I side-eye Joyce as I rise, completely confused and out of my depth. She rushes in, preventing me from saying anything.

"Lady Natalie, this is Sir Christopher Wren. Perhaps you have heard of him?"

Her expression practically begs me to play along. I frown,

searching for a proper 17th century response. "Err, yes. Of course. How do you do, Sir Christopher?"

"I am splendid, Lady Natalie. Absolutely splendid. These Botanic Gardens are a favourite of mine, and I intend to make good use of my time here. I have many herbs to collect now, and mayhap later, I shall have the chance to escort my beloved along these very paths." Caleb beams again, evidently pleased with himself. "Now, if you don't mind, I must excuse myself. I have much to do." He doesn't wait for a reply, sweeping past us to walk deeper into the garden.

Joyce takes one look at my face and laughs. "Sorry about that, Nat. I should have warned you, but honestly, it is more fun to see how people react. Caleb Farrow is a method actor."

"A method actor?" I ask, raising my eyebrow. "Are you saying that he is staying in character throughout the entire shoot, even when he is off camera?"

"On camera, off camera and even when we're on a production break," she admits, still chuckling. "I would not want to be his family. It must drive them around the bend, having to keep up the period lingo for weeks on end."

I can't help but grin as I realise that my months of chatting with centuries-old Eternals might finally come in handy. If anyone can carry on a conversation with a historical figure and keep a straight face, it's me.

We're still laughing when another man crosses over to join us. His shoulder-length salt and pepper hair is pulled back by a leather thong, highlighting his thick eyebrows and ruddy cheeks. The lines around his eyes speak to a life well lived and add to his appeal. Although he is also dressed in the billowy white shirt and fitted trousers common in the 17th century, his introduction is decidedly modern.

"What a ridiculous fool," he mutters, shaking his head with annoyance. "If he were half the actor he thinks he is, he wouldn't need to spend all of his time in Lalaland. He could slip in and out of the role like the rest of us professionals." He pauses, suddenly realising he hasn't introduced himself. "I'm Gideon Pomerance. You must be Harold's niece."

"Nice to meet you, Gideon. Yes, I'm Natalie, but please, call me Nat." I give him a smirk. "Shall I call you Gideon or Wilkins?"

"Gideon, by all means. This is my first time working with Farrow. I'd heard through the rumour mill that he was a method actor, but I didn't expect him to take it this far. Do you know that the man is actually staying in a 17th century farmhouse? It doesn't have electricity or indoor plumbing!"

I pull a face of disgust at the very thought of it, causing Joyce to crack up again. Someone calls Gideon's name, pulling him away before he can tell us anything else. He makes me promise to meet with him once we get to Somerset, curious to know more about my role at Oxford and what insights I can share that will help him in his role of John Wilkins, mentor to Sir Christopher.

"There's only Vivian left to meet, and I expect she is in either wardrobe or make-up. Shall we head in that direction?" Joyce asks.

"Lead the way," I answer. "Thanks for making time to take me around this morning. I imagine you have plenty to keep you busy."

"No worries," she breezes as we wind our way through the field of cables snaking across the events lawn. She guides us towards a long, narrow trailer, stopping in front of the small set of risers in front of the door. "I do have a few things I need to take care of before filming starts. Vivian should be inside. I'll leave you here, if that's okay? We can meet up again when we break for lunch." With that agreed, she dashes off.

I pause before I go in. Caleb Farrow and Gideon Pomerance were certainly sitting at opposite ends of the spectrum. I wonder where Vivian will fall. I take a deep breath and climb the steps into the trailer.

"Hello?" I call out when I fail to spot anyone. Since this is one of the larger trailers, I expected to find a brightly lit, spacious interior. Instead, a row of tall white changing cubicles sit to my right while racks and racks of clothing are crammed together, creating a maze on my left.

"We're in make-up, *bella*," a heavily accented female voice replies. "Come on through."

Looking more closely, I spy a narrow corridor in between the racks and follow it. I emerge on the other side, feeling as though I've stepped through Narnia's wardrobe and arrived in an alternate magical universe.

Staring in wonder, I skim my gaze over all the details. The far end of the room is obviously make-up, with its brightly lit mirrored wall and tall director's chairs. The countertop is covered with every face and hair product imaginable. How anyone makes sense of the mess is beyond me.

But that isn't the strange part. What catches my interest is the sitting area located in between the costumes and the make-up.

There is an elaborate crystal chandelier casting a scattering of light over the deep red tones of the plush Persian rug. Matching armchairs anchor one side of the space, upholstered in royal blue crushed velvet, their ornately-carved legs sinking into the rug. The oak coffee table has a silver platter with two demitasse espresso cups and a bowl of sugar cubes sitting on it. Renaissance prints line the walls. It looks like someone picked up a sitting room from an Italian villa and plunked it down in the middle of a filmset trailer.

"Ciao, *bella*. Can we help you?" the voice asks, pulling me from my reverie. I skim the rest of the trailer, finally spotting the small cluster chatting in the far corner. There is a woman seated, her eyes closed while a man applies liner and mascara. Beside them stand an obviously Italian middle-aged couple. Between their dark hair and eyes, designer clothing and rapid hand gestures, they have no hope of hiding their heritage.

"I'm Nat Payne," I explain, halting my approach when the Italian woman splits off from the group, coming over in a flurry.

"Harold's *nipotina*! *Certo*! Welcome, *bella*." She pauses only long enough to air kiss my cheeks. "I am Ilaria, and that is my husband, Marcello. We are in charge of set design and costumes."

Suddenly, the Italian sitting room makes sense. With their expertise and industry connections, the couple can create any room they want for themselves.

Ilaria wraps her arm around mine and practically drags me over to the group. "Vivian, you must know. She is our lead actress," she explains, pointing to the woman in the make-up chair. "And the genius behind the production's hair and make-up is Joe."

Joe is dressed in solid black, the only colour coming from the pink streak in his hair and the matching neon pink shadow on his eyelids. Even close up, I can't tell whether his cheekbones are actually that sharp or the product of a professional hand. I make a mental note to ask if he offers tutorials.

Somehow, Vivian is the most normal in the bunch, her hair piled high in a riot of curls and her body encased in a fluffy pink housecoat. She flutters open her eyes and says hello, but Joe shushes her. "Your make-up hasn't set yet, Viv! Don't move your mouth!"

She barely manages an apologetic smile and shrugging her shoulders before Joe returns to his task.

"Nice to meet you all," I say, glancing around the group. "Sorry for interrupting. Joyce told me to go on in."

"Nothing to worry about, *cara*," Ilaria reassures me. "Let's have a *caffè* and get to know one another while Joe finishes making our Viv even more gorgeous."

She leads me back to the sitting area, motioning for me to sit on a small loveseat. Marcello settles into one armchair while Ilaria bustles around, preparing espresso in a tiny Italian coffeepot using a single electric hob. The warm scent of fresh coffee fills the space followed by a burbling sound that signals the drink is ready. A third demitasse cup is found, and the three of us are soon sipping away with delight.

Ilaria and Marcello move to the top of my list of filmset favourites. The couple are flamboyant, hilarious, and perfect matches for one another. Half the time, they finish each other's sentences. When we're done with our coffee, they pull me to the other end of the trailer, showing me all the costumes and set decorations and peppering me with questions about the colleges.

Swimming in a sea of bustles and bonnets, I lose all track of time. When someone opens the door and announces the start of the lunch break, I'm amazed to discover two hours have gone by. The colour drains from my face when I realise I completely forgot someone.

H is due to arrive at any moment. He was taking the morning to visit Eternals around town to see if anyone has spotted any signs of strangers but promised to turn up by mealtime. No surprises there. I say my goodbyes to the friendly Italian couple, happily agreeing to visit again in the coming days, and rush outside. Hopefully, I can find my favourite Eternal before he eats his way through Craft Services.

"There you are!" H shouts as soon as I step out of the wardrobe trailer. He dive bombs from his perch on top of a nearby trailer, zooming to land at my feet. "Lor luv a duck, Nat, I'm starvin'! What took you so long?"

"Sorry, H," I cry, reaching down to stroke his head in apology. "I lost all sense of time inside the trailer. I didn't mean to leave you waiting. Let's go to Craft Services. To make it up to you, I'll ask them to make a second plate with whatever you want on it."

H pretends to think about it, but we both know he's going to forgive me for the delay. He flaps up to hover at my side. We mark time in the long line waiting in front of the food trailer, updating one another on our morning activities. Thanks to the magic of Oxford, no one around us thinks anything odd about a woman and a wyvern having a conversation. The magic convinces them they're seeing a woman with a cute black and white cat by her side.

"No luck at all? No one has seen anything or anyone out of the ordinary?" I ask as we near the front of the line.

H pauses his review of the lunch offerings to give me a negative shake of his head. "Nuffin' at all. Oi, do you think they'd let me 'ave both the chicken and the sausages?"

Before I can reply, we're interrupted by a nearby shout. A man's voice rises above the chatter, calling out, "Mates, get a look at that crow! It's huge!"

"It's the biggest bird I've ever seen. Take a photo of it!" another man replies.

An enormous crow sitting here in the Botanic Garden? Crows are not known for living in populated areas. Can it be the crow from the Torture Museum — the one who helped Simon Beadle orchestrate his theft in the Ashmolean's archives? The same bird which sent a man tumbling to his death, moments before Beadle set the building on fire? If it is, H and I have to act fast.

I turn to H, finding him deeply distressed. "Are you thinking what I'm thinking? Is there any chance it is a normal crow?"

His eyes are wide with fury as he gives a furious shake of his head. He is literally steaming with rage at being pulled away from the promise of food to face off against his feathered nemesis.

"Where is it? Let me at 'im!" H screeches, punctuating his words with a jet of flames. His snout twists from left to right, smoke leaking from his nostrils as he searches the treetops for the black bird.

"Wait, H!" I shout. "We should get Bartie and my grandfather." But it's no use. Livid at the crow's incursion into his territory, H backs up and launches himself into a sprint, looking like a fighter pilot racing along the runway as he takes off for battle. And battle it will be if H sinks his talons into his Eternal enemy.

I have no idea what the people around me see. The magic must be working hard to cover up the furious flight of an angry wyvern. H flaps his wings at a rapid pace, his talons outstretched, ready to do their damage. He takes a flying leap and bullets straight into the air.

I call after him in vain. He is singularly determined, his eyes and ears fully focused on the black smudge hiding amongst the leafy green branches of the tall oak tree. I spin in a circle, taking stock of my location. Who's closer: Bartie or my grandfather? I catch a glimpse of the tall black iron gates which mark the entrance. Bartie it is.

"Baaarrrrrrttiiiieeeeeee!" I shout, crossing my fingers as I dart after H. Bartie must have been close because he immediately appears at my side, his eyes wide open at the sight of my madcap dash.

"The crow," I gasp. "It's here."

Bartie disappears and reappears moments later, this time with my grandfather in tow. They jog behind me, all three of us following the sounds of thrashing tree branches pounding up ahead. A blast of orange red flames alerts us to H's location, and we quickly round the corner to catch up.

It *is* the crow from the Torture Museum. Same beady black eyes sparkling with the promise of evil. Same greasy feathers as dark as the deepest night. The crow is even bigger than I remember. He is squared off against H, the two of them perched on opposite ends of a sprawling tree branch, both their chests heaving with exertion. Clearly, the battle started before Bartie, my grandfather and I got here.

The gloating voice, however, is new. The crow's beak opens wide, shrieking an onslaught of insults in a screechy male voice that reminds me of fingernails running down a chalkboard.

When he finishes his taunts, he turns to us and glowers, "Look at you lot, running around like fools. Is this the best Oxford has to offer?" It caws loudly, practically laughing in our faces.

"Look who's talkin', you bird brain," H sneers back. "You 'ave a shamed excuse for a philosopher and a rejected museum director leadin' your pack."

The crow spreads its wings wide, flapping them in anger. It opens its beak, ready to retort, when H strikes

In a blaze of fire, H runs along the branch, tucks his wings in and launches himself, talons spread wide, at the evil bird. The crow flaps furiously, tumbling out of the way and barely twisting its fall into a glide.

Bartie, my grandfather and I stand aghast as the two beastly Eternals take their battle to the air. I wring my hands, nervous that H might get hurt, but Bartie reaches over and pats my shoulder with reassurance. "No need to fear for H, Nat. He's got a clear advantage over the corvid."

"What's that?" I ask, without taking my eyes off the mid-air battle. Before Bartie can reply, H takes a deep breath and sends a stream of fire at the bird, singeing its tail feathers.

The crow realises his miscalculation about the same time. It scrambles higher, darting left and right to avoid the steady flow of flames licking at its clawed feet. For his part, H zooms close behind, offering the bird no quarter.

It is the first time I get to see H in action as a fearsome wyvern instead of my cheeky mate. His yellow eyes glow even in the daylight, his aerodynamic scales helping him slip through any wind resistance.

The two fly higher and higher, their bodies turning into backlit shadows against the bright summer sun. The crow maintains the lead, but that lead shrinks with every second.

"Come on, H. You can do it," I cheer.

Without warning, just as H spews a torrent of fire, the crow twists its flight into a dive, barely evading the flames. His beady eyes survey the landscape, searching for a way to avoid capture. I trace its descent, wondering where the crow will take the battle next.

"Err, I think we have a problem," I shriek, getting Bartie and my grandfather's attention. "The crow is headed straight for the events lawn!" The men do their own math and arrive at the same conclusion, their faces draining of colour. I cup my hands in front of my mouth and pitch my voice as loud as I can, calling out, "H! The film crew!"

Bartie and my grandfather disappear, but I'm left hotfooting it back the way I came. My leather flats slip on the gravel path, forcing me to slow down if I want to stay upright.

I stumble onto the events lawn, my breath heaving and a stitch screaming in my side, to find utter chaos.

The crow has abandoned its attempts to escape and is instead intent on ravaging the film set, causing as much collateral damage as possible. It buzzes the top of a picnic table, sending paper plates flying left and right. Next up is the camera crew. The crow flies figure eights, weaving in and out of the space between the trio, sending them ducking for cover.

H is clearly torn between putting a stop to the bird's antics and helping fix the damage it leaves in its wake. The turning point comes when the crow makes a final pass over the lawn, using its claws to grab a mass of cables. Its wings beat in a maddened frenzy, tugging the cables higher and higher until they eventually sever in half.

As the broken black cables tumble past, H spins in the air, chasing them back down to earth. Then, in a moment of sheer brilliance, he does what only he can do.

He gathers the frayed ends, clutching them tightly in his talons, takes a deep breath and then spews his magical fire over them. The smoke fades to reveal perfect, unbroken lengths, magically made whole once again.

The crow gives a final, distant caw before disappearing from sight.

I bound over to H, heedless of whomever might be watching, and pull him into a giant hug. "Are you okay?" I whisper.

"I'm right peeved," he grumbles. "Iffen that bird brain 'adn't tried to torpedo the set, I'd 'ave 'ad it for sure." H brushes off any further concerns, spinning around to prove he is injury free. Only his pride has been hurt.

By the time I stand back up, Bartie and my grandfather, together with the magic, have managed to put everything back to rights. I hear a few mumbles about crazed cats and devilish birds, but otherwise, no one seems concerned about the battle that just took place.

I escort H back to the Craft Services trailer where, fortunately, there is no longer a queue to be served. H calls out his requests, which I translate for Sam, accepting the heaping plate of sausage rolls, chicken wings and mini wheels of baked brie. After his valiant effort, H deserves a hearty feast.

We're barely seated at the now-empty picnic table when I hear a cry go up from the other end of the lawn.

"The new scripts... they're gone! Someone's run off with the scripts!"

Uncle Harold emerges from a nearby trailer, his frustration evident. As he directs the crew to search the area, I can't help but wonder. Was the crow here to distract us so Hobbes and Beadle could walk away with the scripts? Or did someone on the crew take advantage of the momentary disarray to create more chaos for the production?

Finding out will take more than luck. I roll my shoulders back and steel myself for another investigation.

"Bartie, Grandfather, you'd better alert the others. We need to regroup after work at my place. It's time we put together a plan to determine what exactly is going on here."

Later in the evening, H is comfortably ensconced in our front room, basking in his moment. Mathilde, Harry and Kate sit on the sofa opposite his chair, peppering him with requests to re-enact his battle with the crow. Watching from the dining room, I can't help but think he deserves every minute of his time as the centre of attention.

"Oh, I wish I could have seen it," Mathilde anguishes. "I'd have paid good money to see H give that old crow the what-for. He deserves every singed tail feather you gave him."

"I'm more impressed by your quick thinking with the cables, H," Kate interjects. "You did the right thing by letting the crow escape. Your fiery breath saved the day's filming schedule. Well done, mate."

Harry grabs her handbag and rummages through it, eventually pulling an oddly shaped, wrapped package from its depths. "Every hero deserves a reward, H. Hopefully, you'll find this one to your liking." She passes it over to H, who stares dumbfounded at the gift.

"For me?" he asks, as though he can't believe it. Harry nods and motions for him to hurry and open it. He needs no further encouragement, making quick work of the brightly coloured paper and curly ribbon. His eyes twinkle with excitement as he beholds what is inside. "A wedge of Lincolnshire Poacher cheese, all for me? It's my favourite, 'Arry!"

"I know it is. It's yours and yours alone. You'll need to keep up your strength," Harry replies with a wink.

Sensing a lull in the conversation, I step into the room and set the tray of hot drinks on the coffee table, telling everyone to help themselves. As I look around the room, I feel some of the tension from the day slip away. My grandfather and Bartie have their heads together, sitting near the window, no doubt discussing what additional support the Eternals can offer. When Edward follows on my heels, carrying a bowl of crisps, the group is complete.

Given our penchant for group gatherings, I made the wise choice to furnish the front room with a sofa and several armchairs. When you add in the cushioned seat in the window, there is space for all of us.

"Thanks for coming by on your way home from work. The situation is growing more serious by the day. Our original plan to lure Beadle and Hobbes to Oxford and catch them in the act needs a rethink."

I pause to see if anyone disagrees with my view, but they all sit quietly, with varying degrees of worry on their faces. "I'm not sure how much each of you know, so for the sake of completeness, I'll quickly run through everything that has happened on set and around the centre so far."

As I recount our chase through the covered market, the crashing light, learning about the curse and everything else, the sheer volume of troubles blankets the room. Even Harry, our battle axe, has worry lines wrinkling her forehead.

When I wrap up with the missing scripts, Kate sighs in

frustration. "I hate to admit it, but I think we underestimated Beadle and Hobbes. What I don't know is whether they've had Eternals from the Torture Museum lurking around Oxford this entire time, or if this is a sign they are ramping up their efforts."

"I think they are ramping up," Mathilde states confidently. "There is no way unknown Eternals could pass unnoticed in Oxford. They'd be spotted eventually by one of the Eternal creatures, like H or a ghost. I think our plan worked too well."

I lean forward, curious about her last sentence. "What do you mean?"

"We wanted a lure that Beadle and Hobbes wouldn't be able to resist. And what's better than the chance to destroy part of your enemy's legacy? It caught their attention, but maybe it also aroused their suspicions. If they know we're on to them, they have fewer reasons to try to cover their tracks as they've done before."

"It's true," Kate adds, looking grim. "They've got away with multiple break-ins, stealing items from Iffley, St Margaret, Barnard and the Ash. Perhaps they think they can't be stopped."

Harry harrumphs from her end of the sofa. "That's fine. Let them keep their confidence. People who think they can get away with bloody murder always end up getting nabbed in the end. Their confidence will lead them to make a mistake."

"Let's hope so, Harry," Edward agrees. "Our problem is that we still don't know what their end game is here. Do they simply want to steal enough items to solidify their new connection to the magic? Or do they want to rip our connection away?" He taps his chin, considering all the options. "It could also be as simple as a case of revenge. Maybe this isn't about the magic anymore. Maybe their only goal is to take down Wilkins' legacy and Kate's job at the Ash."

Edward's words land like a lead weight, leaving us all stumped. My grandfather rises to his feet and crosses the room to stand in front of the fireplace. "Bartie and I have spoken with the other Eternals. We all agree that it should be easier to keep an eye on things when the production moves to Somerset College tomorrow." He scans the group, looking Kate, Mathilde and me each in the eye. "How do you three want to play this?"

Mathilde and Kate exchange meaningful glances. Mathilde speaks up. "Not to put you on the hot seat, Nat, but you are our resident planner and the only one of us who will be at Somerset the entire time. Seems only right that you should make the call."

I roll my eyes, unsurprised to draw the proverbial short straw once again. "Planner extraordinaire to the rescue, I guess."

I reach over to the nearby bookshelf and retrieve a pad and pen, weighing our options. "We need to plan two tracks for our investigation. The first priority has to be Beadle and Hobbes. We know they are willing to kill to achieve their ends. That puts identifying the mischief-maker within the film crew in second place. If someone on the crew is trying to sabotage the production, we'll spot them, eventually. Especially if we've got all hands on deck to keep an eye out for Beadle and his murderous crew."

"I'll speak with the Eternals. Given the circumstances, I am sure we can entice a few of them to leave their hallowed college halls and take up a surveillance area," my grandfather offers. Bartie voices his agreement, offering to cover the University Parks in addition to St Margaret.

I make note of the assignments on my pad, checking them against the action plan. "That leaves me with Somerset. H and I will track down Somerset's Eternals first thing tomorrow."

"Don't forget about Trevor," Mathilde calls out. "He is due to visit the set tomorrow."

I brighten up, delighted to have the extra help. "Fab! I wonder what time he is planning to come... Uncle Harold must know..."

Mathilde coughs, causing me to look over in time to see a

flush colour her cheeks. "Um, he said early afternoon."

Her awkward manner and rosy cheeks attract Harry and Kate's attention. Almost in unison, the two of them turn towards Mathilde, displaying the same curious gaze.

Mathilde decides to brave through her embarrassment, pretending it is nothing. "What? I offered to meet him. He had to let me know what time he will be there."

Harry narrows her eyes, unconvinced by Mathilde's offhanded explanation, but Mathilde straightens her shoulders, almost daring Harry to call her out on it. I have to give it to Mathilde. If there is any sort of affection blossoming between her and Trevor, she sure is keeping it close to her chest.

Sensing the need for an intervention, I call Harry's name. "I forgot to mention one key piece of information, which I'm sure will be of interest to you, Harry."

"What's that?" she asks, still eyeing Mathilde.

"I met Caleb Farrow today."

Harry's head spins around so quickly I worry she's given herself whiplash. "Caleb? You met him? Ohh!" she squeals. "What's he like in person? Is he as gorgeous in real life?"

"Even more handsome," I reassure her. "He called me 'Lady Natalie' and bowed when he met me."

Harry practically swoons in her spot on the sofa. Chuckling, Kate grabs a takeaway flyer from the coffee table and fans her.

Hand to her chest, Harry confesses, "I am so excited, Nat. I can't believe he didn't show up on the first day at the garden. Do you know his shoot schedule? I can't wait to meet him."

"I'll check the college filming schedule tomorrow and send you a text. I cannot wait for you to meet him either!"

If only Harry knew how much I mean that! One big question remains — do I warn Harry in advance about Caleb's penchant for staying in character, or do I let her discover this quirk for herself?

Chapter Four

Of all the days to sleep through my alarm, it had to be this one. I had turned in early enough yesterday evening, dropping off into an exhausted sleep within minutes, and I fully expected to wake up this morning in the exact same position in which I'd nodded off.

However, the neighbourhood cats had other plans in mind.

Was it only a few days ago that I cautioned H not to set them on fire? Well, whatever sympathy I had for them is now gone. It had disappeared around two in the morning when they lined up for a chorus on my back fence. Worn out by his battle with the crow, his belly full of Lincolnshire Poacher cheese, H had fallen into a serene sleep in the downstairs reception room. While I had 'enjoyed' a front-row seat at the feline concert, H was blissfully unaware of our visitors.

By the time I make it down to breakfast, I'm seething with rage.

"That's it, H; I am done playing Mr Nice Guy. You have my full permission to unleash your worst on the neighbourhood cats. If the magic sees fit to save them, hopefully it will leave them with enough sense not to return."

H opens his mouth, thinking to calm me down, but decides that in this case, discretion is the better part of valour. He scuttles off to his garden house, breakfast in hand, but pours me a cup of fresh coffee before he goes.

The coffee, together with a plate of eggs and toast, works wonders on my disposition. Feeling somewhat more human, I call H to meet me out front so we can go to Somerset College. Near the Bodleian Library, it's a short fifteen-minute walk from our new home. The day is bright, the sun reflecting off the puddles left by an early morning rain burst. The air smells fresh, the temperature slowly warming up into the low 20s. In England, it doesn't get much better than this.

We pass Barnard College with its ivy-covered walls, stopping to spare a moment to window shop at Blackwell's Bookshop. The Weston Library is festooned with vinyl banners advertising a new exhibition on the journey to the moon. Around the corner, we finally spy the main entrance to Somerset College.

A low stone ledge separates the pavement from a grassy lawn. H and I dodge around a pair of giggling little girls, their pigtails bobbing as they walk atop the ledge, pretending it is a tightrope. H uses his tail to give the smaller one a gentle push when she seems in danger of tumbling off.

Standing before the looming stone facade, I slow my steps, needing a moment to take it all in. Somerset is set back from the street by the grassy lawn. I've walked past dozens of times without ever stopping to take in the magnificence of it all.

The stately building — its perfect symmetry unbowed by four hundred years of wind, rain, and snow — stands proudly, ready to welcome visitors inside. Typical of the older Oxford colleges, the enormous arched doorway lies dead centre, its heavy wooden doors kept closed. It isn't hard to imagine the doors thrown open wide with a king and his train of royals riding regally through the gate. Instead, a small panel is propped open, barely large enough to allow entry without having to duck. It offers tempting glimpses of the gardens hidden behind the impressive facade.

This very building dates back to the beginning of the 1600s. Wilkins, Wren and the other powerful men of their age walked along this same pathway when they entered this very building. I wonder whether they imagined it would still stand tall, serving the same purpose all these years later.

A rush of heat on the back of my legs brings my imagination to a screeching halt. H, who has run out of patience, swats my calf with his tail.

"Come on, Nat. I'm starvin'. Do you think they've got the Craft Services trailer 'ere yet?"

My university badge gets me past the college security desk, and later, past the production guards standing watch over the building stairwell. Donald is kind enough to point me in the room's direction where the crew is setting up for the day's scenes.

Most of the filming will take place in the main building and its centre courtyard. I glance out a window, hoping to catch sight of a member of the crew, but there is no sign of the production team anywhere. I worry but then recall that they are setting up the trailers in the rear gardens, hidden away from both spying eyes and the camera lens. The arched stone entryway on the far side of the courtyard is likely to be a high traffic area over the next ten days.

Somerset's main building is remarkably similar to Barnard, which shouldn't come as a surprise. After all, the two colleges harken from a similar timeframe, and likely took architectural inspiration from one another. Not that they'd ever admit it.

Discreet signs on the walls offer directions to the hall, where filming is set to commence later this morning. Ducking inside, I spot a familiar dark head of hair and lithe form standing near the doorway.

"Francie! Is that you?"

The young woman spins around, gracing me with a bright smile. You'd never know that less than three months ago she stood accused of murder and spent two weeks in jail. As Kate's assistant at the Ashmolean, Francie found herself falling under suspicion for the arson in the museum archives and the death of the security guard. Thanks to Kate's determination and our investigative skills, we were able to prove she wasn't to blame. For a while we worried she might not recover from the trauma, but seeing her now sets any of my remaining concerns to rest.

"Hi, Nat! Isn't this exciting? A film shoot!" she gushes. "Kate sent me over to check all the artwork and to make sure the antique equipment we're loaning is properly displayed."

I cast my eye around the room, hoping to see some of the priceless antiques, but the room looks remarkably similar to the last time I visited. Admittedly, the hall needs little help to turn from dining space to film set. With its wooden tables and high-backed chairs, it seems frozen in time.

Francie notices my survey and explains, "We've swapped out a few of the portraits in here but otherwise left everything as it is."

"Ah, that explains why I couldn't spot any differences! So where have you put the treasure trove of artefacts?"

Francie leads me to a nearby window, pointing to a doorway leading off from the courtyard. "The production crew has staged one of the college meeting rooms to act as John Wilkins' 17th century office and laboratory. Most of the items are down there. With only one doorway and small windows, we thought it would be the safest place to store everything."

I nod sagely, impressed by Kate and Francie's thoughtfulness. It is one thing to dangle the notion of priceless items to Hobbes and Beadle. It is another to make them easily accessible.

The sound of voices in the hallway halts any further conversation. I turn around and am surprised to see my assistants, Will and Jill, make their way in the door.

"Morning, Nat," Will calls.

"Hey, Francie," Jill adds.

"Hiya, Will and Jill," I say, crossing the room to greet them properly. "What are you two doing here this morning?"

The pair exchange confused glances before Jill replies, "We have a meeting this morning. To discuss the party next week?" When I still look perplexed, Jill follows up. "For the cast and crew... Remember? We're supposed to organise it."

Her words kick my brain into overdrive. With everything else going on, I somehow let the wrap party completely slip my mind. How in the world am I going to explain that I forgot about the big event?

Jill must sense something of my distress because she reaches out a hand and pats my arm. "You forgot, didn't you? I'm not surprised. You've been running nonstop over the past month and a half, prepping for the filming and remodelling your house."

Will stifles a laugh before admitting, "Honestly, it is nice to see proof now and again that you're just as human as the rest of us!"

At a loss for words, I shake my head, still unable to believe I could make such a mistake. With perfect timing, Joyce sticks her head inside the door, waving at us. "Ready for our meeting about the wrap party? I reserved one of the small conference rooms for our use."

Will and Jill are still chuckling as we follow Joyce into the hallway. I notice that H chooses to stay behind, his nose in the air as he heads towards the small doorway into the kitchen. Although classes aren't in session, there are still students living in the dorms who need to use the dining hall for its intended purpose. Their hours of access will be limited, but with any luck, H will be in time to sweep up any remainders from breakfast.

The nearby conference room is indeed small and very modern. With clean white walls, an oval table, and a large display, it looks more suited to an office building. We take care of introductions as we get seated. After a minute of shuffling papers and notebooks out of our bags, we're all ready to get down to business.

Joyce starts us off with an overview of the number of attendees and a little about each group. Pen in hand, I sketch notes on my paper. Try as I might to keep my mind focused on the task at hand, every time Joyce switches over to a new department within the production crew, I find my mind wandering off. Could there be a bad egg in that group? Is someone in that team more likely to hold a grudge against Harold or the production overall?

Each time I realise my mind has wandered, I wrench it back to the present. But it is no use. There are simply too many other pressing problems clamouring for my attention. As much as I love a good party, stopping Beadle and Hobbes and helping my uncle are higher priorities.

My subconscious must be hard at work because my mind clears right as my vision lands on Will and Jill. Unlike me, the two are busy taking copious notes, interrupting Joyce with questions as she goes along. I settle back in my chair, watching as the pair expertly guides Joyce through the pre-planning process — gathering information on food preferences, event hours, budget and any other constraints.

Finally, my assistants grow quiet, seemingly satisfied that they have all the background they need to begin work on an event plan. We thank Joyce for her time and put a follow-up meeting in all our diaries before she dashes off to her next task for the day.

With Joyce gone, I clear my throat to capture Will and Jill's attention. "What would you two think about taking the lead in organising this event? As you can see, between helping the production team and managing the remodel, I am overwhelmed. This event would be a fantastic opportunity for the two of you to show-off your capabilities."

"Really?" Jill asks, her voice full of hopeful excitement.

"Really!" I reply with a smile. "I'd love to grow our team and be able to take on more events at a time. It would be beneficial for the university and also give both of you the chance to progress in your careers. Now is as good a time as any for the two of you to demonstrate what you can do."

Their beaming grins are all the answer I need. With that task sorted, I wrap up the meeting so I can move on to my next assignment — tracking down Somerset's Eternals.

❖

I spy H circling over the courtyard and rap on the window to get his attention. I wiggle the latch, barely managing to get it open in time for him to fly inside.

"Spot anything out of the ordinary?" I ask as H lands at my feet.

"Nah, it's all quiet out there, Nat. No signs of birdbrain or any of the torture museum Eternals so far."

"Excellent. Let's see if we can find some of Somerset's Eternals and draft them into helping us keep an eye out. I imagine there must be dozens of them, given how old Somerset College is. Any suggestions on where we start?"

"Let's see..." H scratches his chin with a talon, deep in thought. "There's the 'ead of Eternal Affairs for Somerset, but 'e is kind of a stuffed shirt. All 'e cares about is the college ranking in the academic tables. Not likely to be worried about a film crew, iffen you know what I mean."

"We'll need to meet with him at some point," I note. "However, I can see your point. We need someone more like Harry, who knows everyone and doesn't let a thing slip past her."

H's eyes light up and an excited curl of smoke slips from his nostril. "I know just the woman, Nat. Follow me."

H leads me through the college halls, back down the stairs, and across the courtyard. While he flies overhead, I move more slowly, carefully picking a path between the snaking lines of cables and piles of film equipment. He swoops low, crossing under the arched corridor, which leads to the college gardens.

"Found 'er!" H shouts, waving his arms for me to speed up. I jog across the sprawling grass lawn, moving towards a line of perfectly trimmed hedges. It takes me a moment to find an opening between their leafy branches. On the far side, I emerge into a vegetable and herb garden, cultivated in neat rows.

A flutter of cloth behind a trellis of vines attracts my attention. I take care with my steps, not wanting to damage any of the plants growing in the dirt. When I reach the trellis, I find H chatting away with a stout woman in a light blue dress. At the sound of my approach, she spins in my direction.

Her simple cap and the sturdy cloth of her dress mark her as a member of the servant class. The lines on her face make her seem middle-aged, but I'd guess she is likely younger than she looks. Life in the 17th century took a higher toll on the working class than it does now. Her expression is one of welcome, her eyes twinkling with a hint of humour. She brushes her hands against her skirt, knocking off the dirt, before holding one out in greeting.

Her calloused grip speaks to years of hard work. "Hiya, Nat. I'm Molly, the Laundress. Your grandfather told me to keep an eye out for you."

She waits expectantly for me to reply, but I'm too dumbstruck to formulate a sentence. In sharp contrast with her clothing, demeanour and hairstyle, her accent is exactly the same as my own.

Molly gives a hearty laugh, her voice booming across the peaceful garden. "Expected me to sound like Shakespeare?"

I nod in amazement.

"I may be dead, but there's no reason I can't move with the times. Besides, keeping track of the comings and goings of our staff and students would be nigh impossible if I didn't understand the vernacular." She winks at me, and adds, "Plus, it drives our Head of Eternal Affairs absolutely batty."

Her last comment cracks me out of my frozen shell, literally, when I let loose a snicker. "Molly, I can already tell you and I are going to be great friends."

Pointing towards a nearby bench, Molly suggests we have a seat in the sunshine and get to know one another. Since her plan perfectly aligns with mine, I willingly comply, slipping my sunglasses on as we get comfortable.

"Before we get onto the topic of the college, would you mind telling me about yourself, Molly? I'm embarrassed to admit that I didn't ask H or my grandfather in advance for information on Somerset's Eternals."

H interjects before Molly can reply, explaining, "That's no accident, Nat. We Eternals 'ave an unspoken rule. We don't tell each other's stories."

"Really?" I arch my eyebrow and look at Molly. She smiles and nods, confirming H's statement. "Huh. I guess that makes sense. You have so few opportunities to tell them, it wouldn't be right to deny you the chance. So, Molly, over to you. How does the college laundress become an Eternal?"

"It's pretty simple. When you're the only woman living and working in a college, it tends to be a notable experience in your life."

"Wait, what?" I rock back against the bench. "Can you back up a step? The *only* woman?"

Molly shakes her head, almost as though she can't believe it either. "I heard you spent time with Lady Petronilla at Barnard College, so I assume you know well her role in the college's foundation. Somerset's story isn't wildly different. The Duke of

Somerset may have founded the institution, but it was his wife who ensured the college survived after his death. She set the rules and regulations, determining that no women should be allowed within the walls. The only exception she made was for a laundress."

"Heaven forbid a man should have to wash his own unmentionables," I quip, causing Molly to chuckle and H to snort in embarrassment.

"Exactly right, Nat, although that was far from my only task. I spent most of my time trying to keep that philosophical club from burning down the building or poisoning us all."

"The Philosophical Club?" I sit up straight, feeling a surge of excitement.

H flaps his wings to get her attention. "Do you mean John Wilkins and Sir Christopher Wren?"

"Yes, those two were at the centre of the group of grown men acting like schoolboys with their toys. They were always haring off, chasing after one barbaric notion after another. Wilkins's office was filled with gadgets and chemicals. Tidying up behind those men took a few years off my life, that's for sure."

"Molly, this is wonderful," I exclaim. She wrinkles her brow, unsure whether I'm poking fun at her. "No really, you are exactly the person I need by my side for the next ten days. Do you know why we're all here?"

"Something about a movie or television programme," she replies, waving off the notion. "I like an evening in front of the telly as much as the next person, but these period dramas are not my favourite. I spend most of the show shouting out all the things the productions get wrong." She leans over, murmuring, "It's the curse of living as an Eternal. You know how everything should be, but no one knows to ask you."

I leap to my feet, holding out a hand for her to join in.

"Today is your lucky day, Molly. How would you like to be an unofficial consultant on a series about the life of Sir Christopher Wren?"

"Are you pulling my leg?" she asks, looking skeptical.

H leaps onto the back of the bench, putting himself high enough to look Molly in the eye. "She's tellin' you the truth, Mols. I swear it. Iffen I knew you were so keen to be involved, I'd 'ave flown over sooner."

When she stands up, I ask her where she wants to start. "Costumes? Sets? Scripts?"

Molly waves off all my suggestions. "Let's start with the people. If they don't have the casting right, none of the rest will make a difference."

I send H off on a reconnaissance mission to track down the leading players. Molly takes advantage of the wait to finish up her pruning, looking pleased when I kneel to lend a hand. We make quick work of the remaining row and then store away the gardening tools in the nearby shed. By the time H returns, Molly and I are chatting away like old friends.

"The actor blokes are both in the rear garden, sitting as far apart as possible." H explains to Molly, "No love lost between those two, ya'll soon see. I couldn't find Viv anywhere, though."

I shrug, unconcerned by her absence. "She's probably in the costume and make-up trailer getting dolled up for the day's shoot. We'll catch her later."

Once we're past the hedge, I spot Gideon Pomerance sitting nearby, a script in one hand and a cup of coffee in the other. I point him out to Molly and explain his role. From our position, he can't see me unless he turns his head.

Molly circles around him, her eyes narrowed as she looks him in the face and moves around the check his profile. "Can you get him to say something, Nat?"

I nod and step forward into the garden. "Morning, Gideon.

How are you? I can see you found your way here without too many troubles."

"Hullo, Nat," his voice booms as he flashes me one of his legendary smiles. His bright white teeth gleam in the sunlight. "The security team arranged for a car service. Ridiculous, really, given how close our lodging is, but they aren't taking any risks with us actors."

We continue with meaningless chatter, Gideon none the wiser to Molly's assessment of his fit for his role. I nearly sigh in relief when she gives me the thumbs up, letting me know I can wrap up our conversation.

"Well?" I ask as we walk away, leaving Gideon to his script. "Does he make the cut?"

"His voice isn't exactly right," Molly mutters, looking back over her shoulder. "However, he has the same sense of self-assurance Wilkins had, and he sure is a handsome devil. I suppose he'll do."

Before I can reply, I hear a male voice calling my name.

"Lady Natalie, finest felicitations on this most glorious morn." Caleb Farrow, still very much embodying his role of Sir Christopher, bows in my direction.

I cast a quick glance at Molly, not wanting to miss her reaction. She rocks back half a step, her expression pinched as though she's stumbled upon something rotten. Now I see why Joyce said it is more fun not to warn set visitors about Farrow's predilection for method acting.

"Finest day to you as well, Sir Christopher," I reply, bobbing a curtsey. Molly's expression shifts from pinched to flat out horror. It's all I can do to keep a straight face. "And how is your lodging, Sir? Had you far to travel this morn?"

"I've taken lodging in Woodstock, a small village not far from here. It is a half day's walk on foot, but a short jaunt in the carriage." Farrow rolls his shoulders back, twisting slightly so the sun highlights his best features. This sends Molly's eyes rolling and nearly pushes me over the edge. I make quick work of my goodbye before spinning around and darting into the nearest open doorway. The empty hallway provides me space to let loose my laughter.

"I've heard it said that actors are a different breed from us normal folk, but never in my existence have I seen anything as ridiculous as that," Molly declares, looking practically affronted.

I give her a smirk. "I take it Caleb Farrow isn't measuring up as well as Gideon did?"

"Not hardly," she snorts. "Wren was a fine fellow, humble, his mind nearly always occupied with solving one problem or another." Molly steps around H and motions towards the front door. "That buffoon is about as far from Wren as one can get. I'll see what I can do to help, but I think even an Eternal may find this challenge to be too big to overcome."

The rest of the morning gets swallowed up in conversations with Molly and exploration of the new sets. While Molly might be skeptical of the casting choices, she has nothing but praise for Marcello and Ilaria.

"Now these are people who know their way around the history books!" she exclaims, holding her clasped hands against her chest. "It's as though not a day has passed since I took my last breath. The furniture, the books on the shelf, and this portrait! I'd swear it was the original."

"Err, that is the original," I point out. "Kate, the museum prefect, loaned as many original items as she could find within Oxford's various museum archives. Wait until you see Wilkins' workroom — she found much of the original equipment in storage at the History of Science Museum."

Molly takes another long look around the room, silent as she soaks in the details. "Nat, I'm starting to have hope that this programme can be a success."

Mathilde shows up shortly before lunch, not wanting to miss an opportunity to taste the Craft Services cuisine which H has been waxing poetic about for the last few days.

Upon meeting Molly, she shows the same level of enthusiasm as I did, thrilled to get the chance to speak to someone who knew these near mythical individuals as walking, talking humans. Wilkins, Wren, and the other members of the Philosophical Club left incredible legacies behind that had made them all seem larger than life.

I have to tug Mathilde out of her chair when she settles in and launches straight into a litany of questions. "Trevor will be here shortly for the tour. You can come back and speak with Molly another day. If we don't hurry up and get lunch, we'll miss our window of opportunity."

H growls, threatening to set Mathilde's favourite denim jacket aflame. "Iffen you think I'm missing out on lunch so you can pester Mols with a load of questions, you better use your loaf and think again, missie."

Mathilde's better sense comes to the rescue, but only after Molly reassures her she can pop in and visit anytime she wants. "I'm an Eternal, Mathilde! I'm not going anywhere."

The lunch buffet is a veritable smorgasbord of culinary delights. I cannot figure out how Sam and the other members of the Craft Services team can whip up so many delicious dishes within the confines of a trailer, but clearly they've found a way. I make a mental note to get their contact information before filming ends. You never know when I may need a crack team of chefs who can work their magic in a remote location.

We're sipping a post-lunch espresso with Ilaria and Marcello when Mathilde's mobile buzzes with an incoming text. She gives it a quick scan and announces, "Trevor is waiting at the front entrance. Take your time finishing up. I'll go get him and bring him back here."

She strides off without waiting for any acknowledgement or reply. As we watch her navigate her way towards the arched entry, Ilaria asks, "Is Trevor her boyfriend?"

"Not yet, but I'm wondering if they are headed in that direction," I reply.

Ilaria and Marcello make their excuses, leaving H and I behind to wait for Mathilde and Trevor's return. H is already looking decidedly bored, yawning as he rubs his full belly.

I give his snout a tap when it starts dipping towards the ground. "Mate, why don't you find a quiet spot where you can curl up in the sunshine and have a nap while we take Trevor around the sets?"

"What are you talkin' about, Nat? I'm fit as a fiddle!" H opens his snout to add more, but a yawn escapes instead.

I arch my eyebrow, giving him a stern look. "You've been flying reconnaissance missions over the Botanic Gardens for the last three days and you spent the morning tromping from one end of the college grounds to the other. There's no shame in needing a cat nap, H." When it appears he still plans to argue with me, I add, "If you're worried about the crow turning up, have a quick word with Molly and see if a few of Somerset's Eternals can take up keeping watch."

H seems dubious, but a third yawn renders any further arguments moot. He helps himself to a last chocolate biscuit before flying off to find Molly.

Left at loose ends, I return our dirty dishes to the Craft Services trailer, thanking them profusely for the spectacular lunch, and then head towards the main entrance. I bump into Mathilde and Trevor in the main courtyard.

"Sorry we took so long," Mathilde chirps. "Trevor's name

wasn't on the approved visitor's list. I had to convince the security guard to radio your uncle for approval."

I propose we step into one of the empty conference rooms and agree a bit of plan before we start. Although this is a friendly visit, Trevor is taking the task of viewing the crew quite seriously. After a few minutes of discussion, we decide he might have more luck if he keeps a low profile. We'll skip the introductions, instead lingering near the back of the sets where we can all watch how the crew interacts with one another.

"Have you heard any whispers on the set?" Trevor asks as we make our way to the hall, where filming is due to begin. "Any guesses or suspicions among the crew as to who might be responsible for the problems?"

I shake my head, frowning. "Not even a hint of a whisper. If I had to guess, I'd say that none of them want to believe it could be a crew member. For the most part, they've known each other for years. The film world is relatively small and definitely tight-knit."

Trevor's only response is to nod in understanding.

That settled, Trevor turns to Mathilde, his smile genuine. "You had offered to tell me about the history of the college and how it relates to the production. Are you still up for that?"

"Sure," Mathilde replies breezily, although I can tell she is thrilled he asked. I pause momentarily, letting the pair walk a few steps in front of me. While Mathilde is leading the tour and Trevor is watching the crew, I can keep an eye on the pair of them instead.

True to her word, Mathilde launches into her narrative, showcasing her innate ability at storytelling. As we wander through the building, Trevor hangs on Mathilde's every word. His fascination is honest, and the pair fall into a comfortable conversation, with Trevor interjecting questions along the way.

Before we go through the doors into the hall, Trevor holds out a hand to stop our progress. "Have there been any other problems since we met for dinner?"

Mathilde looks at me for a response.

"The daily scripts went missing while we were still at the Botanic Garden. However, since we've moved here to Somerset, there haven't been any further problems, at least not as far as I am aware. Although I couldn't say whether the calm is due to increased security, the new location, or because the perpetrator is waiting for a good opportunity."

The historic hall is an ideal location for shooting. Its ceiling is crisscrossed by dark stained beams, which stand in stark contrast to the whitewashed walls. Sunlight shines through the imposing stained-glass windows that line both of the long walls. The far end of the room features an intricately carved stone window filled with dozens of panes of coloured glass in the shape of various coats of arms. I imagine Mathilde could identify most — if not all of them — but a crew member shouts for quiet before I have time to ask.

They have pushed the long trestle tables set out for students closer to the back of the room, leaving space near the front for the camera crew to set up their gear. Uncle Harold checks that everyone in ready, and then shouts, "Action!"

Gideon Pomerance, in his role as John Wilkins, sits at the head of the high table. I recognise Caleb Farrow sitting on his right, no doubt basking in the chance to fully embody Wren. Other actors, all dressed in a similar style, claim the remaining seats.

The men laugh and talk, arguing good-naturedly with one another as they break bread and pass around terrines of steaming soup. I get so caught up watching them embrace their roles, I forget to watch the expressions of the crew.

Half an hour of filming goes by without me realising, until

Mathilde taps my arm and motions towards the door when my uncle calls for a short break.

The corridor is busy with people rushing around, making phone calls, and rehydrating in between takes. Mathilde calls for us to follow, leading us up a flight of stairs to Somerset's old library. The room is empty except for a single staff member toiling away at the reception desk. Mathilde gives a quick hello and then continues to the raised seating area at the far end.

"That was so cool," Mathilde gushes as she settles into one of the leather sofas.

I rush to agree. "Seeing all of those thoroughly modern actors sink deeply into their roles really makes you appreciate their talent."

Trevor, however, seems less convinced. "I prefer the final version. All the cameramen and the headsets, the wires running around and behind everything, it took away some of the magic of the end result."

"Period films are almost magical," I agree. "I've always wished I could find a time machine and travel back, talk to the people who lived centuries ago and see what they are really like."

Trevor chuckles. "As a child, I would have paid all my savings for a chance to take a trip on a real pirate ship."

"And now that you are grown?" Mathilde asks, her expression brimming with curiosity.

"As one of the people responsible for ensuring the safety of our population, I can honestly say that I'm glad pirates and highwaymen have faded into obscurity." Trevor laughs at the thought, missing the nervous glance Mathilde casts my way. I give her a subtle nod of encouragement. If we're wanting to test the magical waters with Trevor, this is likely to be our best chance.

Mathilde looks left and right, making sure no one else has entered the room. Then she leans close and says, "Speaking of meeting historical figures, there are rumours that the ghost of John Wilkins haunts these very halls."

"A ghost?" Trevor asks drily.

"Yep," Mathilde replies, in a no-nonsense tone. "They say he appears when students are particularly struggling with a problem or concept. The students say it feels like someone is leaning over their shoulder and whispering in their ear. Shortly after the ghost makes an appearance, the student in question ends up finding a solution to their problem. It almost seems like... well... magic."

Although I know Mathilde's story is fictitious, she's edged as close as she can to the truth of Oxford's Eternals.

To our shared dismay, Trevor's response is to boom with laughter.

"That is an Oxford story if I've ever heard one," he notes, his brown eyes glittering with good humour. "A four-hundred-year-old genius ghost helping students with their homework? Only Oxford would dare to make such a claim."

Mathilde gives me a wry look before huffing in frustration. "You never know, Trevor Robinson. Wilkins could be standing behind you right now, listening to you laugh at the mere thought. You may have missed out on your big chance to solve a problem staring you right in the face."

Chapter Five

I expect Mathilde to depart when Trevor goes, but she asks me to wait while she escorts him out. When she returns, we head into the empty nearby Senior Common Room, aiming to get a cup of tea. As our brews steep, Mathilde shuffles around as if she is nervous about something.

"What's up, Mathilde?" I ask. "You're making me dizzy, wandering around in circles like that."

Mathilde falls onto a nearby sofa, looking like the picture of defeat. "Oh Nat, I'm so disappointed in Trevor. I had hoped he might show some sort of hint, or even a tiny spark of an interest in the supernatural. But you heard him! He scoffed at the mere idea of it."

I don't reply straightaway, focusing my attention on stirring milk and sugar into our cups. I grab a pair of coasters and set the cups on the coffee table before taking a seat across from Mathilde.

I weigh my words but finally decide to speak bluntly. "I can't say I'm surprised. This is exactly why we didn't want to rush into revealing the secret of Oxford's magic to him. As a detective, they trained him to look for facts he can prove, not a supernatural explanation for life's mysteries."

Mathilde grabs a pillow and pulls it into her lap, hugging it against her chest. "I know, Nat. But when Trevor agreed to visit the set, and we decided to suss out the possibility of telling him..."

"You got your hopes up?" I offer, finishing her sentence.

She nods, worrying away at her lower lip.

I take a sip of my tea, using the moment to really look at Mathilde. She's fiddling with a button on her jacket. Her shoulders are tight with stress. Seeing her like this casts me back in time to our first few days at Barnard College. This is more than concern about catching a criminal.

"You like Trevor."

My words hang in the air for a moment, long enough to make me think perhaps I've got it wrong.

Mathilde's breath catches, and she holds it for a second before releasing a heavy sigh. "He's well-read, intelligent, curious, polite and handsome..."

"All true," I agree. "But don't forget about the times we've butted heads with him. Our interactions with him haven't always been positive."

"Weirdly, our past clashes with him only add to his allure. I have no interest in a man who will kowtow to my every word. I know Trevor will take a stand for what he thinks is right, and yet, he isn't so arrogant that he can't admit when he's wrong. Think about how he handled Francie's arrest. He stood up to Kate when he thought Francie was guilty, but as soon as we showed him evidence to the contrary, he helped speed the process to release her."

"You don't have to convince me, Mathilde. I was playing devil's advocate. I may not know Trevor well, but Edward has known him for ages and always speaks highly of him. I trust both of your judgements."

I lean forward and pass Mathilde her tea from the table, coaxing her to let go of the pillow she is still clutching.

"Trevor is handsome, but maybe we're rushing into thoughts about relationships." I give her a gentle smile. "Neither of you are going anywhere, so why not postpone any romantic moves until after we catch Beadle and Hobbes? We should have this all wrapped up within a week or two."

"Trevor invited me out for dinner and suggested we go to the Varsity Club on Monday night."

"I knew he liked you!" I exclaim, causing Mathilde to roll her eyes at me. "But that puts an end to my suggestion of delaying. You have to go, you know."

"Of course, I'm going!" Mathilde mutters. "But how do I handle it? What if I accidentally let slip something about Bartie or H or Molly..."

"The magic will smooth out any mistakes, so don't stress about it." I stop, wrinkling my nose. "Sorry, I know well how easy it is to say don't stress but how hard it is to actually do. I was a frantic mess when Edward asked me out. Remember the time he came to lunch in the library with all of us?"

Mathilde barks out a laugh. "Goodness, do I! Your grandfather dropped the bombshell about finding the origin of the magic seconds before Edward walked into the room, and then H flew in through the upper window. I thought you were going to faint at one point, from the stress of it all."

"I felt my vision fade to black at least once, but somehow I hung on and got through it." I give Mathilde a gentle smile. "Despite all the mishaps, Edward was still determined to put a date in the diary for our evening out. He didn't let anything, including me getting shot, stand in the way of us getting to know one another better."

"And look at you now, preparing to move in and start a life together..." Mathilde's expression grows wistful.

"Yes, just the two of us, plus one cheeky wyvern and a horde of angry neighbourhood cats wailing outside my window. It's a dream life!" I end my sentence with an exaggerated wink, making Mathilde laugh again.

I take another sip of tea before shifting gears. "Shall we move on to more serious matters? We got so distracted with the magic conversation, I forgot to ask Trevor if he spotted any concerning behaviour among the cast or crew. Did he mention anything on his way out?"

"Luckily, I remembered when we passed the camera crew in the corridor. He picked up on Gideon's dislike of Caleb, but when I explained about Caleb's dedication to staying in character at all times, he said he could sympathise with Gideon."

"I dunno, I find it to be pretty hilarious," I confess. "I'm sure it can get to be annoying after a while, and goodness knows the crew has been filming for weeks now, but it is harmless."

"Other than that, he said everyone was professional. No stray glances, no side-eyed looks. It was hard to get any read on Vivian, given she was filming B-roll scenes. All she did was wander around the gardens, walk along the corridor, and stand looking out of the window."

I shake my head, my mouth turned down at the corners. "I've yet to have time to chat with Vivian, which is annoying. Several of the pranks on set, not to mention the falling light fixture, have directly targeted Vivian. Without speaking with her, it is hard to say whether that is on purpose or by sheer chance."

Mathilde looks at her watch and jumps up to gather her things. "Still so many questions, but unfortunately I've got to get back to work. Do you think you'll catch up with Vivian tomorrow?"

"Definitely!" I reassure her as I gather our dirty mugs and

drop them onto a nearby tray. "We've got a journalist from the Oxford Daily coming by in the morning, but after that, tracking Vivian down will be at the top of my list."

Satisfied, Mathilde moves towards the door. Before she can open it, I call her name. "There's still one question remaining."

"What's that?" she asks, looking confused.

I straighten my face into my most serious expression. "Are you going to text Kate and tell her about your date with Trevor, or am I?"

I snuggle deeper into the sofa, nestled against Edward's side, exhaustion settling over me like a blanket. After an impossibly long day wandering from one part of Somerset College to the other, there is nothing I want more than to prop my feet up on the coffee table and tune into one of my favourite programmes.

Flipping through the channels, I plead with Edward, "I'm so tired, but I'm desperate to see who wins this cake decorating competition. If I nod off, will you wake me up?"

"The things I do for love," he grumbles, but I can tell he doesn't really mean it. He still has his own television in his flat at St Margaret, with no one fighting him for the remote. He claims he is staying over to spend time with me, but I think that my television preferences are growing on him.

He wraps his arm around my shoulders and pulls me in tighter. "Is H planning to join us? I know he enjoys baking shows as much as you do. Foodies, the both of you."

"Nah, he's outside working on a master plan to take care of the neighbourhood cats once and for all. He mentioned something about booby traps and asked if he could use some items from the garden shed. I suspect he'll be occupied for a while."

I glance up to see Edward's reaction. Not so long ago, he would have chastised me for indulging H. Thankfully, the two of them have resolved all their differences and we've finally achieved some peace in the house. Edward's silence stretches out, making me wonder. "Are you thinking about ways to trap a cat, now?"

Edward tilts his head down, meeting my eyes. "I might have a few ideas from my younger years... but they can wait until tomorrow. Right now, I don't want to be anywhere but here."

The familiar strains of the theme song fill the room and photos of the contestants and judges flash across the scene. Edward pretends to be interested as I explain who's left in the final round and their strengths and weaknesses. I fall quiet when the episode begins in earnest, my eyes glued to the screen until the first advert break. A cereal ad featuring a mixed-race couple reminds me I haven't told Edward the big news.

"Trevor asked Mathilde out... for a date! A dinner date!"

"Really?" Edward replies. "I thought they barely know one another."

I blow a raspberry and lightly slap his arm. "You didn't notice them eyeing one another when they came for dinner?"

"Huh?"

"Or how Mathilde offered to accompany Trevor on his visit to the set... there was no reason she needed to tag along."

When Edward still shows signs of being genuinely perplexed, I roll my eyes and move the discussion forward. "Anyway... I have it on good authority that Mathilde is interested in Trevor, and given his invitation, I'd guess he feels the same."

"That's nice for them. Mathilde deserves to find a good partner, and she could do a lot worse than Trevor Robinson." Edward turns his attention back to the screen, apparently feeling the conversation has reached its end. But a few seconds later, I feel his back go rigid.

"Is she going to tell him about the magic?"

Sensing that this conversation is likely to last longer than the ad break, I reluctantly lower the television volume. "After our conversation with him today, no, I don't expect her to break the news that Oxford is full of Eternals anytime soon."

Edward shifts over until he can look me in the eye. "What happened?"

I recount our afternoon, starting with the tour and working my way up to our last stop in the library. Edward seems amused at our attempts to hint at the existence of magic.

"That's it? You're basing your final decision off him scoffing at the notion of ghosts?"

Now it's my turn to shift. "He didn't scoff. He literally laughed at the notion, practically insulting Oxford in the process. Even when Mathilde got huffy, he still refused to budge. That man had zero interest in the topic and refused to give it a moment of consideration."

"Cut the poor man a break, Nat," Edward grunts. "How is he supposed to know that the two of you have a magical bloodline running through your veins which allows you to talk with ghosts and fantastical creatures? What sane adult would admit to believing in spirits walking the earth?"

"Harry did. She didn't even blink when confronted with Bartie and Catherine Morgan."

Edward shakes his head, smiling to himself. "Harry is the exception to the rule. To every rule. She is one-of-a-kind. It isn't fair to the rest of humanity to use her as your measuring stick."

I huff and turn my attention back to the television, but Edward isn't done.

"For Mathilde's sake, I hope you'll keep a somewhat open mind."

I spin around, my eyebrows practically at my hairline. "Excuse me?"

"From talking with your grandfather, I know how it has always been done. You prefects keep quiet, and your spouses carry on with their lives, none the wiser to the other half of your responsibilities here at Oxford. But the rules are changing."

I stare in silence.

"Look at Kate. She has Bartie — an Eternal — as her partner. And you, through sheer luck, you ended up with an absolutely wonderful man who happens to be a descendant of Sir Christopher Wren."

I snort, unable to stop the laugh bubbling up.

Edward reaches over and caresses my cheek, looking me deeply in the eyes. "Unlike every prefect in history, you and Kate can share all aspects of your lives with the person you love. Is it fair to deny Mathilde the same chance?"

His words hit like a gong strike in my head. "I never thought about it that way. When did you get so perceptive?"

"In one way or another, you've known about the magic of Oxford all of your life. You never experienced the uncanny awareness that something bigger was taking place. I remember that feeling all too well. Although I was certainly shocked when I woke up from a faint to find your long-dead grandfather standing over me, in a way, it made sense."

I mull over his words. "Do you think that is how Trevor would respond? Are you willing to bet the safety and security of the magic of Oxford on it?"

Edward opens his mouth to reply, but I wave him off. "I get what you're saying, Edward. I really do. But you and Harry had been living with the magic, even if you didn't know it. Consciously or unconsciously, you both had some inkling of an invisible hand."

"I think you're stalling, Nat," Edward replies, twisting on the sofa to again face the television.

I exhale and then tuck back against his side. "I might be, but I can't see any benefit to rushing to a decision. Yes, we need

Trevor's help bringing Oswald Beadle to justice, but we don't have any proof of his crimes yet. As for Mathilde, I think we should let them get past the first date before we assume they're waltzing down the matrimonial aisle."

"Ha! That would be a lot of pressure to put on the chap during their meal."

We fall into a comfortable quiet. I reach for the remote, thinking our conversation is done. But Edward lays his hand on top of mine before I can increase the volume.

"But you will think about what I said, Nat? Maybe you can discuss it with Kate."

"Absolutely," I state, nodding my head as well. "This is a shared decision, and perhaps one where Mathilde's voice should carry more weight than mine or Kate's does. I'm overdue for a girls' night with Kate. I'm seeing her tomorrow; I'll suggest we get together while Mathilde is out with Trevor. That will give me a chance to discuss the topic with Kate without Mathilde feeling pressured into speeding up or slowing down her potential relationship with Trevor. If Mathilde does get serious about someone, Kate and I can be ready to support her, either by hiding the magic or helping her share the news."

Later, as we lie in bed, with darkness enshrouding the room, my mind returns to the conversation. For nearly four centuries, Oxford's magic has been kept hidden, guided by the restrictions our ancestors put into place. Society has shifted, changing in ways which Wilkins, Wren, and the other members of the Philosophical Club likely could never have imagined. Would they make the same decision again?

I drift off to sleep, wishing I could ask them that very question.

Chapter Six

Kate bursts into the conference room at Somerset, juggling a stack of binders in her arms.

"Now I see why you asked me to get the coffees," I quip with a laugh as I rescue one of the binders before it can tumble to the floor. "That is a lot of materials for a press interview."

"I know. I've probably overdone it on gathering up background information. Typically, I'd memorise it all beforehand, but we've loaned so many different items to the film crew that there was no way I could keep all the details straight."

I grab the top binder, flipping through the pages. It is meticulously organised, its length decorated with a line of multi-coloured tabs, all precisely labelled. I open a section at random, landing on a portrait I remember seeing in the hall. There is a large print of the painting, followed by information on the painting subject, the artistic style, and the artist himself. A quick flip through the remaining pages reveals more of the same.

"Take your time getting set up," I instruct Kate. "I'll pop downstairs where I can keep an eye out for the journalist and escort him up here when he arrives. This is your show; I'm here to be the intermediary between the production crew and the university."

"Perfect," Kate replies with a grateful smile, before blowing her hair out of her face. "I've done dozens of press interviews over the years, but somehow this one is rising to the top of the stressful list. It's ironic, as local journalists are typically the most friendly. They share our vested interest in generating enthusiasm about the town and all it offers."

"Let's hope he is enthusiastic about reporting on a bunch of old scientific apparatus and portraits of renaissance men." I dust the table off and toss my empty takeaway cup into the bin. "We've been leaking details of the museum's loan to the production crew for a few weeks now, and it seems to have done its job. Beadle, Hobbes and their group of Eternals are lurking around Oxford."

Kate straightens her binders into a new stack and then looks up at me. "This article is the last step in the plan. If I can push the interview in the right direction, the result should be a shopping list for Beadle and Hobbes. I want them to read the article, get mad, and immediately set off to steal or destroy the items. That should give us the chance to catch them in action. I am determined to see them pay for their crimes."

"Then that's our plan and I'll do everything I can to keep the interview on track. You finish getting settled and I should be back up shortly." Kate nods and sends me on my way.

The day promises to be a hot one, the cerulean sky free of even a hint of clouds. Later on, the cool temperatures of the stone entryway will offer respite from the heat, but for now, I choose to step beyond them and soak up some vitamin D.

Dark shadows flit across the lawn, drawing my gaze up to the sky. H waves from above, where he is circling the college, keeping a watchful eye out for any wayward Eternals. Somerset's guardians have placed themselves around the grounds, adding another layer of protection. No one, alive or dead, is getting onto the college today unless their name is on the production's approved visitor list.

Tourists crowd the pavement, flocking into the city centre to see the wonders of Oxford at their most picturesque. Flowers bloom in carefully tended beds and ivy trellises dip under the weight of the leafy vines. The yellow stone so typical of Oxford glows in soft gold tones under the warm sun. I cross my fingers that the journalist intends to take some photos as well.

A male voice jerks me back to the present. "Morning! Are you Natalie Payne, by any chance?"

A man who looks to be around my age strides confidently up the walkway, a backpack slung over his shoulder and a camera around this neck.

I walk forward, meeting him halfway, my hand outstretched in welcome. "Hiya! Yes, I'm Nat. You must be David Blake from the Oxford Daily."

"I am indeed." He gives my hand a firm shake and then reaches into his pocket. "I brought my press pass and an ID as you suggested. I'm glad you sent me an email reminder. I wasn't expecting to encounter any security blocks."

"Normally I could escort you inside without needing to show any ID, but given the famous names included in the acting crew, the production company isn't taking any chances."

David looks somewhat crestfallen at my explanation. "That makes sense, but I'd be lying if I wasn't hoping there might be a story behind the security."

I force my face to remain serene. If only he knew of the problems we were facing. "Nope, no issues at all. Completely standard security protocols. Let's get inside. Kate is expecting us up in the conference room."

As we wait for the security guard to check David's name against the list, David asks how long I've known Kate. I launch into the official version, explaining we met at Barnard at the start of the year and became friends while preparing for the grand opening of the Ashmolean's newest exhibition.

"I toured it for the paper," David admits. "It was incredible! It is hard to imagine that all of those items were seemingly lost for centuries, all the while hidden away in a secret chamber at Barnard College." He pauses, and then adds, "There was one thing I couldn't quite figure out."

"What's that?"

"Why did Barnard's scholars hide those items away all those years ago? The stuff was cool, but fairly innocuous. If there was something there worth keeping a secret, I couldn't determine what it was." He gives me a pointed look.

I brush aside his concerns, replying breezily, "I always thought of it more as a time capsule, rather than whoever it was trying to keep something from becoming public knowledge."

"A time capsule... hmm." David contemplates the idea. "I hadn't considered that option, but I suppose it is possible." He looks disappointed, undoubtedly lamenting the loss of a potential angle he could exploit down the line.

I decide a subject change might be in order. "I've tried tapping on a few walls here at Somerset, but everything so far has been convincingly solid. You'll have to satisfy yourself with the treasures on display rather than hoping for a breaking news story."

Now outside the conference room, I push open the door and lead us inside. "And on that note, I'll turn the conversation over to Kate, Director of the Ashmolean. Kate, meet David Blake from the Oxford Daily."

Kate and David exchange their hellos and we take our seats. I expect David to pull a voice recorder from his bag, but he sets out paper and a pen instead, explaining, "We're not planning to run this as an interview, so I don't need to get exact quotes. I'll take notes on each of the items and then use the reference materials you sent over to fill in any gaps."

"Brilliant!" Kate beams at David, relieved that she won't have to pick her words quite so carefully. She dives into the material, starting with portraits and paintings and working her way through her stack of binders.

I have to admit, David hangs in longer than I thought he would. But somewhere around the third binder's worth of information, I notice that his writing speed flags, and his eyes glaze over.

"Shall we pause for a break? I can pop out and get us fresh coffees or a cup of tea." I push back my chair and stand up to stretch, forcing the other two into agreeing with my suggestion.

David reaches his arms over his head and leans side to side. "A break would be great... but I wonder if we could shift the conversation into a new direction when we come back."

Kate's expression flattens as she tries to hide any trace of concern. "What do you mean?"

David flips through his notes, frowning as he goes along. "You've given me a tonne of great information about the items on loan, but if I limit the article to what you've said so far, it may come out a bit, err, dry." He shrugs in a silent apology.

Kate's gaze shifts to me, her narrowed eyes making it clear she needs a new idea. We both know how important this article is to catching Beadle. We can't afford for it to die in the middle pages of the daily newspaper.

My brain goes into overdrive, searching for a solution. Uncle Harold was clear that the actors are off-limits, as any interviews have to be cleared with their promotional teams. Who is left? "What about meeting some members of the production crew? Might that work?"

David mulls the offer, nodding his head. "Yes, that might

work. I don't suppose I can speak with Caleb Farrow or Vivian Edgemont?"

"Unfortunately, no," I reply with an apologetic grin. "Their PR teams have strict regulations about any press interviews. However, I was thinking of another couple - Marcello and Ilaria Benedetti, the set and costume designers. They've both won multiple awards for their work, and I'm sure they can provide some colour around why they selected the pieces they did."

"Why not?" David shrugs, taking what he can get. He gathers his paper and pen, shoving everything into his backpack.

"If we're lucky, perhaps they can take us behind the scenes on some sets which aren't in use today." I point at his camera, still lying on the table. "Maybe you can get an exclusive sneak preview photograph to go with the story."

That seals the deal; David looks decidedly more enthusiastic as we leave the confines of the meeting room. When he turns his back, Kate mouths a thank you in my direction.

"Here, let me take the lead, since I know where we're going. The make-up and wardrobe trailer is near Craft Services, so you two can grab a hot drink while I see if Marcello and Ilaria are free."

The gods must be smiling on me because both the Italians are sitting in their home away from home, propping their feet up in between scenes. I barely get the word journalist out of my mouth before they leap up, their arms waving in a flurry of excitement. There is nothing those two love more than talking about their work... except maybe their daily cups of espresso.

"Bring the young man in here," Ilaria demands. "We will tell him all about our vision and inspiration. He will be enthralled, I promise you."

I cross my fingers as I step out the door, calling him and Kate over my way. I need not have worried, as Ilaria and Marcello are in top form. They suck David into their whirlwind, draping costumes over his arms and shoving a parade of hats and wigs upon his head. Kate and I slowly back away, fading into the background while the Italians take centre-stage.

All goes well until someone wrenches open the trailer door — the same door I happen to be leaning against. Kate's quick action saves me from tumbling out as she jerks me aside, opening space for someone else to barge in.

Joyce blasts into the trailer, her cheeks pink and her chest heaving. She looks like she just competed in the one-hundred-meter dash.

She opens her mouth, her words tumbling out. "It's Vivian! She's collapsed! They've called an ambulance."

Ilaria looks at Marcello and gasps. "It's the curse, I know it!"

It is impossible to say which one of us springs into action first, as Kate, Ilaria, Marcello and I all realise that we have a nightmare on our hands and a journalist standing beside us.

Marcello and Ilaria circle around Joyce, preventing her from saying anything else which might damage the production. Meanwhile, Kate and I grab David and practically drag him out of the college. We offer feeble excuses for Joyce's behaviour, saying things like, "Of course, Vivian is fine" and "Joyce likes to exaggerate." Although our voices tell one story, I'm sure our faces are recounting another. Kate's has drained of colour and I've nearly bitten through my bottom lip. But needs must, so we concentrate our efforts on wrapping up the visit and getting David out the door as quickly as possible.

However, there is little we can do other than to wring our hands when an ambulance pulls up in front of the college just as we walk out. David was hoping for a unique angle for his story, and it appears he's got one. When it becomes obvious that the security team is not going to let him back inside, he dashes off to file his story, undoubtedly destined to become the scoop of his lifetime.

"Of all the times for the so-called curse to rear its head," I groan, rubbing my hand over my face. "I really hope Joyce was exaggerating and Vivian is okay."

"Let's get back inside and see if there is anything we can do," Kate suggests, already spinning towards the wooden doors.

By unspoken agreement, we head directly for the hall where the crew had been due to film. However, we don't make it far before we run into the crowd gathered in the corridor, awaiting news on Vivian. No one seems to know anything more than we do, and it soon becomes clear that any hopes we had of getting closer are unrealistic.

I glance out a nearby window and spot H mid-flight on one of his loops over the courtyard and garden. I nudge Kate and nod at the window. She is at first confused, but as soon as she sees H, she gives me a grim smile of agreement. We retrace our path down the stairs and out into the main courtyard.

I cup my hands and shout into the air as loud as I can, "Aitchhh!" His snout flips in my direction and he makes a beeline for us when he sees our waving arms. He soars over the roofline, heading our way. In his eagerness to reach us, he misjudges the distance and ends up tumbling to a halt at our feet.

"What's 'appenin' in the main building, missies?" H asks, dusting his scaly hide. "I keep seein' people goin' in, but nobody comin' back out again."

Kate and I take turns relaying the morning activities, from our interview to visiting Ilaria and Marcello, and finally Joyce's arrival with the terrible news. H's mouth is hanging open by the time we get to the end.

Nervously pacing, I pause long enough to ask, "Did you see anything or anyone out of the ordinary?"

"No, Nat. Nobody came in the front except you and your newspaper man."

"What about sneaking in through the back gardens?" Kate adds.

"I'm tellin' ya, missies. We Eternals 'ave the college locked down. No one is comin' in or goin' out without us seeing them."

I groan in frustration. "We need to find out what happened to Vivian. I'd give my right arm to get into the hall, but there is no way we can get through the crowd in the corridor."

H stares at me. "Why don't you go in through the kitchen?"

"The kitchen? Of course!" I practically slap myself on the forehead. "I completely forgot about it. Do you know how to get to it from here?"

"I don't, but Mols will know." H takes a running start and flies up into the air. Kate and I hear a minor commotion coming from the front entrance. We dash across the courtyard, but there are too many people crowding the entryway for us to see what is happening. H reappears with Molly before we can go investigate further.

"Hello, Nat. H tells me you need to get up into the hall straightaway." Molly smoothes her apron and motions for us to follow her. She leads us across the courtyard, down to a doorway at the opposite end from the main entrance. Inside, we follow her through a maze of corridors and stairwells until we find ourselves standing in a thoroughly modern, stainless steel kitchen. It is empty, no sign of cast, crew or the college cooking staff. On the far side of the room, a swinging door leads into the hall.

I push the door gently, barely wide enough to sneak a peek inside the room. Seeing no one nearby and nothing in the way, I push harder, clearing a space wide enough for us to sneak through.

The hall looks much as it did the day before, when Mathilde and I toured Trevor around the set. The high table is laid out for a meal, although a more intimate one. There are plates and cups for two, the rest of the table bare.

Camera equipment lies abandoned, forgotten in the rush after Vivian collapsed. One camera displays a flashing red light. I point it out to Kate and whisper, "That camera is still recording."

The film crew are clustered at the far end of the room, some standing in small groups, while others are seated at the long trestle tables. They all share the same expression of pinched fear.

Kate leans close, murmuring, "I don't see Vivian anywhere. The commotion we heard coming from the front entrance must have been the ambulance crew taking her away."

I spy a familiar blonde head standing in the group. "There's my uncle Harold. Let's see what he can tell us."

We watch our step as we make our way through the streams of cords and cables, sliding in between the cameras and lights and past a bank of monitors.

"Uncle Harold," I call out, causing him to turn in our direction. "What happened? Is Vivian going to be okay?"

Harold looks like a deer in headlights, his eyes wide and his body frozen. "I don't know, Nat. I don't know what happened to her. We were filming and then she said she didn't feel well. We offered to break, but she wanted to get the scene in the can. Next thing I know, she slumps over and was sick all over herself. I've never seen anything like it."

I meet Kate's gaze, hoping she might have an idea of what to say next. She directs H off to the kitchen to get a fizzy drink and leads Harold over to an empty space at the table. Harold sits on one side, while Kate and I take the places across from him. Molly slides into the chair at his side, gently rubbing his back. He can't see her, but I can tell that her touch helps calm him.

H returns as we sit, passing Kate the bottle. She untwists the cap and hands it to Harold, telling him, "Sip it slowly, the sugar will help."

Harold does as he is told, closing his eyes and massaging his temple while he waits for the sugar to hit his bloodstream. He takes several deep breaths, and finally opens his eyes again, looking much more in control of himself.

"Right. Thanks for this," he says, lifting up the bottle of lemonade. "Vivian is off to the hospital, so there is nothing to be done there until we hear something from the team. Vivian was absolutely right as rain this morning, Nat. She was in fine form when she showed up on set. She and Caleb were chatting away at the dining table, getting into character and reviewing lines."

I think for a moment and then try again. "Does she have any allergies?"

Harold frowns, "None, as far as we know. I suppose it's possible she could be allergic to something, but wasn't aware of it. But given all the other problems we've had, that seems a stretch."

"I take it you don't think she fell ill?" I glance at my uncle and he shakes his head.

I raise my head towards the ceiling, contemplating other options. "Was it something she ate? Or drank? Do you think..." I trail off, not wanting to say the word 'poison' out loud.

Harold flinches. "I don't think we can exclude the option."

Kate clears her throat. "In that case, I think we should phone Trevor. Surely the potential poisoning of a famous actress would warrant his attention." She excuses herself, moving into the kitchen where she can have a private space to ring him. As part of our advance planning, we had all stored his mobile number into our phones.

I scan the room, making note of who is still inside. The numbers have dropped even further as the crew scatter to their trailers to rehash what they saw. The swoosh of the swinging door precedes Kate's return, attracting my attention. I spin in my seat, looking at the opposite end of the room, still sitting ready for someone to say, "Action!" That thought quickly leads into another.

"Uncle Harold, I noticed one of the cameras is still running. Do you think there is any chance you may have captured something on film?"

Harold considers my question. "It's possible, Nat. The camera crew would have been filming well before we started running scenes, checking light levels and angles. Only one way to find out."

Kate, Molly, and I fall into step behind him, with H bringing up the rear. I notice Harold's shoulders drop into a more relaxed position as he moves into familiar territory. He checks the cameras, turning off the one which is still rolling, and settles into his director's chair. He grabs a small keyboard out of a pocket on the side of the chair and begins typing commands. "The screens in front of me are connected to the cameras. Give me a minute to find the right files, and we can see if we spot anything unusual."

He clicks open a couple of files before finding the one he wants. "I've set it to display the video on both screens so we can all see it."

Harold and Kate watch the screen on the left, while Molly, H and I keep our eyes on the one to the right. The video runs at fast speed, crew and cast members rushing in and out of view. Marcello and Ilaria pass through first, the pair working in silence as they straighten the place settings and rearrange the dishes. With their backs to the camera, it is impossible to see everything they are doing.

Caleb and Vivian arrive next, pulling back their respective chairs and taking a seat. This is a much easier task for Caleb than for Vivian, with her dress bustle and train to consider. Joyce strides up, offering a hand. When Vivian is settled, Joyce does a final check of the table, facing the actors as she places spoons into the dishes and brushes crumbs from the tablecloth. When she departs, Caleb helps himself to a basket of bread, waving his hands and sending crumbs flying. He must be saying something funny as Vivian throws her head back, laughing. The two actors chat happily as they wait for filming to start.

More members of the crew come in and out of focus, checking make-up, touching up hair, shifting the candelabra. If we must consider everyone who came near the table, our list of suspects stretches long.

Finally, someone holds a clapper board in front of the camera, marking the date, time and take. Caleb and Vivian sit alone at the table, appearing to be a couple deeply in love. Harold speeds through too quickly for me to make out any of the dialogue, but the body language alone tells the story. The lovebirds pick up their enamelled wineglasses, raising their hands in a toast. But before Vivian takes a sip, she fishes something out of the glass with a finger, brushing it off onto the underside of her plate. To give her credit, she stays in character, gamely taking a quick sip before Uncle Harold must have called cut. Could that have been poison?

None of us moves as we speed through more footage. The same people move in and out of frame, resetting the table and emptying and refilling Vivian's cup. After that, it is more of the same.

I straighten up, staring at the table. "What did she fish out of her glass, back at the beginning?"

"No one touched the plates." Harold waves me forward. "Go check her dish and see if there is something on the side of it."

Molly accompanies me to the table, equally interested in what we might find. I pick up the heavy ceramic plate, which is set before Vivian's chair. Sure enough, there is a small purple blossom stuck to the side of it.

Molly comes closer, her eyes narrowed. I reach out a finger to flatten it out, but Molly slaps my hand away before I can touch it.

"What is it? Do you recognise it?" I whisper, glancing at her.

Molly covers her mouth with her hand, her eyes open wide with shock. "Monkshood. I'd know it anywhere. My word, the lady will be lucky if it doesn't kill her."

Terrified that I might damage the key piece of evidence, I stand frozen with the plate in my hand. I repeat Molly's words so that my uncle can hear them. "It's monkshood, Uncle Harold. Highly poisonous."

The hall door swings open before my uncle can respond, revealing Trevor Robinson. His expression is as severe as the black suit he's wearing. Even though we're now on a first name basis, I call out his title by mistake. "DCI Robinson, I mean Trevor, thank goodness you're here."

He takes in the scene, Harold, and Kate at the director's chair, staring at a screen, and me at the high table, carefully holding an old-fashioned plate, my eyes wide with anxiety.

He skips the pleasantries and goes right to the heart of the matter. "I got here as quickly as I could. You look like you've found something. What is it?"

Kate steps aside and indicates Trevor should take her place. Harold gives Trevor the background information as he preps the video to play again. When the two men are engrossed in the film, Molly takes the plate from my hands and carefully places it back on the table, upside down so as to not damage the flower. I dash into the kitchen with an uncontrollable urge to wash my hands. I know I didn't come close to touching the plant, but Molly's worried expression has me terrified.

I emerge into the hall to find Trevor, Uncle Harold and Kate around the table, staring down at the plate.

Trevor twists around, looking at me. "How do you know this is monkshood, Nat?"

"Err," I stall for time, not having given my knowledgeable pronouncement any thought. Molly whispers in my ear, offering me a lifeline. I repeat her words. "It's a common plant, but highly poisonous. I saw a display about it at the Botanic Garden when we were there filming."

"Are you sure?" Trevor gives me a hard look. "I've got a detective on her way to the hospital. If you are confident in your identification, I'll text her so she can pass along the message to the medical team."

Molly nods furiously, with not a hint of self-doubt in her response. I follow suit, telling Trevor that I am 100% positive that the purple blossom is indeed monkshood. Kate waves her phone in the air, adding, "I searched up a photo and it does look very similar. Check it yourself."

Trevor takes a quick glance at the phone and the plate and then pulls out his own mobile to fire off a text.

"In the interest of time, I am going to treat this as an attempted murder investigation for now. I'll call for a team to come over and begin gathering evidence." Trevor gives me a pointed look. "Please don't touch anything else. I'm going to need to speak with everyone who was in this room today, and particularly those who had access to Vivian's cup and the table."

Harold groans in misery, "That will be most of the cast and crew."

"Sorry, Harold," Trevor murmurs, patting my uncle awkwardly on the shoulder. "I'm also going to need to know more about Vivian, who got along with her, and who didn't."

❖

As soon as the investigative team clears Kate, she waves a hurried goodbye and departs for her office at the Ashmolean to deal with the work piling up there. H and I are left behind, tasked with the challenge of trying to lift Harold's spirits. We drag him outside, laying claim to the comfortable bench near Molly's vegetable garden. I make sure the police know where we are in case we're needed, but otherwise keep our hideaway a secret. Harold needs peace and quiet.

I sit quietly at his side as he makes the necessary phone calls. First, he rings the studio to give the bad news. Next up are the executive producers who are backing the production. He answers the same questions over and over again. No, he doesn't know what happened to Vivian. Yes, he hopes she'll make a full recovery. Yes, she had a few scenes left to film.

My moral support is barely enough to keep him going.

"Ugh, still one call left to make," Harold groans, stretching his back before hunting up the number. When he stands up to pace around the garden, I nudge H and whisper, "H, I think it is time for us to call in the cavalry."

H quirks an eyebrow up and snorts a ring of smoke. "Eh? Who's that, Nat? Edward?"

I shake my head. "Dominic."

Dominic picks up right away, listening as I provide him a quick update on our morning. When he finishes haranguing me for waiting so long to ring him, he says he'll drop everything and makes me promise not to move a muscle until he arrives.

Harold is still tied up with his call, leaving H and I to debate what to do next. Going outside the college grounds is out of the question.

I slump on the bench, grumbling, "I wish there was somewhere we could go to grab a drink and try to take Harold's mind off the production."

H takes my request seriously, tapping his snout as he ponders the options. "There is one place we could go, Nat. It 'as beer on tap and, best of all, it won't cost you a thing."

I sit up, intrigued. "What is this wonderland of which you speak, H?"

"The Junior Common Room!"

"Of course! You're brilliant, H, absolutely brilliant." I pull him into a tight squeeze before he can stop me, and not letting go until he threatens to burn his way out. H pretends to be disgusted by my overly fond behaviour, but I know he secretly loves it.

I hear Harold wrapping up his call, which is my cue to grab my handbag and lead him to our next stop. "Uncle Harold, can I buy you a drink?"

He wipes his forehead, sweating under the summer sun. "That would be wonderful, Nat, but we can't leave the college. Remember?"

"We don't need to, Uncle Harold. Follow me and I'll introduce you to one of the great institutions of an Oxford College — the Junior Common Room. Dominic is on his way. If you can message one of the security team members to show him where we are, he can meet us there shortly."

With H in the lead, our trio circles around the back way, avoiding running into anyone else. We slip into an unmarked door, H confidently striding along the corridors until he reaches the room we need. A sign on the wall proclaims all are welcome, and I couldn't be more grateful when we go inside and see a line of draft beer taps lining the bar.

Harold scans the room, his eyes wide with wonder.

"The Junior Common Room is where students go to relax and hang out." I point towards the big screen TV. "When term is in session, most afternoons you can find students competing with one another on the X-Box and Playstation games. There are rooms like this in all the colleges. In fact, Edward and I watched the boat race between Oxford and Cambridge in St Margaret's

JCR. It was way more fun to cheer with the students than to watch it on our own at home."

"I should have gone to Oxford," Harold mumbles under his breath. "Are you sure it is okay for us to be in here?"

"Oh yes, definitely. The college included it in your rental agreement. I thought we might have a cast and crew drinks night, but I forgot about it with everything else going on."

I take Harold's drink order and then shoo him over to the leather sofa with instructions to relax. Feeling extra generous, I include H in my drink prep, pouring him a half pint of stout in addition to our drinks. H can hardly believe it when I place the glass in front of him, and promises to be on his best behaviour. I'm not sure I believe him, but at least I know I can safely leave him in the college overnight if he overdoes it again.

We're halfway through our pints when Dominic comes hurtling into the room, his arms waving in a frenzy. I pour him a glass of white wine while he babies Harold, hugging him close and making sure he is all right. I wait until he is settled at Harold's side, his arm tossed around Harold's shoulder, before I pass him his drink.

Somehow Dominic knows that what Harold needs most is to talk through the situation. He asks dozens of questions, pulling the truth of Harold's worries and fears out into the open where we can address them.

"Hopefully tomorrow things will look brighter, because right now, all I can see are roadblocks," Harold moans. "Poor Vivian! She has to recover; I can't even contemplate the alternative. We had a few scenes left to film with her, and now those will have to be rewritten. It doesn't sound as though she is likely to recover in time to shoot them before we have to leave the college grounds. The college has a hard stop next weekend because they have a conference coming in after us."

H mutters under his breath, "If she recovers..." I give him the evil eye and say a silent prayer of thanks that my uncle and his partner can't understand him.

"Don't worry, *mi amor*!" Dominic's voice oozes positivity. "You and the writing team will have those scenes sorted in no time. You've dealt with worse problems in the past."

Harold refuses to feel better. "We can change the script, but to what? I don't have time to do more research into Wren's history."

Dominic is undeterred. "So, make something up. I know you like to be as accurate as possible, but the programme is fiction."

Harold shakes his head. "Even if I make up something, where will I find a new actor or actress? There's no one, Dommie. And we don't have time to do a casting call."

It is probably the beer talking, but a potential solution pops into my head.

"I could do it, Uncle Harold."

Both men snap their heads up, staring at me in surprise. Harold recovers first. "You? Why would you... what would make you... who would you be?" he splutters.

I set my glass on the coffee table and shift forward, putting my elbows on my knees. "While you two have been discussing the production challenges, I've been running through the possible suspects. I checked with security. No one entered the college who wasn't part of the crew, other than Kate and the journalist. Given they were both with me, I know they aren't our poisoner. So, it has to be a member of the crew. Or Caleb Farrow. They were the only people who had access to the film set this morning and could have planted the flower in Vivian's drink."

Harold's face crumples in despair. "I know, Nat. I've realised that truth as well. But I still don't understand why you would want to get even deeper involved, particularly now."

"As soon as word leaks out about the poisoning, Somerset College is going to be tarnished by association. My first worry is you, Uncle Harold. I want your programme to be a huge success. Next, as your liaison with the university, part of my role here is to protect the reputation of the college. The sooner we figure out who is behind these terrible acts, the better it is for everyone."

Dominic tilts his head, assessing me with a thoughtful gaze. "Our Nat might not be a trained actress, but we've been to enough of your events to know that you can command a room. With the right direction, I think you could pull it off."

With Dominic now on my side, Harold knows he has lost the battle. "But who would you be? From what I recall reading in the writer's research packet, there were no women allowed in the college. That's why we didn't bring any female extras along with us."

H realises where I'm going. He snorts out a cloud of black smoke, shaking his snout and mouthing the word, "No!"

I ignore him.

"There was one woman allowed in the college, Uncle Harold. A laundress. You could name her Molly."

Chapter Seven

"*Buongiorno, cara*!" Ilaria exclaims when I stick my head in her open trailer door the next morning. "Come in, come in. We need to get you measured and see if there is something in here we can make work for your wardrobe."

I step hesitantly into the trailer, feeling much less confident this morning. Yesterday afternoon, when I came up with the harebrained idea to join the cast, all I could think about was catching our poisoner. While my uncle made calls to the head writer and the costumer, letting them know of the new addition, I was busy preparing my list of suspects and deciding whom to interview first.

With Edward at his own flat working against a research deadline and H sleeping off his afternoon indulgence in his garden house, I had been left to my own devices. I stayed up late planning my interrogations after rewatching the crime footage, agonising over the lengthy list of potential suspects. I was *not* thinking about what would happen when it was my turn to set foot in front of the camera. That reality had come crashing down when I arrived at Somerset this morning and the security guard directed me to report to the costume trailer for my fitting.

Ilaria looks absolutely delighted to have a new cast member to dress and offers me no opportunity to escape. She practically drags me through to the racks of costumes, talking nonstop. "How *fantastico*, darling! Harold says you will be a laundress. I've been sketching since he phoned, and I had more fabric sent up from my warehouse in Buckinghamshire."

"I'm sorry I've put you to so much trouble," I mumble, feeling overwhelmed within the claustrophobic space. Unlike my first visit to the set design and costume trailer, now the towering racks of costumes loom over me, the corset strings and dress laces threatening to bind me to the racks.

Ilaria, caught up in her work, takes no notice of my nerves. "Don't apologise. To be honest, dressing the lower class is so much more fun than designing costumes for the hobnobbers. The coarse textures of the inexpensive fabrics must be wrestled into submission to produce a gown which is at once both practical and flattering. This is where my genius sings, *cara*!"

I paste a wobbly smile across my face and remind myself again why I am doing this. The producers have millions of pounds riding on the show and Somerset College will hardly appreciate being associated with the near-death of an A-list actress. The only way to stop the scandal rumours from becoming larger than life is to identify the culprit as soon as possible. And to do that, I need an excuse to be right in the middle of the action — even more so than I've been to date.

Ilaria has me strip down to my skivvies so she can take measurements, and before long, she is tugging layers of clothing over my body. Stockings and under-skirts are paired with a billowing blouse. I shut my eyes and suppress a groan when Ilaria holds up a tightly laced bodice.

Needing a distraction, I launch into conversation. "Where's Marcello this morning? I didn't see him on my way through the courtyard."

Ilaria pulls a stick pin from her mouth and jabs it into the thick fabric, barely missing my waist. "He is off working on set revisions. He had not planned to show any of the domestic side of college life, but not to worry. He, too, has hundreds of set pieces stored away. He'll have everything he needs in place by this afternoon."

"I'm sure my uncle appreciates all the extra effort you are putting in."

She waves away my comment. "This is nothing. We are as vested as Harold in our desire to see the production be a success, and perhaps winning another BAFTA for our shelf. But even if there was no chance of an award, we would still bend over backwards to help Harold. He is a good man, a *tesoro*!"

"That he is," I say with my first real smile of the day before shifting to a more serious expression. "What do you make of yesterday's events? Do you think someone is trying to kill Vivian?"

Ilaria frowns, her brow heavy. "Before yesterday, I wouldn't have said so, but now I am not so sure. Early on, the problems were minor annoyances. We assumed someone was playing a prank, or perhaps it was nothing more than a series of unconnected mishaps. Costumes get misplaced. Footage can be lost. None of the events themselves were outside the realm of possibility."

"When did you realise there might be something more afoot? Was it when the crew began referring to it as the curse?"

"Hmph, no, certainly not then." She chuckles, explaining, "Cast and crew members are notorious for their superstitions. Filming goes well, then it must be my lucky socks or some other nonsense. When things get misplaced, we are doomed by a curse. My mother raised me to ignore this sort of nonsense, which abounds in Italian culture. If you want to talk about the curse, you'd be better off speaking with Marcello."

Ilaria passes me a kerchief to tie around my neck. "When the lighting rig went toppling down at the Botanic Garden, that's when I knew it was a flesh and blood person committing the crimes."

I shiver, remembering all too well the sound of the scream sending the birds scattering from the trees. "Once again, Vivian was the target."

"Vivian or Joyce," Ilaria corrects me.

"That's right!" Her reminder tickles a memory from the back of my mind. "Joyce seemed annoyed with Vivian when I brought it up the next day. Do they get along?"

"Vivian and Joyce?" Ilaria repeats the names, considering my question. "They barely know one another, as far as I can tell. No, I suspect that was a simple case of envy. When Vivian leapt out of the way, she shoved into Joyce and sent her tumbling into a flower bed. Poor Joyce came up spluttering dirt, but everyone rushed to check on Vivian. It was nothing personal, but I doubt Joyce could see it that way at the time. The stars of the show are always at the top of the list. It is the reality of working in the film industry."

"Yes, she mentioned having to go home and change." I stick my arms out from my sides, letting Ilaria thread a ribbon through the sleeves. "Looking back, it seems likely that Vivian was the intended target. When she avoided injury, whoever was behind this decided to take their efforts to a new level."

Now it is Ilaria's turn to shudder. "It is horrible. Absolutely horrible. Poor Vivian, lying in a hospital bed, fighting for her life, from what I hear."

"Do you know her well?"

Ilaria shakes her head. "No, this is our first time working with her. She is approachable... but not overly friendly. You could chat with her about the weather, but she isn't the type you'd gossip with while you're waiting for the kettle to boil. Added to that,

Vivian only has a few scenes in each episode, so her time on the set is limited."

"Any complaints about her? Anyone's nose tweaked out of joint?"

Ilaria shrugs. "What can I say? She has been purely professional. She shows up on time, plays her part and then leaves. Compared to those actresses who run riot on the set, I'll take a cool professional any day."

I nod my head in understanding. "Okay, so she isn't a diva. How did she get the role as Wren's love interest?"

Ilaria taps her chin, searching her memory. "The role was originally meant for another woman, but she had to pull out at the last minute. Something about an opportunity in Hollywood." Ilaria waves her hand. "You know how these things go. Harold asked around the set to see if anyone knew a British actress who might be available. I think it was Caleb, or maybe Gideon, who suggested Vivian. Harold made a few phone calls, and that was it."

I debate mentioning the camera footage, but then remember Trevor asked us to keep quiet about its existence. As far as the cast and crew know, Vivian drank something which made her sick. If someone outside of our small group mentions the word monkshood or references the dinner scene set-up, they'll earn a one-way ticket to the top of the suspect list.

However, that doesn't mean I can't fish around and see what Ilaria might let slip. "You must have seen Vivian a fair bit yesterday, between costuming, hair, and make-up. How do you think she was poisoned?"

Ilaria cinches the apron strings around my waist before stepping back to admire the result. She tilts her head, the corners of her mouth turned down, somehow not yet satisfied. She spins around, bending over to dig through a plastic bin full of wigs. I can barely make out her reply.

"Where is that thing?" she grumbles, pulling out hairpieces

and tossing them aside. "Poisoning Vivian, you asked? Not that I've given the topic much thought, but it wouldn't be that difficult. She's always drinking some specially made kombucha or aloe water. Compared to everyone else's soda cans and teacups, her drinks definitely stand out."

Ilaria stands up and turns back to me, a white lacy object in her hand and her nose scrunched up in disgust. "She made me try the kombucha once. *Disgustoso*. I'll stick with my espresso." She passes me the white doily, instructing me, "Here, put this on your head."

As I unfold the item, I realise it is a small woman's cap, exactly like the one Molly wears. That thought prompts me to look at myself in the mirror for the first time. I'd been avoiding it before now, not ready to face the result. My eyes grow wide as I take in the full picture.

Despite having only hours' notice, Ilaria has produced a costume which looks straight out of Molly's wardrobe. The tan-coloured skirt pairs perfectly with the dark blue bodice, setting off the bright white apron and undershirt. With the lace cap on my head, even my modern cut somehow looks old-fashioned.

I meet Ilaria's gaze in the mirror, beaming with excitement. "This is incredible, Ilaria. I can't believe you threw this together so quickly."

Ilaria winks at me. "If you think this looks authentic, wait until Joe has a go at your hair and make-up. By the time he's done, even your friends won't recognise you."

"Friends?" I squeak. "Oh my goodness, I forgot Harry is coming on set today. She is going to lose her mind when she finds out I've been tasked with laundering Caleb Farrow's dirty underthings."

"Don't you mean Sir Christopher Wren?" Ilaria asks, winking again, causing me to burst into laughter.

❖

The ringing of my phone cuts through our laughter. I bend over to retrieve my handbag, only to discover that it is impossible to even lean with so many layers of clothing on. Helpless, I have to ask Ilaria to find my phone and pass it to me.

"Hiya, Harry. Are you here? Did you make it past the security checkpoint? Great. Why don't you meet me in the rear garden where all the trailers are located? See you in a minute."

"Go, go," Ilaria gestures to the trailer door.

I hold out my skirt, reminding her I'm still in costume. "Wearing this? But I can barely move in it. Aren't you afraid I'll mess it up?"

"No, *cara*. Keep it on. It will take you a while to learn how to move around with a bodice and a bum roll on. You don't have much time before shooting starts, so straight into the deep end you go."

I'm delighted to discover my dress has pockets. I shove my purse into one and my phone into the other, leaving my handbag in Ilaria's care, and promise to be back in hair and make up immediately after lunch.

Getting out the narrow trailer door also proves tricky, forcing me to turn sideways to avoid tearing my skirt. I can't help but feel like a dog trying to run into the house with a giant stick in its mouth. I pause on the stairs, using my hand to shade my eyes as I search the lawn for Harry's familiar figure. Her white-blonde pageboy cut glows silver in the sunlight, catching my eye as soon as she emerges from the arched walkway. I call out to her, but she breezes right past me, completely oblivious to my presence thanks to my elaborate costume.

I have to hold back a snicker when she huffs in frustration, failing to spot me anywhere amongst the people milling around. She reaches for her handbag, likely to ring my mobile, but she spots the Craft Services trailer and decides to get a coffee and wait instead.

"Perfect," I mumble under my breath as I hold on to the stair rail with a death grip, terrified of getting my feet tangled in my skirts. Harry's attention is fully focused on the coffee menu, causing her to miss my stilted walk across the lawn, still not yet comfortable in the tightly laced bodice and old-fashioned footwear.

I tiptoe close behind her, waiting until I am one step away to say, "Pardon me, madame. Can I take your handbag and put it away in the cloakroom?"

Harry grips her handbag tightly, spinning around to see who would ask such a question. She stares at me for several seconds before the proverbial lightbulb switches on and she realises it is me.

"Oh my! Nat! Look at you! Have you been playing dress-up in the wardrobe department? I hardly recognised you for a moment there."

"Do you like it?" I ask, twirling around so Harry can get the full picture. "I hope it comes across well on film."

"On film?" Harry wrinkles her brow, perplexed. "Do you mean? Are you... are you going to be in the show? Why didn't you tell me they were looking for extras?"

I point to the steaming takeaway cup. "Take your coffee and then follow me. I have so much to tell you."

In her rush to get to Somerset this morning, Harry had skipped her morning ritual of perusing the daily news. She wanted to pop into her office at St Margaret and square away a few items so she'd be free to hang around the set as long as it took to meet her hero, Caleb Farrow. Thus, she completely missed seeing the front-page feature on Vivian's collapse.

We retreat to the far end of the garden, well away from any

listening ears, and I update Harry on the last twenty-four hours. By the time I'm done, Harry's mouth is hanging open.

"My word, Nat. I don't know how you do it," she gushes. "Tell me what you need me to do."

"Just stay by my side and keep me company," I reply. "And if I get nervous, distract me."

Harry rolls her shoulders back, taking my request seriously. "I'm in. Where are we off to first?"

We grab a quick bite to eat before I have to report into hair and make-up, taking extra care to ensure I don't spill a drop or a crumb on my voluminous skirts. Harry does her best to keep a straight face, coaching me as I struggle to sit down and stand back up again.

Joe greets us back at the trailer, pointing me towards the raised chair positioned in front of the make-up bar. When I nearly fall over trying to get into it, he offers to remove the bum roll and a layer of petticoats so I can sit comfortably for a while.

Joe drapes a towel over my shoulders to protect the dress. As he lays out his brushes, he warns me, "Normally, people expect to leave my chair looking more gorgeous than before. However, I need to turn you from an English beauty into a worn-out, middle-aged laundress."

Harry drags a chair over, not wanting to miss a minute of the show. With Ilaria and Marcello off at lunch, the three of us sit in absolute quiet as Joe works his wizardry. Instructed to keep my eyes closed, Harry's gasps are the only clue I have about my transformation. When Joe finally passes me a hand mirror, my stomach is a ball of nerves.

The face staring back looks nothing like my own. Wrinkled brow, cheeks weathered from too many hours working under the sun, and bags under my eyes. Even my pores seem larger. "Joe, you are a genius. My own mother wouldn't recognise me, which is for the best since I wasn't planning to tell anyone about being cast."

Looking pleased as punch, Joe sends us on our way. I check the time, surprised by how much has passed. "We need to go straight to the set. Uncle Harold wants to walk me through my motions before they take some test shots."

"Oh, Nat. I am so excited!" Harry squeals. "What are you meant to be doing?"

"I'm the laundress, Harry. Last I heard, the writers were planning to have me tidy the room and fetch a tray of drinks for the men."

My uncle calls my name as soon as we walk into the study they've commandeered to act as Wilkins's office. I leave Harry standing out of the way, her face glowing with excitement. Caleb Farrow and Gideon Pomerance are deep in conversation at the far end of the room, glowering at one another as they speak. I can't tell whether they are running lines or truly butting heads. I type a quick note into my phone, reminding myself to ask when I have time to speak with them individually.

After that, I push everything out of my mind except for my uncle's instructions. "Walk across the room with the tray of drinks," sounds easy enough, but between my pinched toes in the borrowed shoes, my wide skirts, and the narrow space behind the men's chairs, it is much harder to navigate with any dignity.

We make multiple attempts where I nearly brain Caleb Farrow with the tray, spill the empty glasses into Gideon's lap, and get my skirt caught on the edge of an end table. Each time, my uncle yells cut, forcing everyone to start again from the top. I'm close to tears of frustration when I hear a friendly voice shout out an offer for help.

Unbeknownst to the others, Molly stands in the doorway, her eyes twinkling as she gets a good look at my outfit. "You look like you could be my sister," she says, laughing. She squints her eyes as she checks my make-up. "My older sister, that is."

Gideon takes pity on me, asking my uncle for a ten-minute

break. As cast and crew shift their attention away from me, I plead with Molly to help. "Please tell me you know how to walk across this room without spilling the tray of drinks or ripping a hole in my clothing?"

"I could turn cartwheels in here, if you'd like, but we'll keep things simple until you get more comfortable in your garments."

The first thing Molly does is loosen my bodice laces. "Only the upper class had someone to tighten their strings this much. The rest of us had to tie our own and do what we could with our own brute strength." She guides me through retying the intricate knot, and I take my first deep breath in hours.

"You are a star, Molly. Now, how do I avoid getting my skirt caught in the narrow spaces?"

"That will come with practice, but I can give you a couple of tips to help you get through this scene. First up, walk slower. You likely don't realise it, but you are so nervous, you're practically running across the set. A good servant fades into the background, remember?"

I roll my eyes but catch her meaning. "Okay, walk slower. Erm, how does one do that without looking like they are in slow motion?"

"Let me see if I can explain this to you. Step closer to me and look at the set. What do you see?"

"I see two chairs, an end table and a stack of books."

Molly nods her head, not surprised in the least by my response. "Let me tell you what I see. Over near the door is a pile of dirt which fell off someone's shoes. Further along, the books on the shelf are half-pulled out of place. There's dust on the mantle and crumbs on the end table. All the men notice is me coming into the room, taking the drink request, and coming back with the tray. However, I'd have dealt with all the messes along the way. You need to think like a servant, Nat. Look for the insignificant details, fade into the background and only let them notice what they specifically ask to see."

I mull over her words, rolling them around in my head until they settle into my brain. "No offence, Molly, but I don't think I'd have survived very long as a domestic. How did you keep from yelling at the men for all the messes they made?"

"Oh, I didn't keep too quiet, my dear. But mostly, I waited until they left the room before I let my frustration show." She cackles at the thought.

I spy Harry waving from the back of the room and motion for her to join us. After a quick introduction to Molly, Harry looks at me surreptitiously and whispers, "Do you think it would be okay if I went over to say hello to Caleb Farrow now?"

I scan the room, finding Caleb standing alone, sipping water from an old-fashioned mug. "I don't see why not, but keep it short. We're due to restart filming soon."

Harry bolts off before I can say another word. As I watch her cross the room, her face brimming with excitement, I have a moment of doubt about my decision not to tell her about his penchant for method acting. I cross my fingers and mutter, "Oh no, I hope this goes well."

Harry slows her steps as she nears Caleb, smoothing her gait into a more refined motion. "Good day, Sir Christopher. I do apologise for approaching you without a proper introduction, but I absolutely had to say hello."

My mouth drops open as Molly elbows me, wondering, "How did she know to call him Sir Christopher?"

Caleb grins in utter delight, clearly thrilled to have someone play along with his game. "My dear woman, no need to apologise. Have we met before?"

I stare as Harry bows her head and performs a perfect curtsy as she introduces herself. Her eyes twinkle with mischief as she segues straight into the conversation with Sir Christopher. "No, good sir. I'm Harriet Dalrymple. I am well acquainted with your sister, Susanna. She had intended to join me here today to make the introductions, but I fear she was waylaid by a request for help from some poor ailing soul. She is such a godsend for these poor people."

Caleb rocks back half a step, his eyes wide with disbelief. "Why yes, I do have a sister named Susanna. And you know of her, you say? Why, this is brilliant." Caleb raises his voice, announcing to the room, "Friends, please give a fine welcome to Harriet Dalrymple, a friend of my sister Susanna."

Almost as one, nearby crew members turn their heads, eager to see who has caught Caleb's attention.

What happens next will undoubtedly live in infamy. Caleb, accustomed to being barely more than humoured in his attempts to stay in character, finds himself pitted against a woman who somehow seems to know more about Wren than he does. What starts as a nice chat quickly devolves into a battle of one-upmanship, with both Caleb and Harry determined to show they know more about Wren and 17th century Oxford than the other. All the while keeping in character with their language.

"How long do you think Harry has been preparing for this meeting?" Molly asks in a whisper.

"We had six weeks' notice that the film production crew would head our way. I'm thinking Harry used all of them to memorise the history books in preparation for this very moment."

We grow quiet, following the back and forth between Harry and Caleb... or should I say Harriet and Sir Christopher. As the rest of the crew trickle back into the room, they are quickly shushed and encouraged to watch the battle of wits taking place before us.

Molly nudges me again. "I personally knew Wren, spent years with him underfoot, and I would swear that Harry is more familiar with him than I was. I think she's actually getting the better of Caleb Farrow." Molly and I giggle quietly, thoroughly entertained by the impromptu performance.

Their voices grow louder, with facts, dates and names flying furiously back and forth, until finally Caleb opens his mouth to retort and finds himself at a loss for words. He stands flummoxed for a moment, causing all of us to hold our breath. Then he booms out a laugh and pats Harry on the shoulder.

"My good woman, you are a bright sun on a rainy day."

Harry replies with a shallow curtsy and a very self-satisfied smile. "Thank you, Sir. If it isn't too much, might I beg of you a small boon?"

Caleb gestures magnanimously. "I could hardly refuse you, madame. Please, what can I do?"

As Harry and Caleb pose for photos, Gideon Pomerance slides up on my left, asking, "Friend of yours?"

I nod a yes, explaining, "She's keeping me company today. I promised to pay her with a chance to meet the cast and maybe even get a few autographs."

"I don't normally allow photos and autographs while on set, but for the woman who beat Farrow at his own game, I'm willing to make an exception." He winks and grins.

When Harry takes her leave of Caleb, the rest of us break out into spontaneous applause. Even in a room with some of the most famous celebrities in England, Harry somehow outshines them all.

Filming runs long into the afternoon, late enough for me to decide to send H home ahead of me with a request for Edward to prepare dinner. I change back into my own clothes and breathe a sigh of relief after I wash off the heavy stage make-up.

With no one to keep me company for the walk home from Somerset, I ring Kate to let her know how my first day of filming went.

"I'm a terrible servant, Kate. Seriously, the worst," I groan.

"Don't feel bad, Nat," Kate replies, chuckling. "According to Bartie, I wouldn't fare any better. Women in his lifetime didn't rely on takeout and microwave dinners to feed their families, and they definitely don't switch to paper plates when the dishwasher goes on the fritz."

I speed up, rushing to cross the street with the pedestrian light. When I'm safely on the opposite side, I confess, "I always thought I'd jump at the chance to take a trip in a time machine, but now I'm not so sure. Now that I've had a taste of it, I'll stick with my equal rights and modern appliances over the chance to meet any historical figures."

"Ha!" Kate guffaws. "So says the woman who spent her day getting acting lessons from a nearly 400-year-old Eternal."

"Fair point, Kate! Perhaps I shouldn't be so quick to question other people's choices. Moving on..." I say excitedly "You will not believe what Harry did today."

"What? Was it today she was due to visit the set?" Kate gasps, "Did she meet Caleb Farrow? How did she react to his alternate personality?"

"Turns out she didn't need any warning. Lady Harriet Dalrymple was more than prepared for her introduction to the infamous and great Sir Christopher."

Kate shrieks with laughter. "Lady Dalrymple? Back up and tell me everything."

It takes me the rest of the walk home to recount the story. Kate can hardly speak she is laughing so hard, particularly when I get to the part where Harry asked for a photograph with Farrow.

"You should have seen her, Kate. She had Farrow eating out of the palm of her hand. He even promised to leave one of his top hats behind for her when production wraps up next week."

"She'll have it sitting in a place of honour on her mantle, I'm sure." Kate drawls.

"When Harry finally made her way back to my side, she was flabbergasted to discover I was unaware of Farrow's acting method. She said it had been extensively covered in the tabloids, so of course she was prepared to react accordingly. I don't know whether to be in awe of her, or very afraid."

"Both," Kate chirps. "We're lucky Harry is happy with her life in Oxford. If she woke up one morning and decided she wanted to be the Queen of England, I have no doubt we'd be drinking tea in Windsor Castle before the week was out."

Snorting with laughter, we wind up our conversation with a discussion on where we should go for our girls' night out while Mathilde is off on her dinner date with Trevor. Our plans settled, I say goodbye just as I arrive at my front door.

"Hi, honey, I'm home!" I call out, but no one answers. I drop my handbag and shoes near the door, wandering into the front room. A light shines through the doorway into the dining area, drawing me in for a look.

Edward and H sit side by side at the dining table, engrossed in a video playing on the tablet. Printed photos and loose sheets of paper full of scribbles cover the rest of the table.

I knock lightly on the wall, startling them both so much that H accidentally sets the tablet case on fire. While H attempts to stifle the flames, Edward swipes his hands across the table, pulling the papers into a messy pile.

I wait for them to return to a semblance of calm before asking, "What are you two watching?"

Edward mumbles something, garbling the words until it is impossible to understand him.

"What? I didn't catch that?"

"'Home Alone,' I said." Edward stares at me, daring me to make a comment. I open my mouth to crack a joke, but stop myself before speaking. It is the middle of the summer, so why would a grown man and a wyvern be watching a children's holiday movie? "Wait a minute, are you working on a plan to run off the neighbourhood cats? Are you getting ideas from the movie?"

H flies onto the tabletop, standing with his hands on his hips. "It's a man's right to defend his territory, Nat."

I choke back my laugh, knowing H won't appreciate it. I force my face into a serious expression. "Absolutely, H. You've been more than generous with those other cats, inviting them around and trying to make friends. Enough is enough." I slide my gaze over to H's partner in crime. "And you, Professor Edward Thomas? I'm surprised to see such a distinguished gentleman as yourself plotting a crime."

"Self-defence, Miss Payne, is not a crime."

I roll my eyes at the pair, quickly realising in this case, it will be easier to go along with it. At least with Edward involved, there is hope the plans won't involve setting the back fence on fire. Magical repairs or not, I don't want to have to explain a cat war to the local fire department.

I settle into a chair and reach for the stack of papers. "Can I see what you have planned so far? I've had plenty of experience with building things in my years of organising events. I might have something to add."

"Oh no," Edward stutters, pulling the stack against his chest. H furiously shakes his head, sending wafts of smoke across the table. "We're all set, Nat. Very well planned, nothing left to chance. Your offer is appreciated, but we'll take it from here."

I arch an eyebrow, wondering why the two men in my life are acting so strange, but my stomach grumbles and a wave of exhaustion hits before I can muster the energy to investigate further.

Hearing the rumbles coming from my side of the table, Edward leaps to his feet and offers to retrieve my plate from the warming oven. H lends a hand, and soon enough I've got a full meal and tall glass of cold water sitting in front of me.

Seeing the two men squirming in their seats, I send them off to entertain themselves. "I'm going to eat this food, have a hot shower, and then fall into bed. The garden is yours to defend. All I ask is that you keep it down to a dull roar."

"Done!" H shouts and then darts out of the dining room as fast as his wings will carry him.

With the men occupied in the garden, I turn the tablet in my direction and scroll through the video options until I see something of interest. A nature documentary on deadly predators seems oddly appropriate. I hit the play button and tune out the sounds of Edward and H huffing away in the garden while I enjoy my dinner.

Edward tromps through the room once, carrying a load of wooden scraps on his way back. I go to my zen place, forcing myself to ignore whatever is happening outside.

After I finish, I move onto the next step in my plan. Heated shouts and banging noises abound, overpowering the pitter patter of the shower head. The noise takes me back a few months, to the evening Edward and I attended a high table dinner at St Margaret. Who'd have thought that only a short time in the future, Edward and H would be working together, fighting against a common enemy... or that it would be a huddle of tabbies and marmalade cats living in our neighbourhood.

The setting sun casts a reddish light into my bedroom as I slip into my pyjamas. I open the window, letting the cool evening air into the room. Curiosity gets the better of me.

Leaning out of the window, I search the garden, finally spotting Edward and H hiding beside the garden shed. "Everything all right down there?"

"Ssshhhhh!" they reply in unison. H hovers above the ground, scanning the area for any intruders before flying up to greet me. "We got everything set up, Nat. You need to be quiet. We don't want to scare the tossers off from coming by, especially now that we 'ave our defences ready."

When I look confused, H explains, pointing around the garden. "See that bucket over there? Iffen those muggins leap onto the fence, it'll tumble over. That will pull the string you see and cause the water 'ose to turn on and spray everywhere. After that..."

I flap my hands, halting him there. "I think I'll sleep better if I don't know how many traps you've put out in the garden. If you're done, is Edward coming to bed soon?"

H flaps back, affronted by my question. "Goin' to bed? Not bloody likely, mate. We'll stay out 'ere all night iffen that's what it takes."

I shake my head, laughing to myself and wondering whether Edward knows the siege will go on for hours. "And on that note, I'm off to find my earplugs. Have fun defending the castle."

Still hovering in front of the window, H clicks his heels together and executes a perfect salute.

I fall asleep with a smile on my face.

Chapter Eight

I wake up, morning sunlight streaming in through windows. Edward's side of the bed is cold, the covers still neat and tidy.

"Did they actually stay out all night?" I ask the room, but no one answers. Avoiding the creaky step, I tiptoe downstairs and into the front room. The blinds have been drawn, leaving the room dark.

I spot Edward first. He's stretched across the sofa, his feet dangling over the edge, snoring away like a steam train. I check H's cat bed, but it is empty. Worried, I search the room, creeping across the wooden floor so I can see every corner. Finally, I spot a trickle of smoke trailing into the air. Little H has practically disappeared, his body rolled into a tight circle to allow him to fit between the sofa cushion and Edward's bent knees.

I think to myself that a loving partner would drape a blanket over their sleeping forms, but I immediately discard that idea for a better one. My handbag sits abandoned at the front door, exactly where I left it. A quick rummage through yields my mobile. I have to bite my lip to keep from giggling as I take a photo of the pair and post it in my group chat with Kate,

Mathilde, and Harry. The emojis I get in reply confirm I made the right choice.

Not wanting to disturb my valiant defenders, I decide to skip breakfast and go straight back to my bedroom to get ready. After a final glance to reconfirm they are still asleep, I slip out the front door and turn towards Somerset.

It is early enough that the roads are still quiet. A haze hangs over the city, obscuring any view of the crinoline towers of the colleges. It matches my mood. Although I got a goodnight's rest, I'm no closer to figuring out who could be the poisoner.

On the walk into the centre, I weigh my options on whom to interview next. Caleb is a top choice, but getting him alone and out of character won't be easy. There's also Joyce, a couple of the lighting techs, and Marcello to consider. Although the video footage has helped narrow the list of potential suspects, it is still longer than I'd like, particularly given I've got to fit interviews around my work and filming schedule. And what if it turns out to be a red herring? I'll have wasted so much time looking in the wrong direction. I need more information than what the camera captured.

Thinking about the footage triggers a thought in the back of my head. "The camera crew! Of course! Anything the camera caught, they may have seen as well. If they were moving around, potentially they had an even better view."

Donald is once again standing guard at the front entrance, his wide shoulders enough to make any intruder have second thoughts. We're on a first name basis by now, but he still checks my ID against the approved list before letting me inside.

"Any word on Vivian?" I ask as he scans the list of names.

He glances up and gives me a weak smile. "Still hanging in there, as far as I know. From what I heard through the grapevine, there isn't much the doctors can do except keep her comfortable.

Only time will tell whether she can fight off the effects of the poison."

His words cast a pall over our friendly banter, each of us, in our own way, feeling responsible for Vivian's desperate situation. The sad look in Donald's eyes compels me to reach across and lay a hand on his arm. "She'll recover, Donald. She just has to get better."

Donald gives me a grateful nod and then shakes off the doldrums as we hear another group of people coming up the front path. "You're all set, Nat. Go on in."

I beeline across the inner courtyard and through the arched stone walkway. On the far side, the back garden is still relatively quiet. Sam waves from the Craft Services trailer and holds up a coffee cup. The thought of coffee distracts me from my plan to go directly to the camera crew trailer. I justify the delay by deciding a jolt of caffeine will make me a better interrogator.

As Sam steams the milk, I eye the lavish display of fresh pastries and muffins. The sheer volume of options overwhelms me.

"Here you are, Nat. One extra hot latte. You're here early this morning."

"Thanks, Sam. I was hoping to catch the camera crew before they set up today's shoot. I'm desperate and also terribly nervous to see yesterday's takes so I find out how I did."

"You must have inherited that gene from your uncle. He also likes to start the day with a review of the prior day's footage. If I'm not mistaken, he's in their trailer now."

"Really?" I debate whether to wait until my uncle leaves, but decide having him there might be a help. "Have they had any breakfast yet?"

"No. Want me to plate up a selection of pastries for you to take in with you?"

"Yes, please," I say, pleased to not have to decide which item I want. "Put a few extras on there in case people want to have more than one."

Sam gives me a knowing look, not at all fooled by my attempt to cover up my desire to gorge myself on the fresh pastries. But he leaves the snarky remark unspoken, passing me a heaping plate, and sending me on my way.

It takes me a second of juggling to manage the coffee, plate, and the trailer door handle, but somehow, I manage. Indeed, my Uncle Harold is sitting dead centre in the room, the camera team spread on either side of him. The camera trailer is one of the smaller ones, and most of the space inside is taken up by displays and equipment storage bins. All eyes turn my way as I breeze inside, annoyance quickly turning to delight as the smells of fresh croissants fill the tight space.

"Why am I not surprised to see you here this early?" Harold asks, motioning for one of the men to pull up an extra chair. "And delivering breakfast as well. You remind me of your grandmother. She was always feeding everyone."

I give my uncle a wink. "If I promise not to tell Dominic you cheated on your diet, will you let me watch yesterday's takes in exchange for a pain au chocolat?"

He pretends to mull over my question, but we both know he is a sucker for the flaky, gooey pastries. "Andy, pull up the clips!"

Before long, the trailer is filled with lively banter, as the camera crew pokes fun at my failed acting attempts. Thank goodness I have no dreams of achieving fame on the big screen, because most of my takes range from mediocre to downright horrendous. One of them is so hilarious, I make Andy edit it into a meme for me so I can send it to my friends.

When the laughter dies down, Harold gets serious. "Now that you've seen what has been left on the cutting room floor, do you want to see the end result?"

I cross, uncross, and recross my legs, so nervous I can barely nod.

Andy closes the outtakes folder and navigates to a different part of the screen. A couple of clicks later, the video player opens, starting with a close-up of Caleb and Gideon, puffing on pipes in their roles as Wren and Wilkins. The scene unfolds, the camera gradually sliding back to allow a wider view of the screen. A knock sounds at the door and Wilkins calls out a command to enter. It's a servant woman, with a dusty bucket and rag in hand. Wilkins waves her into the room, with an order to be quick about her work.

I can't take my eyes off the servant, even though I know it is me. On screen, I move silently around the room, the men immediately forgetting about my presence as they return to their discussions. I can hear Molly's voice in my head as I watch myself dust the shelf and straighten the books before moving to the table in between the men. Wren is the one who makes the request for a drink. Moments later, I reappear, keeping my gaze low as I deposit the tray on the table and back out of the room, dismissed.

"If I didn't recognise myself, I would swear you replaced me with a real actor. How did you manage it? It must be the magic of the editing room. You can tell me the truth; I won't be offended."

Harold chuckles. "Your early takes were terrible, as you've seen for yourself. But after Gideon asked for the ten-minute break, things improved dramatically. I think part of the problem was in the scripting. The instructions to cross the room were too abrupt, and you kept distracting the viewers from the focus of the scene. What made you decide to add in those extra touches — dusting and straightening the shelves and that sort of thing?"

I shrug, taking my time before answering and coming as close to the truth as I dare. "I don't know what happened. Maybe I channelled the original laundress or something."

My uncle searches my face, somehow sensing that I'm hiding

something from him. He knows me too well. I make extra sure to keep my expression completely neutral. Eventually, he huffs, "Well, whatever you did, do it again, but ideally sooner, okay?"

"Ha! Will do, Uncle Harold." I help myself to another croissant, making it clear I'm not quite ready to go yet. "Speaking of yesterday's shoot, I noticed Gideon and Caleb exchanging harsh whispers. Do Wilkins and Wren have a falling out planned in the script, or has Gideon finally had enough of Caleb's method acting?"

My uncle gives me a strange look, wondering where I'm going with this discussion. I wag my eyebrows at him, silently communicating for him to play along. I expect my uncle to reply, to keep the conversation going, but it is Andy on the camera crew who pipes up instead.

"I agree there is something going on between those two, but I don't think Caleb's annoying behaviour is causing it."

Sabrina, the camera woman sitting beside Andy, throws her hands in the air, grumbling, "Not again with your conspiracy theories, Andy." I narrow my gaze, glaring at the woman into being quiet.

I twist my chair, turning until I'm looking straight at Andy. He gulps as I lean forward, subtly inviting him to confide in me. "Tell me what you think is going on, Andy."

Andy rubs the back of his neck and shifts in his chair, glancing at my uncle for approval before responding. "Back me up here, mates. When we started blocking scenes early in the production, Caleb and Gideon got along just fine. In between takes, they were always running lines and walking through their movements, remember?"

Sabrina rolls her eyes, but doesn't contradict him.

Empowered by Sabrina's silence, Andy sits up straighter in his chair. "Gideon would grumble about Caleb, but it was always a good-natured complaint. He'd never admit it, but I think Gideon actually appreciated how reliable Caleb was. Haven't you all noticed that Caleb never flubs a line? His method might seem unorthodox, but it clearly works for him."

"That's true," Uncle Harold adds, giving Andy another boost of confidence. "I knew all about Caleb's preferred way of working before we cast him. He throws himself into his roles and the end results speak for themselves."

"Okay, so things started off fine, but presumably changed at some point." I shift my focus to Andy. "I guess this is where your theory comes in?"

"Shortly after Vivian joined the cast, their dynamics changed. I noticed it in Gideon first. I was getting the camera ready for filming, adjusting the lens and that sort of thing. I happened to zoom in where Gideon was standing. He was staring at Vivian and Caleb, with his jaw clenched so hard you could see it tick. I elbowed Sabrina, to show her, but by the time she glanced over, his expression was back to one of casual indifference."

Sabrina throws her hands in the air. "I'm sorry, Andy, but I think you are seeing things. I've watched Gideon enough. We all have. I've seen plenty of signs of his annoyance with Caleb, but outright hate?" She shakes her head and flattens her lips.

Sensing a potential dispute, Harold steps in and points out the time, reminding us we need to get back to work if we want to make call time. As I gather up the plate and dirty napkins, my mind is spinning. Sabrina may think Andy is imagining things, but I believe him. The interaction I saw between the two actors yesterday did not look like a case of simple annoyance. Nor do I think Gideon would waste his breath trying to convince Caleb to abandon his approach to acting.

I'd been thinking about speaking with Joyce next, but Gideon Pomerance just moved to the top of my list.

❖

I wonder if fate has a different plan in mind when Joyce flags me down as soon as I exit the camera crew's trailer.

"There you are! I've been looking everywhere for you." Joyce sprints up beside me, thrusting a bunch of papers at me so she can massage a stitch in her side. She swipes her long fringe out of her face and explains, "I've got your next batch of scenes from the writing team. They thought you might appreciate having a full day to practise before shooting begins."

"Wow, twenty-four whole hours! Yes, please." I resist the urge to flip through the pack, instead rolling them up and shoving them into my handbag. "Thanks for going to such an effort to find me."

"No worries, it's literally my job." She straightens up, breathing normally again, and pulls her phone from her pocket to check her next task.

"You don't happen to know the filming schedule for today?"

"Yes, I do," she replies, opening another app on her phone. "Let me see... Gideon is up first this morning, filming his solo scenes. We've got an hour break for lunch and the afternoon is marked off for Caleb's solos and finally more B-roll shots."

"Perfect!" I say something else, but Joyce looks up from her phone with a grimace and makes her apologies for having to dash off.

I check my phone, but there's no word yet from Edward. He and H must still be recuperating from their nighttime antics. My calendar is empty until early afternoon, when I'm due to regroup with Will and Jill to see how they are getting on with their event plans. I wing off a quick message to Edward, telling him I expect a full report when he comes to pick me up for lunch.

With Gideon tied up in filming, only one thing remains to be done: my scenes. After grabbing a coffee refill from Sam, I settle at one of the picnic tables and unfurl the roll of papers.

The sight of the thick stack of papers makes my throat go tight, but I soon realise it isn't as bad as it seems. Most of the text is the dialogue. I fish a pack of hi-lighters from my handbag, using the bright colours to break out my actions from those of everyone else. Skimming over the colour-coded lines, I soon grow bored. The actions are bland and obvious. 'Carry a basket of laundry' or 'Hang clothing on the line'. Even though I'm nothing more than an insignificant extra in the film, Molly the Laundress deserves better.

A spark flickers, turning to a full-on fire in my belly. This simply won't do and there is only one way to solve it. I crumple my empty takeaway cup and toss it into the bin, striding off to track down the woman herself.

I find her in her vegetable garden, sitting on her knees with her hands in the dirt, mumbling under her breath words of encouragement for her tiny green sprouts, newly shooting from the ground.

"Morning, Molly. I can see you're busy with some very important tasks, but I wonder if you might spare an hour or two for me."

Molly leans back on her heels, squinting her eyes against the summer sun. "I've been talking to these plants for generations, so I suppose they can survive for a day without me babying to them. What do you need?"

I size up the shady bench, but the call to absorb some vitamin D is too strong. Instead, I stake out a small patch of grass nearby, stretching my legs out. "Tell me what you did when you were the laundress. Alive, that is," I clarify.

Molly tilts her head, wondering where I'm going with my question. "I gathered up the linens and washed and dried them.

Sometimes I'd tidy up after the men and boys. On special occasions, I helped out in the kitchen."

I swat her words away. "That sounds like a Wikipedia entry, Molly. One written by a man, I might add." I cock my head and then shake it. "You don't become an Eternal by washing someone's trousers. You were the only woman living in the college. You must have had an incredible influence over the young men studying under Wilkins' tutorage. Don't boil your existence down to a few throwaway lines, Molly. Tell me what you really did here."

Molly's gaze drops to her lap as she slides sideways, balancing on her hip, her hands flat on the ground. For a moment, I'm sure I crossed an invisible line by pushing her too hard.

When she finally raises her head to look at me, her eyes are bright with unshed tears. "Do you know, Nat, that no one - living, Eternal or Prefect - has ever asked me that question?"

I don't dare move my eyes from hers as I pull a pen and the stack of script papers from my bags. She watches as I flip the packet over and uncap my pen. "Well then, it is long past time that someone did."

It takes a few halting starts, but soon enough Molly opens up to me, unleashing a torrent of information. She tells me stories of the times she played mother to the boys sent to Oxford to study. As the only woman, they expected her to bandage wounds and dry tears besides reminding them to pick up their clothing. Wilkins may have been in charge, but Molly's backbone of steel often made her the winner of their arguments. Her stories bring the pages of history to life, taking the flat characters and rounding them into real people, flaws and all.

I cover page after page with notes, automatically organising the information into sections so I can more easily study it later. The shadows, which stretched long before me when I first sat, creep closer and closer until they disappear. They signal the arrival of midday as efficiently as any clock.

When I finally put the cap back on my pen, massaging my wrist, Molly sits serenely in a puddle of sunshine. She brushes off my thanks and sends me on my way, content to remain alone, drifting in a pool of fond memories.

I arrive at the front entrance, apologies tumbling from my lips. "Edward, I'm so sorry I'm late. I was deep in the zone and didn't even hear my mobile buzz."

"No need to worry," he says reassuringly as he steps to the side to reveal Jill and Will standing with him. "I ran into your star assistants and they were updating me on the plans for the cast party."

I pause, dusting off my skirt and tidying my hair. "Hiya! What are you two doing here so early? Our meeting isn't until after lunch."

"We wanted to chat some ideas through with the crew and we thought it might be easiest to catch them over lunch break," Jill explains, exchanging looks with Will.

I lower my head and study the two. "And I suppose the buffet at the Craft Services trailer has nothing to do with it, right?"

"Definitely not," Will cuts in, but his cheeky smile confirms my suspicions.

Try as I might, I can't stop the snort from slipping out. "Since the two of you are working on a Sunday, I think the least the production can do is feed you a free meal. I heard something about a full roast dinner, including Yorkshire puddings."

"Well, since you insist," Jill shrugs, "I guess I could eat a little something."

"Excellent! I'll be back in time for dessert," I promise. "We can enjoy fresh strawberries and cream while we discuss how the plans are coming along."

After the pair takes their leave, Edward slips his hand around mine, tugging me out of the door. "Don't worry, Nat. From what I heard, it sounds like Will and Jill are organising an event you won't soon forget."

❖

My meeting with Will and Jill after lunch wraps up sooner than I expect, leaving me absolutely delighted with their work. The pair have fully embraced the challenge of organising a high-profile event on their own, and it shows. When I run out of questions, the two beg my leave, wanting to chat about the event with a couple more crew members before they call it a day.

Left alone in the college meeting room, I decide to take advantage of the quiet and catch up on my emails. I sort, file, reply and delete as needed until my inbox is cleared in advance of the coming week. I wrap up with a quick glance at the coming week's activities.

That's when it dawns on me just how quiet Beadle and Hobbes have been. After a flurry of initial activity, there's been no sign of them since we arrived at Somerset. We tightened our lines of security, but maybe we did the job too well. If we want to catch them stealing or damaging the priceless portraits and antiques, they will need a way inside.

I double-click the calendar, adding a reminder to discuss the matter with Kate. As the prefect responsible for the safety of those items, she will have to be on board with any plan which might put them at risk.

My work life once again in order, I close my laptop and leave my quiet space. I open the door in time to see a group of people ambling by, the voices cheery as they chatter away. Joyce lags, lost in thought, but quickly returns to the present when I call her name.

"Oh, hi, Nat. I didn't see you there. Where've you been all day? I've barely seen you."

"Here and there," I chirp as I fall into step beside her. "I spent the morning reviewing the scripts you gave me, skipped out for lunch, and then caught up with Will and Jill."

"I had lunch with them," she comments in reply. "They are both so lovely. They crack me up, always finishing one another's sentences."

"That's them. They're really excited about the wrap party. I appreciate you and the others making time to answer their questions."

"Happy to do so... speaking of making time. DCI Robinson was here earlier and was asking about you."

I startle, looking at her askance as I wonder whether he has any news on his investigation. "Do I need to ring him? Did he say what he wants?"

"Something about Mathilde? I don't think it was anything serious. He was smiling when he asked if I knew where you were."

I sigh. "Probably something for his date with Mathilde tomorrow night. I was hoping he might have an update on Vivian."

Joyce shrugs her shoulders and gives me a wan smile. "Viv is still touch and go, from what I've heard. You might ask Caleb, though it isn't easy to get a straight answer from him."

Caleb? He would not have been my first choice for information on her, for a number of reasons. "Why Caleb? Are they friends?"

Joyce halts her step, letting the rest of the group pull even further ahead. "I don't normally gossip, Nat, but since you're Harold's niece, I know I can trust you not to take this information to the tabloids. I'm fairly certain that Caleb and Vivian are more than friends, if you know what I mean."

I rear back in shock. "But Caleb has a long-term girlfriend!"

Joyce shakes her head, looking as disappointed as I am. "You know what these showbiz types are like. The moral standards apply to everyone but them. I wouldn't put it past either of them. Caleb will probably say it was all part of his method acting, and Vivian, well, she is known for doing whatever it takes to get ahead."

Joyce and I go our separate ways when we reach the courtyard and this time, I'm the one deep in thought. Could this be the reason Gideon was so angry with Caleb? But why would he care about what the other actors were doing, if it didn't impact the production?

There's only one way to find out.

I march past the picnic area and crew trailers, looking for the right one. Gideon's trailer is the last one in a long row. The door is propped open, allowing the fresh air to circulate inside.

"Knock, knock. Anyone home?" I peer into the doorway to see Gideon's head pop out on the other side of the small kitchenette. He spies me, rising to welcome me inside.

"Come in, Nat. How lovely to see you." He leads me to a small circular table, and I slide into the far side of the curved bench seat. Loose newspaper pages are strewn around the table, with a half-filled water glass sweating a perfect circle onto one of them.

"I hope I didn't interrupt anything," I murmur.

"Not at all! I was taking advantage of the afternoon break to relax. I have a thing for crossword puzzles. My assistant bought copies of the major papers and I've been off in my own world of mystery solving. What brings you here?"

"I'm following up on some clues myself, if I'm honest."

Gideon takes his reading glasses off, pushes his salt and pepper hair back, and then leans back with his hands behind his head. "Really... and you've come to see me? I'm intrigued. Do tell."

I think for a moment before deciding where to start. "It's my Uncle Harold. He's a bit of a wreck, worrying himself about the production. Although he's kept it to himself, the pranks had him concerned. He'd asked me to keep my eyes open when you all came to Oxford. I've had some experience with catching criminals recently, and he thought, as an outsider, I might spot something the rest of the security team was overlooking."

Gideon gives me an assessing look. "A well-known event planner and an amateur sleuth? You're a woman of many talents."

I bark out a laugh. "Emphasis on amateur, I assure you." I wait until his chuckles subside before returning to the subject. "When I arrived on set yesterday, I couldn't help but notice you and Caleb talking to one another. It seemed heated. Is everything okay between you two?"

Gideon's face tightens as he shifts from his relaxed pose, bringing his hands down to cross them over his chest. He gives a pained sigh, his mouth tilting downwards at the corners. "Farrow," he practically spits the name. "He and I are not on the best of terms, but we're both professional enough to keep our problems off the screen."

Gideon's expression is stony, closed off enough that a normal person would probably get up at this point and make an abrupt departure. But after everything I've been through since arriving in Oxford last October, a grumpy movie star is the least of my worries.

I lay my clasped hands on the table and hunch over them, making it clear I'm not going anywhere just yet. "I'm not the only one who noticed your dislike of Caleb. From what I hear, the problems started when Vivian arrived on set. Now she's lying in a hospital bed, and you want me to believe that all is fine with you and Caleb?"

Gideon matches my stare, hardly moving. His shoulders are tight with pent-up emotion. There is clearly something more to his arguments with Caleb.

"I'm not looking for gossip, Gideon. Whatever you tell me, I'll keep private. I promise."

Gideon turns his head to the window, staring blindly while he fights an internal battle. When his shoulders drop, I know he's ready to tell me the truth.

"This goes no further than you and Harold, okay? Do you understand?"

I nod.

"We don't make a big deal out of it, but Vivian is practically my goddaughter. I knew her father well... he was a cameraman; did you know that?"

I shake my head this time, confused by his words.

"I watched her grow up, and I helped her get her foot in the door at the BBC when she decided she wanted to be an actress. Her father refused to help her, you see. He didn't want his daughter entering the harsh world of movies and television. He'd spent too many years watching the industry chew up and spit back out aspiring actors."

"So, she came to you for help? Is that what happened with this show? Did you recommend her?"

"Oh no, that was all Caleb," Gideon shudders. "I told you before I had heard rumours of Caleb's tendency to fully embody his characters. What I didn't add is that he sometimes takes it beyond the set and into the bedroom. Says it makes the love scenes that much more realistic."

I wrinkle my nose at the thought. "Gross, but what? You thought he'd pressure Vivian into doing something she didn't want to do?"

"Normally? No," he replies, sighing, "but her father passed away suddenly last year. His death hit her hard, made her more determined than ever to break through into Hollywood. She won't admit it, but I think she is still trying to prove her father wrong. She accused him of wanting to hold her back, but all he wanted was to protect her. With him gone, I'm doing my best to shoulder the responsibility of watching over her. Farrow's next role is to play superhero in a big budget production. I was worried she'd fall prey to him in the hopes he'd take her along to Hollywood."

I settle back into my seat, tapping my chin as I process my thoughts. "How far would you go to protect Vivian? Did you start with smaller pranks, hoping to discourage her from the role? When that didn't work, you had to go bigger. Maybe you didn't mean for her to get as sick as she did?"

"What?" Gideon stares at me, his eyes wide in disbelief. "No, of course not! I would never, ever do anything to hurt Vivian. I saw how badly things went with her father and I wasn't about to make the same mistake. I didn't breathe a word of my concerns to her..."

"But you did speak to Caleb." I finish his sentence.

Gideon wipes his hand over his mouth, his face flushed. "At first, he laughed at me. Dismissed it completely. But I'd catch him chatting her up in between takes. When I overheard him invite Vivian back to his place, I confronted him. Caleb called me an old man, told me to mind my own business. Said if anything happened, it would be between two consenting adults, and nothing to do with me."

"Did anything happen?"

Gideon grows quiet, but his fists are clenched in his lap. "I don't know. There was only so much I could do. I couldn't ask her outright, and Caleb refused to speak on the subject. There was no one else to ask without arousing suspicion. And that was the last thing I wanted to do."

I gulp, feeling terrible for Gideon and his predicament. "Do you think he poisoned her? If he propositioned her and she refused, maybe he wanted her out of the way so he could find a new actress to take on her role."

Gideon remains silent, lost in a quagmire of what-ifs.

I check my watch, dismayed to see how much time has passed. I slide out of the booth and stop beside the table, tapping on its wooden surface to get his attention. "If Caleb is responsible, I promise you, I will make sure he doesn't get away with it."

Chapter Nine

After a brief reprieve, the next day heralds my return in front of the camera. Molly's insights have made a transformational difference to how I play my role, at least according to Uncle Harold — that's the upside. The downside to my improved acting abilities is that he had also added in more scenes, including some B-roll of me alone.

Throughout the day's shoot, Molly and H stick close to my side, calling out suggestions and coaching me when I stumble through an action.

"Do that thing again... where you shoo the cat out of the room, Nat. That was brilliant!" Harold cries from his director's chair.

H smirks as he swishes his spiky tail in the air, not realising he is waving a red flag in front of the bull. I don't have to pretend annoyance when I grab the old-fashioned twig broom and threaten to launch him out into the garden. Molly cackles, invisible to everyone except me and H, safe from any risk of being roped into the action.

If that isn't bad enough, my filming breaks prove even more frustrating. Caleb Farrow is completely incommunicado, and his alter-ego of Sir Christopher crumbles into tears anytime I attempt to bring up Vivian's name. "My beautiful fiancée," he moans, sniffling into a handkerchief.

The problem with interviewing talented actors is I genuinely cannot tell whether Caleb is truly broken up over the mere mention of Vivian's name, or is simply acting the way he believes Sir Christopher would in the same circumstances.

Either way, after two failed attempts to corner him on the set, he actively avoids me for the rest of the day. When Uncle Harold announces our dismissal late in the afternoon, I practically sprint to the wardrobe to rip off my heavy costume in favour of the sundress I stashed away this morning. The hangers screech as I shove costumes aside, searching frantically for the floral pattern of my dress. It is nowhere to be found.

"Has the production bandit struck again, this time targeting me?" I mutter to myself before raising my voice to ask, "Ilaria, have you seen the sundress I left in here this morning?"

"*Sì*! I spotted it hidden away amidst my costumes this morning." She circles around the clothing rack, frowning at me. "It simply wouldn't do, Nat. The fabric was cut against the bias and the seam bunched near the hem. I practically broke out in hives when I saw it."

I shake my head and blink several times, too dumbfounded to offer a response.

"But don't worry, *cara*. I fixed it for you. Wait there, I'll bring it around." She flutters off, her hands in constant motion as she lists off the improvements she's made. Like a whirlwind, she swoops back seconds later with a garment bag draped over one arm.

"But... but it was my favourite," I moan, still coming to grips with the fact that this woman kidnapped and disassembled my dress, without asking.

"It *was* your favourite," Ilaria agrees, "but trust me, it won't hold a candle to my new and improved version. See for yourself!" With a wink, she passes me the bag and pushes me into a changing room.

Too nervous, I keep my back to the mirror as I pull the dress over my head and smooth it down.

"Come out, *cara*. Let me see how it looks on you now."

I gingerly open the door and shuffle into the centre of the room. Ilaria takes a deep breath and then shrieks in delight. "I am a genius, no? Open your eyes, Nat, and look at yourself."

I peek out of one eye and then open the other. Gone is my empire-waist maxi dress with the spaghetti straps. I inch closer to the mirror, starting at the bottom and clocking all the changes. The dress no longer swishes around my ankle, instead hitting me just below the knee in a ruffle of matching fabric. The skirt tapers at my waist, switching to alternating stripes of sheer midnight blue and brightly coloured floral, wrapping around my mid-section until just below my chest. There the original fabric remains, but now it is cut in a heart-shaped halter. The peekaboo stripes and flattering neckline provide a tantalising hint of sexiness while still somehow staying workplace appropriate.

"I take it back. This is my favourite dress. Ever. In my whole life." I twirl around, watching the ruffle flare in my reflection.

"*Brava, cara! Brava!*" Ilaria reties the halter, letting the straps fall artfully down my back. "Let me tell you what was wrong with the original version, so you will never make that same mistake again."

My day and my outfit rescued by Ilaria's wizardry, I leave the wardrobe trailer floating on cloud nine. Outside in the garden, I answer my ringing mobile with a breathy hello.

Kate's voice greets me. "Hiya Nat, you sound out of breath. Have you just finished shooting? I guess you will want to go home and change before we meet for drinks. Shall we say 7pm, at the restaurant bar?"

I glance down at my feet, encased in gold leather gladiator sandals on loan from the Costume department. "No need to wait. I'm ready now. I was thinking, maybe we should go by Mathilde's flat. Make sure she's not feeling too nervous before her big date. What do you think?"

"Ooh, that is a good idea. I'll meet you there."

I swallow back a laugh when Kate's taxi pulls up in front of Mathilde's house, seconds ahead of me. "I knew I should have walked here," she huffs when she sees me standing beside her car door. "I forget how terrible traffic can be leaving the centre. I was stuck at the big roundabout at The Plain for ages."

We ring the bell and beam at Mathilde when she opens the door. "What on Earth?"

"Hi there! We thought you might be nervous about your big date, so we came over to provide moral support," I explain as I push past her, striding confidently inside.

"Is that what you're planning to wear?" Kate asks after she kisses Mathilde's cheeks in hello. "Speaking of clothing... Nat, that dress is fabulous. Where did you get it?"

To give Mathilde her due, she accepts our interruption without complaint, but can't stop herself from rolling her eyes at us as she leads us to her room. After I model my new dress, I plump up the pillows and perch on the bed. Kate claims the desk chair and both of us turn to Mathilde.

"Got any other new clothes hiding away?" Kate asks, tilting sideways as she attempts to peer around Mathilde. "Show us everything you've got. We'll help you choose."

Mathilde remains firm, crossing her arms and tapping her toe. "Are you two here to help, or is this a spy mission to see what else I bought during my makeover shopping spree?"

"The second one," I admit with a broad wink. Mathilde throws her hands in the air but does as she's told.

As Mathilde spreads options on the foot of the bed, Kate scrutinises her. "Where is Trevor taking you tonight?"

"I'm meeting Trevor for drinks at The Varsity and then I assume we'll go somewhere else for dinner." Mathilde replies as she gamely tries on a few options with us quickly vetoing them.

I clear my throat as she straightens a shirt on a hanger. "Are you going to drop any other hints about the existence of the magic?"

Mathilde frowns, but doesn't reply until she finishes pulling a new shirt over her head. "I don't know, Nat. I feel as though I should, but I don't want to risk ruining our first date. Would it be wrong of me to ignore the topic all together?"

Kate steps in smoothly before I can respond. "Not at all, Mathilde. First dates are stressful enough on their own. Set all our current worries aside for an evening, and just enjoy yourself. You deserve a night of fun."

"We all do!" I chime in, making everyone laugh. "While you're off on your big date, Kate and I are going to retreat to the Head of the River pub for a dinner of our own and bask in the warmth of the summer evening."

"Head of the River pub?" Mathilde pauses, hairbrush in hand. "I love that place. They have the best fish and chips platter."

I lift a single eyebrow and cock my head, meeting Mathilde's gaze in the mirror. "You could always skip your date and come with us..."

"Ha! No thanks, I'll stick to my original plans." Mathilde spins around and sends a hairband flying in my direction. "Go off and have your girls' night. If you two stay here and keep up this act for much longer, you are going to make me late. Go!"

"Fine, fine. We're going," I fake grumble as I rise to my feet. "But you better text us the very moment you get home and tell us everything."

"Everything," Kate echoes. Mathilde picks up an abandoned

shoe and threatens to launch it at us, sending us scurrying out of her room and down the stairs to the front door.

"Bye, Mathilde. Have fun on your date," I shout up. "Ring us if you need anything!"

"Don't wait for my call," Mathilde replies cheekily.

Laughing, Kate and I stroll along the pavement, making our way to the pub for a much-needed evening of relaxation.

The restaurant hostess leads us to a picnic table in the garden and hands us a stack of menus, daily specials, and wine lists. Overlooking the River Thames, every table in the garden is taken. The gentle lapping of the water melds with the hum of conversation, creating a relaxing soundtrack for our evening meal.

Kate flips through the menu, her sleek, dark hair reflecting the deep red tones of the evening sun. "Shall we start with a pitcher of Pimm's and some appetisers? I'm not in any rush."

"Sounds good to me. Now that I've finished filming my scenes, I feel like a small celebration is in order."

We flag down a passing waiter and place our order, sighing with relief when he returns moments later with two icy glasses and a tall pitcher, fresh fruit floating atop the amber liquid. As the first sip goes down, I'm reminded why this is practically the English drink of choice for a hot summer's day. It is at once both refreshing and soothing, with only a hint of the spicy gin at its core.

"Tell me about the house," Kate orders, as we nibble on a bowl of crisps. "Are you nearly done with the remodel?"

"We're getting there, but every time I think we're close to being done, there is another decision to be made or another construction delay." I take another sip of Pimm's to settle myself. "On the positive side, my Uncle Harold's partner Dominic has offered to help with the interior design. You haven't met him yet, but I'm positive you two would be thick as thieves together. His eye for art is legendary."

"Really?" Kate drawls. "Then you absolutely must arrange for an intro. I've been wanting to change a few things at my place; perhaps he could help. If I wait until I have free time, I'll never get around to it."

"Speaking of free time, I haven't heard you mention anything about a summer holiday plan. Are you going to get away at all?"

Kate gives me a long look over the rim of her glass, her eyes heavy with emotion. It almost looks like sadness. I freeze in place, replaying my last words in my head, wondering what I said wrong.

"I wanted to go away, someplace warm and exotic like the Maldives or Malta."

"But?" I ask, prodding her to explain.

"I'd have to go without Bartie."

Her words hang in the air.

"Oh god, Kate. I'm sorry. I didn't think... of course he can't leave."

Kate's head snaps up. "He can leave."

I rock back on the bench, catching myself before I tumble off. "What do you mean he can leave? I thought the Eternals were bound to remain within the borders of the magic. If he can travel, why can't he go with you?"

"It doesn't work like that, Nat," Kate says, shaking her head in dismay. "Oxford is the only place where the magical world and our world align. For the rest of it, I guess the easiest way to explain it is to imagine two concentric circles that overlap at a single point — here in Oxford. Bartie can go to his Malta, but he can't come to mine."

"Wait. So, are you saying that the Eternals have their own little universe, for lack of a better term? But if that is the case, then why could Edward and I take H with us to London?"

Kate shrugs. "You know as well as I do the creatures are different from the ghostly Eternals like Bartie. Their spirits are anchored to live animals, which allows them to eat and move around, but also get tired and need to rest. They didn't live and die and therefore don't have the same connection to the Eternal realm."

I stare at Kate, my mind spinning. "Wow. I mean, I never... but wow. And also, that sucks, Kate. I'm so sorry that your relationship with Bartie has these constraints. It hardly seems fair."

Kate gives me a wan smile. "Don't pity us too much, Nat. We've found one another, which is no mean feat. Who cares about the beach, anyway? All that sand gets stuck in everything."

"Oh, definitely," I agree. "Sand is the worst."

Having run out of words, we both sit in silence. I use the moment to top up our drinks and call the waiter over to take our dinner orders. Kate takes a fortifying sip of her Pimm's cup, forcing the melancholic thoughts from her mind.

"Let's talk about something nicer. How about you and Edward? When is his big move into the house scheduled?"

I feel a smile bloom. "August. We're hoping to get away for a few weeks in July, after the production wraps up. He wants to be completely out of boxes and living comfortably before term starts in October."

"That's quite a whirlwind romance you two have had, Nat," Kate cracks. "From enemies to friends to partners-in-crime-fighting, and soon, official housemates. What's next? Marriage?"

She laughs at her own joke, but I choke on my drink.

"Oh no, what did I say?" Kate says as she passes me napkins and fans my flushed face. "Marriage? Are you getting married?"

I finally stop coughing long enough to get a word out. "Goodness no, not as far as I know. Not that I'm opposed to the idea. But it would be really too soon, right? There's no need to rush; we've got plenty of time and no pressure and now we've got the house." I force my mouth closed, feeling a blush creep up my neck. "I'm babbling, aren't I?"

Kate snorts, "Completely babbling, but in the most lovely, endearing way. And you are right. There is no rush, and besides, if you are living together, will a piece of paper really change anything?"

"No," I shake my head, but inside, can't help but wonder if I'm telling the truth.

Our food arrives, its steaming heat sending wafts of delicious smells all around us. By the time the waiter finishes laying out the dishes and cutlery, topping up drinks and asking if we need anything else, the conversation moves on.

Something tells me, though, I'll be mulling over Kate's question later. If marriage is what I want, I don't have to sit back and wait for it to happen. But first, we've got a house is finish remodelling, Edward has to move in, and life must settle down to something approaching normal. Once all of that is in place, I'll think about what I want next.

Over dessert, I remember the other topic I wanted to discuss with Kate — Mathilde, her future love interests, and the secret of the existence of Oxford's magic. While thinking about how to phrase the question, I scrape my bowl, getting every hint of cream remaining from the Eton Mess I ordered, and plop it into my mouth.

"Do you want me to look the other way so you can lick the bowl clean?" Kate asks sarcastically.

I wink at her as I threaten to make one more pass with my spoon, earning a snicker in response. Setting the empty bowl aside, I swap my relaxed grin for a more serious expression.

"There was one more thing I wanted to mention about Mathilde, something Edward pointed out to me, if you can believe it."

"Edward?" Kate scrunches her forehead, completely stumped.

"We were chatting about Mathilde and Trevor's date. Unsurprisingly, Edward used it as an opportunity to bring up again the question of telling Trevor about the magic of Oxford."

Kate shifts sideways, propping her chin up with her hand. "Have you changed your mind about telling him?"

"No, not at all. However, Edward made the point that someday, whenever Mathilde finds the person she wants to commit to, we may face the same question. Every prefect generation before us kept the magic a secret from their partner. But then you found love with an Eternal, and I stumbled upon another descendant..."

"And Mathilde is left out." Kate finishes. "Hmm, I hadn't thought about this at all. And you say Edward was the one to bring it up?"

"He said he knew all too well what it was like being the odd one out. Even if he and I weren't in a relationship yet, he was around us enough to know that something weird was there." I tap my fingers on the table, still considering the question. "History dictates that Mathilde should keep quiet, but it's hardly fair to hamstring her relationship if she picks someone outside of our inner circle."

"Have you talked to Mathilde about this?"

"No, I wanted to discuss it with you first." When Kate looks at me askance, I hasten to add, "Not because I want to stand in her way... far from it. But if you disagree, or if you see a problem I'm missing, I didn't want us to end up arguing about it in front of her."

Kate sits upright and places her hand back on the table. She looks me in the eye and smiles. "What is it they say about love, Nat? Something about when you find it, you want everyone around you to experience the same? That's how I feel about Mathilde. There is nothing I would say or do to stand in the way of Mathilde making a full and honest commitment to her special person. Whoever he or she might be."

I open my mouth to add my agreement, but a nasally male voice intrudes before I can.

"Hear, hear, Kate. Mighty generous of you. Too bad you don't feel the same about everyone else."

Kate rears back in shock as a middle-aged man drags a chair over and plonks himself down at the end of our picnic table, uninvited. I squint my eyes in confusion, but soon enough, the light bulb goes on. The paunch, the sallow complexion and the thinning dark hair are all things I've seen before, in a photo on the wall of the Torture Museum.

"Beadle," Kate seethes, forcing the words from between her teeth. "What are you doing in Oxford?"

"What are you doing in Oxford?" he mocks her, repeating her words in a falsetto. He sits back comfortably in his chair, his mouth turned up in a sneer. He ignores me as though I wasn't even there. His attention is laser-focused on Kate. "Do you have any idea what it is like to work for something your whole life and then have it ripped away from you at the last minute? The Directorship should have been mine! It was mine. Everyone knew it!"

He clenches his hand into a fist, his face florid with anger. "I had bled my heart and soul into the Ashmolean. And then you swan in at the last moment and have the hiring board eating out of your hand."

"Swanned in?" Kate squeaks, livid.

Oswald Beadle cuts her off, refusing to give Kate an inch. "Everyone expected me to bow to the decision. I spent years earning their respect, and instead, I end up getting nothing but looks of pity. *Poor Oswald, passed over for promotion,*" he mimics in a high-pitched voice. "The only reason I stayed was to make sure you failed. I wanted the hiring board and everyone else at the museum to see you, the new golden girl, flop spectacularly. And instead, you tossed me out to the kerb like a piece of rubbish."

I watch as Beadle's words crash onto the table. Kate's eyes practically glow red. I reach over and lay a hand on her arm, reminding her we're in public.

Beadle huffs, "As I was being escorted from the building, without even the chance to gather my things, my mind was spinning. How could you possibly get rid of me?" He raises a hand and points a finger in Kate's face. "You should have been bowing down and thanking me for showing you how to do your job."

He lowers his hand, his sneer growing into an evil grin. "And then I found out your secret. You didn't deserve the job. You weren't more competent. It was magic. Bloody magic. Your only advantage over me was winning the genetic lottery."

Kate glares daggers. "That is not my only advantage, I assure you. You were too egotistical to realise the truth, Oswald. You were never going to get the Directorship. But tell me, how did you find out about the magic of Oxford?"

He smirks, ignoring Kate's insult. He is only too happy to tell us about his discovery. "I came back to the museum after hours. All I wanted was to take what was rightfully mine and to make you pay for what you had done to me." His tone rises in anger as he says, "Pay for the shame of being frogmarched out of the building! I crept into your office, dug through your drawer. I found the old key to the cabinet. When I stuck it into the cabinet lock, I felt the bolt of lightning all the way up my arm."

Kate stares him down, refusing to show any further hint of emotion. "Yes, we guessed as much. And so you discovered Oxford's secret."

His eyes glitter, making me realise how much Beadle is enjoying this moment. My presence at the table is irrelevant.

Beadle has clearly been fantasising for months about confronting Kate. I can perfectly imagine what Kate's first week must have been like. Working alongside this atrocious man. I'm sure he lugged his superiority complex into every meeting. It must have been hell.

I remain still, not wanting to draw his attention. I subtly squeeze Kate's arm, holding her back from interrupting. The longer we let him go on, the higher the chances he'll let some critical piece of information slip out.

That said, listening to his squeaky, patronising voice makes me want to scream.

"I left your office, rubbing my elbow and none the wiser of the dramatic change I'd just wrought in my life. I crept down to the basement to take one last walk through the museum... my museum... an old man was waiting for me there. At first, I thought he was a homeless man, snuck inside to look for a place to pass the night."

"Hobbes, I take it?" Kate interjects. She leans towards Beadle, goading him into revealing more. "What a disappointment you must have been! He waits nearly four centuries to speak to a descendant, and he ends up with a snivelling rat."

Beadle's face turns beet red, his eyes growing wide. "You'd like to believe that, wouldn't you, Kate." He shifts his gaze to land on me for the first time. "Or you, Natalie Payne. Oh yes, I know who you are. I know all the Prefects, each of you less deserving than the next. The magic must be scraping the bottom of the barrel if you lot are the best Oxford has to offer."

I seethe but refuse to rise to the bait. "What do you want, Oswald? Why are you here? Aren't you nervous about being caught for your crimes?"

To my horror, Beadle laughs, sending a braying sound echoing across the restaurant patio. I duck my head as the people nearby turn to look in our direction.

He slaps his hand on his knee, acting as though I've said the funniest thing he has ever heard. "Oh, Natalie... can I call you Natalie?" He carries on before I can reply. "What crimes? What risk? I know you and your little miniature dragon came to my museum weeks ago. I had a moment of anxiety, but then, nothing happened. Where are the police? If I'm guilty, why am I walking freely through the streets of Oxford?"

Kate points her finger at him, once again drawing his attention. "We know what you've done, Beadle. The thefts, the fire and even your role in Andrei's death. You won't get away with any of it."

"Won't I, though?" Beadle smirks cruelly. "The magic is helping me, Kate. I can waltz in and out, take anything I want from here, and who is going to stop me? It is as much my birthright as yours, Kate."

My hand clenches into a fist. I imagine rearing back my fist and then bloodying his nose. But I force my fingers to loosen before I lose all control. Oswald is determined to provoke us. I may be seething inside, but I'll be damned if I let him see it. He'd love nothing more than a chance to play the victim.

Kate fluffs her hair out of her face, releasing her pent-up frustration. She rolls her shoulders and sighs, once again in control. She cannot, however, hide the fury in her eyes when she turns to Beadle and asks, "What is your goal here, Beadle? To steal enough of the magic to make your little museum of horrors into a reputable institution?"

Oswald leans forward, getting in Kate's face. "Once again, you're underestimating me. I've already accomplished that task. My little museum, as you call it, now has visitor numbers which would rival yours. Our event bookings are sold out for months. And as for donations, I've got enough raised now to move to a larger building."

Kate and I rear back in shock.

"Surprised? The magic works fast. I'm not here for my gain. I'm here for your loss. Grandpa Hobbes is right. Oxford has benefitted from a magical advantage for far too long. While I've been building up my connection to the magic, Hobbes has been working on a way to strip yours."

"You won't get away with it, Beadle," Kate growls. "There are too many of us here. We will stop you, and we certainly won't let you hurt anyone else."

Although Kate's voice drips with conviction, Beadle merely arches an eyebrow at her. He rises from his chair, still chuckling. "If there is one thing I've proven beyond a shadow of a doubt, Kate, it is that there is nothing you or any of your ridiculous Eternals can do to stop me."

He turns his back and walks away, but halts, as though suddenly remembering something. He twists around and calls out one last remark.

"Enjoy your time with your new boyfriend, Kate. Bartie, is it? Your lifetime together might not be as Eternal as you think."

Chapter Ten

Oswald Beadle breezes out of sight, leaving Kate and me sitting shellshocked at our table. My breath shudders out as I struggle to regain my balance. How could a simple dinner out turn into such a moment of horror? And how did Beadle even know where to find us?

I spin in my chair, frantically searching the surrounding area for any signs of the crow or Beadle's other Eternals. By now, the restaurant garden is packed with locals and tourists enjoying the warm evening. I rise from my seat, angling for a better look at the far side of the garden, but I wrest myself back down. If an Eternal is following us around, realistically, what can we do about it? It isn't worth driving myself around the bend worrying about.

The clink of the ice in Kate's glass attracts my attention. She takes a shaky gulp, also struggling to find her own inner calm. As she carefully places the glass onto the table, she mutters, "God, Nat. That was awful. *He* was awful, even more so than I remembered."

"I suspect he's got worse, Kate," I sigh. "If you thought he was a self-entitled, boorish jerk before, I can't imagine that the magic has wrought any improvements in his personality."

Kate frowns glumly. "I need to tell Bartie..." her voice trails off as she covers her mouth with her hand. "Bartie! Do you think Beadle meant it when he said he intends to rip the magic from Oxford?"

"I'm positive he meant the words, but whether he can do it... that's the million-pound question." I snatch up my handbag and extricate myself from the picnic bench. "Let's go, Kate. We need to speak with the others right away. We can pay our bill on the way out and regroup at my house. Do you know where Bartie is now?"

Kate slips her handbag strap over her head, draping it across her body as though it is a sword, and she is heading into battle. Her gaze is murderous. Whatever fear and shock she felt initially has been completely replaced with her inner fire. "Bartie should be at my house. I'll stop by there and get him and then we'll meet at yours. What about Mathilde? Should we call her?"

The question throws me for a loop. "Err, no?" I reply, making it more of a question than an answer. I grapple with conflicting thoughts, shoving them into some semblance of order. "No," I say, more confidently this time. "This isn't urgent enough to justify interrupting her date, and anyway, what would she say to Trevor to make her excuses? We'd be putting her in a no-win situation."

Kate groans, "Ugh, you're right. I'll text her later and ask her to call me."

Out front, we split up, heading in separate directions. If there was ever a moment in which I wished I had the power to blink myself from one location to another, this would be it. Instead, I've got a twenty-minute walk in front of me.

The itch between my shoulder blades convinces me that walking the mile and a half home alone might not be the wisest choice. I take a moment to find my mobile within the depths of my handbag, pressing the button to call Edward as I fall into step behind a large group of tourists chattering away in a foreign language. The singsong lilt of their voices wraps me in a cocoon of safety while I wait for Edward to answer.

I muffle my voice with my hand, murmuring a quick explanation to Edward and asking him to send H off to find my grandfather. With any luck, we'll all arrive at my house at the same time. Edward promises to leave right away and turn on the kettle. When facing a challenge of epic proportions, any reasonable English person requires a strong cup of tea.

Next on my list is Harry. I half hesitate, my finger hovering above my mobile screen. She isn't a prefect. Is it right for me to drag her even deeper into the situation, particularly if there is a risk of danger? The beeping of the crosswalk lights hammers into my brain.

"What would Harry want me to do?" I ask myself under my breath.

She'd want me to call her. Obviously. And she'd probably be annoyed that she was second on my list. I let my finger fall onto the screen, landing on her name in my favourites list.

When she answers the phone with a breezy hello, I can hear a canned laugh track in the background.

"Sorry to drag you away from your television, Harry, but there's been an urgent development in our situation with Beadle and Hobbes and we need to meet up. Can you come to my house? Now?"

Something in my tone must hint at the seriousness of my request, because Harry doesn't ask questions. I hear the creak of the chair as she stands up. "Let me get out of my pyjamas and I'll be on my way."

I spare half a second to wonder what she'll tell Rob, her husband, before deciding it isn't worth worrying about. Harry is quick on her feet, and will no doubt spin some tale of relationship woes or party planning catastrophes while sashaying out the door.

My walk takes me past the Ashmolean, its grandiose facade lit in a shower of spotlights. Although several months have passed, I cannot look at the building without thinking of that night of the fire, and the frantic dash of the firefighters as they rushed towards the burning building. Nor can I forget the tears and terror on Francie's face when Trevor and the other detective led her out of Kate's office.

There must be a way to not only stop Beadle, but to see him pay for his crimes, and Hobbes must be punished as well.

My mind skips a beat. How do we stop an Eternal? Kate hinted at a larger magical world, one which extends beyond the boundaries of Oxford. Does it have courts? Jails? A police force of its own? Question after question overwhelms me. I struggle to rein my thoughts back in.

How far will Beadle and Hobbes go to achieve their revenge on the town and the people who ruined their lives? The video footage from the Ashmolean warehouse proved Beadle had zero remorse for his role in sending Andrei to his death. Did he rationalise the cost of Andrei's life, thinking it a fair reward for Andrei's bad actions? Or was it simpler than that? Has Beadle been pushed so far that he doesn't care who gets hurt?

I speed my steps, my mind jumping from one horrible outcome to another. Bartie, my grandfather and the other Eternals — gone from our lives forever. H, permanently trapped inside a cat's body, no longer able to communicate with us. Kate, Harry, or Mathilde injured.

My hand shakes as I try to slide my key into the lock. Edward must be standing nearby and hear my attempts. He throws the door open and pulls me into his arms. I sink into his embrace, not caring that we're spotlighted in the open front door.

When my heart stops racing, I blink back my tears and peel myself off his front. Edward closes the door, blocking out the world, while I rid myself of my handbag and shoes. Together, we move to the sofa, Edward sliding an arm over my shoulders after I curl up, leaning against the armrest.

"Are you okay now?" Edward asks, his tone gentle. I nod, savouring the warmth and safety of his arm. In a moment, I will go back to being the strong and determined woman that I am, but first I need a second to gather myself and block the video of terrible outcomes playing in my mind.

We sit in silence, Edward somehow understanding that I don't need platitudes or empty reassurances. Nor am I expecting him to take charge, dictating tasks for the rest of us to do. Without me saying a word, he knows that the only thing I need right now is a partner.

Gradually, I feel my fears slip into the background, my head clearing enough to remember I have another urgent task. By the time the doorbell rings, I'm back to my normal self, paper in hand and pens at the ready. There are plans to be made.

Beadle can be caught. Hobbes can be stopped. Kate, Mathilde, and I are the prefects. With the power of the Eternals standing behind us, we can accomplish anything.

Darkness falls. My grandfather leans over, drawing the curtains closed. He's sitting at his favourite spot on the window seat, with his back against the cushions and his feet propped up. I imagine us here on the weekends this winter, a fire roaring in the fireplace, him at his perch and Edward in his armchair. H and I curled up on the sofa, all of us immersed in one book or another.

My grandfather's stern expression reminds me that now is not the time for wool-gathering. I let my eyes scan the room, checking that everyone is ready to begin our strategy planning session. Edward sits across from me, one leg crossed over the other, confident in his leather chair. Kate and Bartie practically cling to one another on the sofa, while H stands at attention on the armrest. Harry is closest to me, looking ready for battle despite her hastily assembled outfit. There is an empty seat on the sofa where Mathilde should be, but I imagine she's here in spirit, if not in form.

My grandfather taps his knuckles against the wall, bringing us to order. "Alright, Nat. We're all here now and I've closed the drapes against any spying eyes. Start from the top and tell us everything you can remember from your conversation with Beadle."

Taking turns, Kate and I piece together the conversation, filling in the gaps for one another when our emotions cause us to draw a blank. H digs his talon into the sofa in his rising fury, while Harry grows more determined, the angles in her face sharpening as she tightens her jaw.

When we finish, the silence is so profound, you could hear a pin drop. H is the first to break it, shooting sparks from his nostrils.

"Tossers, the whole lot of 'em. Don't you worry, Nat. They won't get past me, Mols and the other Eternals at Somerset."

I hold up a hand to halt him before he can go any further. "Actually, I think that might be part of our problem."

My grandfather gapes at me. "What do you mean?"

"We all know that Oswald Beadle is responsible for the theft of antiques and paintings from Iffley, St Margaret, and Barnard Colleges, as well as the fire in the Ashmolean's archives," I tick the break-ins off on my fingers. "However, we can't prove it. We can't prove any of it. He's identified every weakness in our security systems and exploited our lack of awareness to turn Oxford into his personal playground."

"All the more reason to plug the gaps, Nat," my grandfather replies.

"If we wanted to stop him from taking anything else, you'd be right." I shift my gaze to Kate. "But Beadle told us tonight that his goal isn't to stretch the magical border — it is to rip it away completely. If it were him alone, I wouldn't be much concerned. However, he has Thomas Hobbes to help him."

I pause, gathering my thoughts before continuing. "The university has loaned dozens of scientific apparatus, artefacts, antiques and paintings to Harold's production — all of it dating back to the time when Wren and Wilkins discovered the magic of Oxford. We dangled their names, assuming Hobbes would want to damage their legacy. But what if it is more than that?"

Kate tilts her head, her gaze assessing. "What do you mean?"

"I keep running through Beadle's words. He didn't threaten us with thefts, fires, or anything else which might damage the priceless works on display."

"You're right," Kate agrees, sitting up straighter. "His only threat was to rip away the magic from Oxford. And he said Hobbes was working on a way to do that."

I nod, pleased she's catching on. "We know from reading Wren's journal that it was an experiment gone wrong which led to their discovery of the magic in the first place. What we don't know is how they stabilised the connection. There has to be something more than using metal rods. What if the answer lies within the equipment or artefacts sitting in Somerset right now?"

Edward leaps to his feet and begins pacing. "It would certainly explain Beadle's confidence. If Hobbes thought he knew how to create his own magical border, and to undo whatever it was Wilkins and Wren did, Beadle would leap at the chance to confront you two. He'd want to make sure you knew he was behind your lost connection to the magic."

"Since the film production moved from the Botanic Garden to Somerset College, we've had no sign of Beadle, Hobbes or even the crow." I nod at H, still seething on the armrest. "H and Somerset's Eternals have done too good a job keeping them out of the college. Beadle needs us to make a mistake, so he can find a way inside."

"And that's why he barged in on our dinner this evening," Kate adds. "He wanted to throw us off-balance. He threatened Bartie, likely hoping we'd split some of our security away from the college to protect him instead."

"I don't need any protection," Bartie states, stone-faced in his determination. "I won't hide in fear from a snivelling weasel suffering from delusions of grandeur. None of us will."

Wanting to break the tension in the room, I shuffle through my stack of papers, picking out the one I want. "I'm sure none of you will be surprised to know I've been jotting down some ideas."

As I hoped, everyone chuckles.

I skim through my notes, finding the place to start. "We've been protecting the right thing — the magic — but we've been going about it in the wrong way. We need to loosen our security at Somerset and give Beadle hope that he and his team of Eternals can get inside. We have to be able to catch them in the act."

Kate wrinkles her brow but doesn't disagree immediately. She does, however, raise an important question. "So, we set the trap, let them inside, and then hope it all goes off according to plan? That might work for capturing Beadle, but not Hobbes."

I hold up a finger, stopping her. "That's where the second part of my idea comes into play. And I have you, Kate, to thank for it."

"Me?"

I nod, explaining, "It was our discussion about summer holiday plans. It never dawned on me that Eternals could be somewhere other than Oxford. I always assumed that it was a 'what you see is what you get' kind of thing."

Edward and Harry both spin their heads my way. Harry stares as Edward asks, "Wait. It's not?"

This time, Bartie steps in. "We have our own plane of existence, and Oxford has, for lack of a better term, a door into it.

A door for us, that is. We can cross through here, thanks to Wilkins' and Wren's discovery. But we aren't trapped in these places."

I jump in before Edward can ask another question. There's plenty that come to my mind as well, but for now, we need to stay focused on the matter at hand. "Exactly! Wilkins and Wren lived some of the best years of their life here in Oxford. They died knowing that Eternals exist. I'm willing to bet that when death came for them, they found a way to remain behind. Just like you did, Grandfather. Somewhere in that other world, Wilkins and Wren are likely to be still around... and we should try to find them."

My grandfather rubs his chin, deep in thought. "My word, Nat. How did we not think of this sooner? I can't imagine you're wrong."

H flaps his wings, lifting above the sofa in his effort to leap into the conversation. "Iffen your right, Nat, 'ow are we goin' to find 'em?"

"Grandfather? Bartie?" I glance between the two, hoping one of them will have the answer.

"They could be anywhere," Grandfather mumbles, still rubbing his chin.

"I wouldn't have the first clue where to look," Bartie comments, frowning in frustration. "We need an expert historian. Mathilde, maybe?"

Harry shoots up from her chair, her eyes wide. "Not Mathilde. Molly! Who better to find them than someone who knew them personally? We've heard her talk. She likely knows those men better than they know themselves."

I flip through another couple of pages, snagging one and holding it into the air. There is one word written on it, in large block print. "Molly!"

Harry leans over and pats me on the back. "Great minds think alike, Nat."

Edward stops his pacing but doesn't sit. Instead, he stays at the front of the room, leaning against the bookcase. "If Molly can find Wilkins and Wren, I feel confident we can prevent Hobbes from doing any lasting damage to our connection to the magic. After all, they know better than anyone how Oxford's connection to the magic works. But we still have the problem of Oswald Beadle. Yes, we can give the appearance that we've loosened the security around Somerset, but catching him? You're talking about a sting operation."

"I'll sting 'em, Nat. Just watch me, eh?" H shouts, shadowboxing in the air.

I snort at the sight, but Edward remains straight-faced. "Your help is much appreciated, H, but we need evidence — *incontrovertible* evidence — we can use in a court of law. I know you don't want to hear it, but Nat and Kate, please. We need Trevor."

Kate glances at me, biting her lip. I take care to make sure my expression gives nothing away as I once again return to my notes. When Edward sees the next page in my pile of notes, he rolls his eyes and groans.

"I don't know why you make us go through this farce of a planning session if you've already figured everything out," he grumbles, but his smile lets me know he isn't serious.

Kate clears her throat. "We delayed bringing Trevor into the group for as long as we could, but like both of you, I can't see a way forward, which doesn't require his help. The question now is who will be the one to tell him? And how?" Kate turns to me, "Nat, have you got the answer to this problem solved as well?"

I shake my head and explain, "This was as far as I got before you all arrived. I don't have any preference for who tells him, other than to vote that it *not* be Mathilde."

"I agree with that," Harry says, still standing by my chair. Almost as one, Kate, Harry and I all point our eyes at the front of the room. Edward freezes in place, uncomfortable to find himself the centre of attention.

"Me? Why me? I'm not even a prefect."

I rise from my chair and cross the room, reaching out a hand to squeeze his arm. "In this case, I think we need to worry more about the connection to Trevor than to the magic itself. You know Trevor better than any of us, Mathilde included. You have a history with him, and he knows you well enough to know you wouldn't joke about such a thing."

Edward leans away from me, shaking his head. "But I don't know where to start or how to make him believe me."

"Take Bartie with you," Kate chimes in. "You've both been arguing for weeks that we need to tell Trevor about the magic. Well, now you've got the approval to do it. Seems only right that the burden should fall on the two of you."

H guffaws, accidentally lighting a nearby stack of magazines on fire. My grandfather hops up to help him put out the flames and then dust the ash away. When all is set to rights, Grandfather stands tall, commanding our attention.

"Now that we've sorted all the questions, let's restart the discussion from the top. We've only got a few days left before the filming wraps and all those antiques and artefacts go back into storage. If we're going to pull off a sting, capture the criminals and save the magic, we're going to need a proper plan in place."

Harry, Edward, and I return to our chairs, all of us crowding around the coffee table. As our task list grows and timelines fill in with details, so too does my confidence. Beadle and Hobbes have no idea what's in store for them.

Chapter Eleven

I arrive at Somerset College the next morning with a clear head, a solid plan, and a task list in hand. As a bonus, I've brought along my favourite sidekicks — H and my grandfather.

The day is overcast, the weak sunlight fighting a losing battle against the cloud layer. Despite the dreary chill, I'm determined to keep a positive attitude. As soon as we're through the front entrance, I pull H and my grandfather aside and begin assigning our tasks.

"Kate is phoning Mathilde this morning, and Edward is planning to stop by the police station to see Trevor later. So that leaves the Somerset tasks to the three of us." I open my calendar app, double-checking what is first on our list. "H, would you mind doing a quick lap of the grounds to check for wayward Eternals and to see if you can find Molly?"

"Don't worry your loaf, Nat. I'm on it. Where do you want me to bring Mols iffen I can find 'er?"

"Hmm. We need someplace private where there is no risk any of Beadle's Eternals might hear our conversation. We don't want them to have even a hint of what we're doing. How about the meeting room upstairs I've been using? It should be free."

"Got it!" H calls, already flapping his way towards the sky. "We'll meet you there in a flash."

Without waiting, my grandfather spins around and moves to the stairwell. He glances over his shoulder, asking, "I take it we're going straight up?"

"Not so fast. I've got one pressing task to do before we lock ourselves into that room."

My grandfather quirks up an eyebrow, silently asking me to fill in the blank.

"Coffee. I need a latte, and I know just the place to get it. We should have time for a quick pass by the Craft Services trailer before H and Molly return."

Grandfather rolls his eyes, but doesn't complain. He knows better. A strong caffeine boost is the secret to my morning productivity.

The film crew is slowly beginning their own morning assignments. I wave, say hello and nod as we stride across the inner courtyard. While the grey sky might not be to my liking, it is ideal for filming the outdoor scenes. The clouds filter the sunlight, eliminating awkward shadows and too bright spotlights. I spy the camera crew setting up their equipment in the corner of the courtyard and slow my steps for a quick chat.

Andy, the more outgoing of the trio, tosses a friendly hello when I get close.

"Morning, Andy. Guess you're filming the courtyard scenes today. Any chance you know the shot order? I haven't seen Joyce yet to get the daily schedule."

"Morning, Nat. Yes, we'll be out here all day, and I am most definitely looking forward to the fresh air. We've been cooped up inside for far too long. As for the scenes, we've got Caleb and Gideon, along with some of the supporting actors, on call for the whole day. Depending on how the weather holds, we'll see how many scenes we get through."

My question answered, I make my excuses, needing to hurry if I want to get a latte from Sam. I wander off but have to backtrack when I realise my grandfather isn't with me.

At first, I think he's disappeared completely, but then I spot his white head hidden in the midst of the camera crew. I hesitate to interrupt, curious to see what has caught his eye.

Andy and the other man and woman on the crew are busy with their tasks, oblivious to the old man beside them. As they check camera angles and lighting levels, my grandfather watches their every movement. His gaze shifts left and right, peering over their shoulders as they turn dials and press buttons, and then glancing at the video screens to see the result.

The only thing he can't do is peek through the viewfinder. Try as he might, one of the camera crew members is always in his way. I have to hold back a snort when his frustration reaches his max, and he finally remembers he is a ghost. He bends over, shoving his head through the middle of Andy's chest, leaning towards the camera. He squints, one eye closed, and checks for himself, even going so far as to adjust the lens.

He stands upright, looking like a child who has just discovered a new toy. Fearing we'll be here all day if I don't stage an intervention, I quietly call his name, hoping to get his attention. Once, twice, but no luck. He is too engrossed in the machines.

I raise my voice and try again, hoping the magic will prevent the camera crew from wondering who I am talking to.

"Grandfather? Alfred? Hello? Are you going to stay there all day?"

"Oops, sorry, Nat. Those cameras caught my eye when they pulled out all the equipment on the first day at the Botanic Garden, but I was always off patrolling the grounds whenever they were using them. I wanted a chance to see how they worked for myself, and now seemed like as good a time as any."

Chuckling, we keep our chat going as we cross the courtyard, walk under the arch and out into the back garden. I send my grandfather off to relax at a table while I wait in line for a coffee. It moves quickly and before I know it, I'm standing at the counter requesting my regular.

As Sam sets the drink in front of me, I feel a tap on my back. I take a quick look see over my shoulder and find Joyce. Her eyes shift left and right as she bites her cuticles. Although Joyce is often frenetic, darting from one task to another, this time she looks agitated.

"Hiya, Nat. Can I talk to you for a second?"

"Um, sure," I answer, grabbing my coffee and following her to the edge of the trailer. It is just far enough away from the window to put us out of earshot of everyone else. I expect her to launch into whatever is bothering her, but instead she opens and closes her mouth a few times while wringing her hands.

Perhaps a gentle prod is in order. "Joyce, did you need something?"

She takes a deep breath and replies in a hoarse whisper. "Normally I'd go to Harold if I thought anything was amiss, but he isn't on set yet. And really, maybe it isn't a big deal... but I thought no one was supposed to be in her trailer."

Alarm bells go off in my head. "Whose trailer?"

"Vivian's," she stammers, still twitching nervously. She mumbles, half-trying to convince herself. "Maybe it's fine. He doesn't have his own trailer, but still. DCI Robinson said we shouldn't..."

I lose my patience with her babbling and ask pointedly, "Who, Joyce? Who is in Vivian's trailer?"

"Caleb."

My eyes grow wide. "You saw Caleb Farrow go into Vivian's trailer? Even though the police warned everyone to stay out of it?"

She nods, chewing on her lower lip.

I reach out my free hand and lay it on her arm, squeezing

gently. "You did the right thing by telling me, Joyce. I'll go see what he's up to in there. Can you go wait at the front entrance and watch for Harold? Bring him over as soon as he arrives, okay?"

She nods again, sighing in relief. "Thanks, Nat. I was sure you'd know what to do."

I wait until she darts off before turning around and scanning the picnic tables, looking for my grandfather. Our eyes meet, his eyebrows raised in a question. A split second later, he is by my side.

"Something's come up. Can you find H and Molly and wait for me in the meeting room?"

"Of course, dear. I knew something was wrong as soon as I saw that young woman's face. You run along, and I'll catch up with the Eternals."

That sorted, I hightail it over to Vivian's trailer, walking as briskly as I can without sloshing my coffee or garnering too much attention. The last thing I want right now is an audience. It's high time I had a word with Caleb Farrow himself... and not his alter ego.

My mind races, coming up with theory after theory as to why he would be inside. Could the rumours of their affair be true? If so, he could be in there right now, erasing all evidence of his relationship. Or maybe it is even worse. What if Vivian brushed off his advances and he didn't take it well? Is there proof of his threatening behaviour hiding inside?

Scraping through my memories, I try to recollect whether Trevor and his detectives searched the trailer. I rationalise that they must have made at least an initial pass. However, there must be a reason why it is still off-limits to the cast and crew. I debate ringing him, but there simply isn't time. A phone call after the fact will have to do. I'm sure he'll understand once he hears my reasons why delaying isn't an option.

Vivian's trailer is located at the far back of the lot, on the opposite end from where Gideon's is located. Someone has dressed it up for her with a line of potted flowers lining either end of the steps up to her trailer door. I tiptoe up, not wanting to give Caleb any warning of my arrival. If I'm lucky, I'll catch him in the act of whatever nefarious task he is doing.

The police tape flaps loose, haphazardly stuck back up by someone in a hurry. The door handle twists smoothly in my hand. Thankfully, it doesn't make a squeak. I slowly push it open, just wide enough to peek one eye inside. There's no one in sight, but I can hear the sounds of drawers being pulled open further in.

Emboldened, I open the door wider and slide past, not bothering to replace the police tape dangling off one edge of the door frame. After all, I rationalise, the damage is done.

Inside, the layout is the same as Gideon's trailer — a galley kitchenette followed by a circular booth dining area. Deeper along the wall sit a love seat, armchair, and television. However, while Gideon's trailer was a study in masculine minimalism, Vivian's trailer is the opposite. There are cosy cushions on the love seat, a bright cotton rug on the floor, and striped curtains hung on the windows. If this place wasn't roped off, I bet there would be a crush of people trying to lay claim to it.

But for now, there is only one person nosing around inside. I recognise the male voice right away, having listened to it on set for hours. It is Caleb's voice — and for once, he isn't using old-fashioned language.

"Come on, mate. Where are you? Where'd she put the bloody things?"

More scraping sounds and clatters abound from the far end of the trailer, presumably from Vivian's private dressing area. I slink through the kitchenette, past the table, and into the living area. Unfortunately, due to the angle of the door into the back room, I still can't see what Caleb is doing.

I count to three in my head and then step through the doorway.

Whatever brilliant line I had in my head flies out the window when my eyes land on Caleb's bare backside. I screech out something incoherent and nearly tumble over in my effort to get out of the room. The backs of my knees hit the armchair and I fall into its open arms, slapping my hands over my mouth as I dissolve into a stress-induced case of the giggles. I struggle to get them under control, reminding myself I came here for a reason.

In the other room, Caleb curses under his breath, and I hear him ripping the blanket from the bed. His pounding footsteps are the only warning I have before his muscular form fills the doorway. His broad shoulders and firm pecs narrow at his waist, which is currently wrapped in a pink and yellow floral quilt.

He runs his hand through his wet hair, flexing his bicep, and his gaze is thunderous as he glares daggers at me. He takes a shuddering breath as he rolls his shoulders back, and then he stands tall, resuming his standard Sir Christopher posture. I stare, hardly daring to blink.

Surely, standing in nothing more than a feminine blanket, Caleb won't revert to character. Right?

He contorts his face, shifting his expression to one of profound disapproval. "Lady Natalie! Whatever are you doing here? This is highly inappropriate!"

My mouth drops open. "Good grief, man! Are you seriously going to stay in character right now, while standing half-dressed in an off-limits trailer?"

Before Caleb can reply, another deep male voice booms from the trailer doorway. "That is exactly what I want to know as well."

I rock sideways, shifting to see who has come in. To my shock,

Trevor is standing in the kitchenette, looking official in his dark suit and crisp white shirt. His gaze pierces into me before sliding over to Caleb.

I know Caleb must recognise Trevor. After all, Trevor questioned every member of the cast who was on set at the time of Vivian's collapse. Indeed, Caleb's left eye twitches, and the colour drains from his face. Nevertheless, he seems determined to brazen through the situation... in character.

"This is my fiancée's home. I have every right to be here." He draws himself tall and looks down his nose at us. "How dare you burst into her private domain! I must insist you leave immediately."

If Trevor were a wyvern like H, he'd have smoke streaming from his ears by this point. His voice deepens sending shivers of fear down my spine. "Farrow, you have two options. You can either get some clothing on and then come back out here as yourself, or I can haul a half-dressed Christopher Wren down to the station. Which is it going to be?"

Caleb must sense the truth of Trevor's words, because he skedaddles back into the bedroom and slams the door shut behind him.

I push myself to my feet and knock some imaginary dust from my trousers, feeling fairly pleased with myself. That is until I glance at Trevor and find him glowering at me.

"Do you want to tell me what you are doing inside a trailer I specifically said was off-limits?"

I flinch at his harsh tone. "Joyce came to me this morning, telling me she'd spotted Caleb sneaking into Vivian's trailer. I was planning to ring you, Trevor, but I didn't want to risk missing the chance to catch him in the act," I explain.

His eyebrows soar up his forehead, his disbelief evident. "The act of what? Showering?"

Caleb throws the bedroom door open and stalks out before I

can reply. Fully dressed, with his hair dripping down his back, he flops onto the loveseat, slouching over with his elbows on his knees and his head in his hands. His voice is barely audible.

"I just wanted a shower, mate. Is that too much to ask? I'm living in a rundown cottage with no electricity or running water."

Trevor appears unmoved by Caleb's explanation. "So what? You think your body odour justifies tearing down police tape and letting yourself inside?"

At this, Caleb lifts his head, his expression pleading. "Everyone knows I'm a method actor. It is part of my mystique, a quirk my adoring fans love. But this is the first historical production I've done, and I did not know what I was signing up for. Do you think I enjoy talking like a romance novel hero all the time? Or living like a hobbit? I went to the one place where I thought no one would catch me out of character. Cut me some slack, mate!"

Trevor wavers, the lines in his face softening. Caleb's wet hair and hastily dressed appearance certainly align with his story. But it doesn't explain why he was rummaging in Vivian's drawers, searching for something.

Fearing Trevor will let Caleb off with a warning, I interrupt. "If all you wanted was a shower, why were you pawing Vivian's things? I heard you opening and closing her drawers."

"Pawing her things?" Caleb squawks. "I just wanted some cotton wool to clear my ears! Besides, there's nothing back there except expensive make-up and scented hand cremes."

I ready my retort, still unconvinced, but this time Trevor gets in the next word.

He raises a finger and points to the door. "Get out, Farrow. Get out and stay out of here until I personally tell you you can come back inside. Do you understand me?"

Caleb doesn't need to be told twice. He swipes his shoes from the floor, slides past Trevor and dashes out the door. Trevor turns to follow, but I stop him with a question.

"Why did you let him go?" I ask, once Caleb is out of earshot.

He looks at me, incredulous. "Let him go? What was I meant to do, Nat? Throw one of Britain's leading actors into the nick because he wanted to shower in secret?"

Hands on my hips, I rise to his challenge. "How do you know the shower excuse wasn't a cover for something else? Caleb and Vivian were having an affair. Did you know that? Maybe he poisoned her to keep her from telling his partner."

"Having an affair?" Trevor's tone rises. "Surely you don't believe that ridiculous rumour..." He shakes his head, looking at me in dismay.

I rear back as though he struck me. "How do you know it is nothing more than a rumour? My uncle's production is at stake here, Trevor. Someone has gone to extreme lengths to stop it. We have to investigate every potential lead, even if it ends up being nothing more than gossip."

Trevor exhales, his expression softening. "I know you mean well, Nat, but you need to leave investigating to the professionals. Do I have to remind you what happened at Barnard College? You went off on your own, headstrong, and you got shot!"

My cheeks flush at the injustice in his words. "I didn't go off on my own. Edward was with me when that happened. I can't sit back and wait. There are other factors in play here, Trevor. Things you can't understand."

"Then tell me, Nat. Make me understand. Let me do my job."

Our eyes meet, neither of us blinking. I stare deep into his eyes, searching for a clue of what will happen next. We need Trevor's help. We had planned for Edward to tell Trevor the truth about the magic. But now he is here with me. I wrestle with the options and finally settle on one.

I blow the air from my lungs and throw my hands skyward.

"Edward wanted to be the one to tell you. We all agreed. But you're here now..."

Trevor cocks his head to the side, confused by the turn of the conversation. "Tell me what, Nat?"

"About the... the existence of..." The words escape me. "It's easier if I show you."

Trevor remains quiet as he follows me out of the trailer and across the back garden.

When we cross under the arch, his curiosity gets the better of him. "Where are we going, Nat?"

I don't reply, too busy hunting for the best way to reveal the truth. With Harry, I told her we were meeting a group of actors. In Edward's case, I let the key work its magic, unlocking his own capabilities. Clearly, neither of those is an option with Trevor. He is a man of facts. He will need evidence, not an explanation.

I lead Trevor inside the main building and up the stairs, heading towards the meeting room where my grandfather, H and Molly await my arrival.

"If you're wasting my time, Nat," Trevor growls.

"I'm not wasting your time," I say, soothing him. I twist the handle, opening the meeting room door to reveal the trio inside. Trevor follows on my heels. I wave him to take a seat and close the door behind us.

Trevor surveys the mostly empty space. Unable to see my grandfather or Molly, his eyes land on H. "Your cat? You drug me across the college grounds to see your cat? Is this some kind of joke?"

"No, there is something else I need you to show you. I'll explain, but it is better if you see for yourself first." I turn to the other end of the room and give my grandfather a grim smile. "Grandfather, I know we planned for Edward to tell Trevor about the magic of Oxford, but the situation has changed. We need to tell him now, and I need your help. Can you and Molly please reveal yourselves to Trevor?"

Trevor sucks in air, my only clue that they have done as I asked. Since they always look and feel solid to me, I can't tell any difference.

I take a deep breath, closing my eyes to centre myself, and then launch into the truth, releasing a torrent of words.

"This is my grandfather, Alfred Payne, and the woman is Molly, a laundress from the 17th century. They are ghosts, Trevor — or Eternals, as we call them. I am a prefect, tasked with responsibility for protecting the magic of Oxford."

Trevor blinks, caught completely off guard. "The what?"

"Oxford has magic. It is as real as you and I are. It dates back centuries, discovered right here at Somerset by none other than John Wilkins and Sir Christopher Wren. There are Eternals — ghosts and creatures. They walk the halls unseen, lending a helping hand to all who enter the college walls."

"Is this some kind of movie magic? Wilkins and Wren? Ghosts?" Trevor scoffs. "More like holograms. Are you having a right laugh, Nat? I'm not impressed."

"This is no prank, Trevor. I'm trying to tell you the truth. Magic exists, and in fact, it is at risk of disappearing. Edward was planning to tell you today."

"Edward?" Trevor barks. "You've conned Edward into believing this madness? About ghosts and goblins?" He halts, shaking with a sudden realisation. When he speaks again, his voice is low. "Does Mathilde know about this? Is this why you two were asking me about ghosts and time travel the day I came for the tour?"

I freeze, inadvertently giving away the truth.

"You, Mathilde, Edward, and even Kate... all of you? Did you dream up this farce as repayment for me locking Francie up? Was my date last night all part of the act?" Trevor motions at my grandfather and Molly. "And this? Some kind of special effect you brought in, to add credence to your ridiculous tale?"

I tug at my hair. "There is no equipment in this room, Trevor. Look around you! You're being purposefully obtuse. There's no great revenge plot going on."

Trevor fights the urge, but eventually gives in, scanning the walls looking for a projector. The only one in sight dangles from the ceiling, its fan and lights off.

I grit my teeth, wondering what else I can do to show him. My gaze lands on H.

"If you won't accept the ghosts, perhaps seeing a creature will convince you this is real."

H glides across the table, his spiked tail twitching angrily. He stops exactly halfway between me and Trevor, within an easy arm's reach of us both.

"Please, Trevor. Trust me," I plead, my voice dripping with sincerity. "Take my hand and I will show you." I hold out my right hand, beckoning him to take it. He looks wary, but something in my expression must get through to him. He rests his hand in mine.

I act fast, before he can change his mind, reaching with my other hand to grasp the end of H's tail. In turn, H reaches out a paw and places in on Trevor's other arm. Trevor jerks in surprise as the current of energy races across our arms, giving him the ability to see H for what he truly is — a wyvern.

Trevor tugs his hands back, checking to make sure they are uninjured, before lifting his gaze back to me and H.

H flaps his wings, barely lifting off the table, and then shoots a carefully controlled jet of flames in Trevor's direction. Trevor's arms windmill backwards as he throws himself out of harm's way. He lands on his hands and knees on the far side of the table.

Wide-eyed, he stares at H in utter horror.

Undeterred, H matches his glare with one of his own, his vivid yellow cat eyes sparkling in fury. "Lor luv a duck, mate. Use your loaf. The missie 'ere isn't telling tall tales. Magic is real, and we need your 'elp."

H's words have the opposite effect of what he intended. Trevor backs until his feet hit the wall and then cautiously, slowly creeps up to standing, never taking his eyes off H.

H swoops over, landing beside me, his tail wrapped protectively over my arm. My grandfather and Molly shift slightly, preparing themselves for whatever comes next.

His breathing is ragged. Trevor glances wildly around the room, his mind fighting tooth and nail to hold on to any rational explanation for what sits before him. We wait for him to calm down, to see reason and to accept the truth.

Unfortunately for all of us, he chooses the opposite. With no warning, he flings himself towards the door, banging it open and sprinting out of sight.

"That did not go well," I blurt in shock, stating the obvious.

Seeing how upset I am, my grandfather's expression softens and Molly slides from her chair, moving to sit at my side. She rubs my back, murmuring, "There, there, dear. It will work itself out somehow."

My grandfather echoes her words, but I can tell he does so half-heartedly. There is a chasm between where Trevor stands and him accepting the existence of the magic. A chasm which I inadvertently opened up when I revealed H's true identity.

H nuzzles my hand as I choke back tears provoked by the rush of emotions crashing over me.

"I better call Edward and warn him." My hand shakes as I pull my mobile from my handbag and search up his contact. The call fails to connect. Instead of Edward's voice, I'm greeted with an automated message telling me the person is out of reach. I hang up and try again, but don't have any better luck.

"Send 'em a text," H suggests, tapping a talon against the phone case.

I dash off a cryptic note, not knowing how to put everything that has happened into a simple text. "Urgent. Find Trevor today. You have to speak with him."

"What do I do now?" I look around the room, hoping for a flash of inspiration.

My grandfather braces his hands on the armrests of his chair, leaning back and sighing. "We do what we can, Nat. And in your case, that means returning to our tasks for the day. We have a lot to accomplish, not the least of which is asking Molly here for her help."

Intellectually, I know my grandfather doesn't mean to sound harsh, but the words lash about my shoulders, flogging me for my gross misstep. I gulp audibly.

Molly pats my back. "Let me get you a cup of tea. Your coffee has grown cold. Then you can tell me what you need. If it is within my abilities, I will make whatever it is happen."

Molly's cup of tea and ready agreement lift my spirits as well as anything can. I force all thoughts of Trevor out of my head.

I get through the day by focusing on one step at a time, moving around the college grounds. Do this task. Then do the next. Don't think. My mobile is silent. No messages or updates. But also, no angry voices on the line. I choose to view the quiet as a positive. Surely if Edward's talk with Trevor went worse than mine, Edward would get in touch. He knows I'm not filming today.

If I'm quiet and introspective, no one else seems to notice. The cast and crew are too busy, desperate to get their scenes in the can before they lose the light. Will and Jill stop by, abuzz with their plans for the wrap party. They are so caught up in showing me the menu, the decorations, and the musical options, they fill in all my gaps of silence.

I trudge home at the end of the day, shoulders slumped and gaze downcast. By now, H has abandoned all efforts to cheer me up. When we reach home, he flies off, going straight to his garden house and leaving me to face Edward alone.

Inside, Edward's bass tones trickle out from the kitchen, singing under his breath as he prepares dinner. His off-key notes warm my heart, giving me hope that perhaps all is fine. Surely the man wouldn't sing if the world was falling down around our ears. I hasten to drop my bag and shoes at the door.

"Hiya Nat!" he calls from the back of the house. "How was your day? I think your phone is off. Mathilde's been trying to get in touch with you."

I spin around and retrace my steps. My phone is in the depths of my bag, the battery dead.

"Battery drained out," I explain, holding up my phone as I head to the charging station on the kitchen counter. "Did she say what she wanted?"

Edward grabs me for a quick kiss. "No, but I didn't talk to her. She sent a text, and I told her you'd be home soon enough."

My phone screen lights up with the dead battery symbol. As much as I want to ring Mathilde, I'll need to wait a few minutes for the battery to reach a minimum charge.

"Did you catch Trevor today?" My voice cracks awkwardly as I ask the question.

Edward, unaware of my stress levels, continues stirring a steaming pot. "Hmm? I went by the station, but they said he was out. I left a message there and another on his phone."

I must make a whimper because Edward drops the spoon, looking at me with worry. "Is everything okay, Nat? If it's about Trevor, I wouldn't worry too much. He might have been in court today. I'll catch him tomorrow, for sure."

"I caught him today," I whisper.

"What? You seem upset. What happened?"

The doorbell rings, preventing me from answering. I push off the cabinet and quick step to the door. When I open it, I find Mathilde standing on my doorstep, tear tracks traced across her cheeks.

I reach out an arm to pull her inside, but she pushes past me, striding to my sofa. Edward steps out of the dining room in time to see her collapse onto the seat.

"What have you done, Nat?" she chokes out. "Trevor showed up at my flat. He was livid, full of accusations. He accused me of being part of some master plot to make a fool of him. He said you'd confessed it all."

"Eh?" Edward walks up behind me, offering moral support. "What's this?"

Any other time I'd appreciate him standing behind me, no questions asked. But not tonight. I rock in place, rubbing my arms. Edward moves around the room to face me.

"I didn't mean for it to happen, certainly not the way that it did. Trevor showed up on set and was annoyed with me for investigating on my own. I tried to tell him something bigger was at stake... he demanded to know what. I told him about the magic of Oxford."

Mathilde gasps, fresh tears tumbling down her face. Edward goes still, almost as though he is a hunter facing a particularly dangerous animal. He slides carefully over to the armchair and sits without ever taking his eyes off mine.

"Start from the beginning, Nat," he instructs me, his tone gentle. He makes it seem less like a command and more like a way out of whatever trouble I've got myself into.

I slump into the other chair and recount again everything that happened. Joyce's concern, Caleb's secret mission to shower. That, at least, earns an involuntary snort from Mathilde.

My cadence grows faster the closer I get to the moment of truth. I blurt the last bit out in a torrent of words, letting them trail off at the end. A hush falls over the room.

Edward glances left and right, his gaze darting from me to Mathilde. It's obvious that Trevor made his way to her next.

"That explains a lot of the holes in what he told me," Mathilde finally says. "He said he'd been wandering around for hours, waiting for me to get home. That poor man..."

"I'm so sorry, Mathilde. Believe me, hurting either of you was never my intention. If I could go back in time, brush Joyce off when she first approached me... I would. In a heartbeat, I'd do it."

"I know you would, Nat, but the damage is done." Mathilde sniffles, twisting a tissue round and round her fingers. "We had a great date last night, you know? We started with drinks and then dinner. We talked until they closed the restaurant. Neither of us wanted to go home at that point, so we went for a walk and ended up sitting in South Park, talking late into the night."

"That's great." I give Mathilde a soft, hopeful smile, my eyes crinkling.

She gives a tiny shake of her head. "It should be... but when you confronted him, forcing him to see the magic..."

She pushes up from the sofa, gathering her bag. She turns back before she reaches the front door. "We talked for hours, but I never once mentioned anything about the magic. It makes everything else I said last night look suspect. I don't know where we might have ended up, but from the anger and disappointment in his face when he walked away from me tonight... I don't think I'll ever find out what might have been."

"Mathilde, wait!" I call out, scrambling to my feet, but she walks out the front door without another look back.

Edward still sits in his chair in the front room. I stand before him, my arms at my side.

Finally, after what seems like hours but is probably mere

seconds, he wipes his hand over his mouth and frowns. "What an utter mess, Nat. I know you didn't mean for it to turn out this way, and that you thought you were doing the right thing..."

I blink furiously, fighting tears of my own. He rises and crosses the room, coming to a stop at my side. He squeezes my arm gently. "I'll find Trevor tomorrow. If there is a way to repair the damage, I swear I will find it."

"I can help," I whisper.

Edward kisses my forehead, lingering for a moment. "I know you can, but right now, Trevor needs to see someone else. You can still do your part — find Wilkins and Wren and figure out a way to stop Hobbes."

Chapter Twelve

I toss and turn throughout the night. There is no respite in my dreams, each one more nightmarish than the previous. When a pale stream of sunlight peeks out from behind the curtains, I drag my body from underneath the bedcovers. The mirror reveals deep bags beneath my eyes, and their normal spark is dimmed.

How did the situation with Trevor spiral out of control so quickly? My reflection has no answers. I glare at the mirror, unwilling to accept there is nothing I can do to fix the damage I caused between Trevor and Mathilde. Trevor will come around. He has to!

Needing to clear my head, I pull a set of running clothes from my drawer, taking care not to wake Edward. He mumbles in his sleep before rolling over and dozing off again. I move into the guest bedroom to get dressed and tiptoe downstairs in search of my running shoes. I leave a short note on the coffeemaker, letting Edward know where I have gone, and then I let myself out the front door.

The weather seems to have aligned with my troubles. The sky is grey, and the air is heavy with moisture. Patches of fog float along the street, giving the sense that the sky is falling.

This deep in the neighbourhood, the streets are empty. No cars or bicycles pass along them so early in the morning. I am isolated from everyone and everything. Even the curtains are closed in every house I pass.

I eschew my normal path through Port Meadow, the one which takes me past the gazing cattle and sheep who call the field home. Instead, I jog towards the Thames River path, my feet pounding against the beaten dirt path. I pass by one houseboat after another, wondering which one Harold and Dominic are calling home. The urge to text them and suggest we meet for a coffee crashes over me, but I shove it backwards. I'm not ready to face more questions, not while I have no answers for them.

Could Trevor be right? Am I rushing to sleuth out a suspect without any real clue of what I'm doing? My mind flashes up memories from my interrogations. Ilaria and Marcello had nothing to add and no reason to dislike Vivian. If Gideon is telling the truth, his only goal is to protect her. Joyce pointed me towards Caleb... I grit my teeth as I realise I still haven't got a straight answer from him about his relationship with Vivian.

Andy on the camera crew was convinced there was more happening than met the eye. What was it Trevor said yesterday? He could hardly drag a major celebrity down to the police station. Could Trevor be turning a blind eye to the possibility Caleb is behind all the problems on set, the falling lighting rig, and Vivian's poisoning?

I can't walk away from my search for the poisoner. I know I can help. If I keep talking to the cast and crew members, something will shake loose. The important thing is to have an open mind and to look at the situation from every angle.

With that thought, my mind veers off in a new direction. Could *Caleb* be the target instead? Perhaps someone on set was hoping to catch his eye, but then Vivian arrived and ruined their chances. If that is the case, then I've been asking all the wrong questions.

My watch buzzes as I complete another mile, pulling me back to the present. By this point, I am surrounded by open fields, only the quiet burble of the placid river providing any noise. My steps slow, my breath coming out in great gasps. Frustration rises inside of me.

Why did Trevor come to Somerset yesterday? Why did he have to find me in Vivian's trailer, question me, and goad me into revealing the truth of the magic? He asked me to tell him what secret I was hiding so that he could help me. But where is he now? He crashed out of the room, driven by his fear. He should be here with me, discussing motives and opportunities. I should be his inside man on set, probing for information an outsider or officer would struggle to find.

I ball my fists and release a scream of frustration, sending a flock of birds scattering. It doesn't help and I'm not surprised. I keep using Trevor's name, but the person I'm most angry at is myself. I knew better than to throw him into the deep end, and yet that is exactly what I did. I should have kept quiet, phoned Edward, or sent Trevor on his way.

I didn't stop to think — I acted. And I let everyone down.

A crow caw and a flapping sound attract my attention. The black bird swoops from the sky, landing in the middle of the now empty field. For once, it is an average, ordinary crow, and not a magical creature mocking me. Nonetheless, its presence reminds me of my priorities. Even if Trevor is angry with me, he can be trusted to do his job. If anything, his refusal to acknowledge the magic will make him even more determined to resolve the question of who poisoned Vivian. He will leave no stone unturned in his effort to find the person responsible.

There is nothing to be gained from me tracking Trevor down. Edward is right; I need to leave it to him to resolve the situation with Trevor. Edward is more likely to have a chance of getting through to him.

I coax my feet back into motion, retracing my steps towards home.

I'm drenched in sweat by the time I arrive. The house is silent and empty. The coffeemaker is decorated with a second note, this one from Edward. He has gone back to his flat at St Margaret to get ready for the day, and H has gone along with him, hoping to meet up with his girlfriend Princess Fluffy.

Armed with a plan and feeling more like my normal self, I shower and get ready at record speed. I toss my handbag into my bicycle basket and take off for Somerset. Unlike earlier this morning, traffic has picked up. It takes all my attention to weave around parked buses and oblivious pedestrians.

I pass in front of the Museum of Natural History and Rhodes House, finally seeing Somerset's expansive wings and crinoline central tower before me. Bystanders crowd the pavement in front and news vans line the street. I pull on my brakes, slowing to a stop at the back of the pack.

A group of locals cluster nearby, standing beside their bicycles as they attempt to peer around the crowd. I approach them, wondering if something has happened.

"What's going on here? Why are there are so many news vans?"

A middle-aged man with an oversized delivery service backpack weighing on his shoulders is the first to respond. "Word is they're filming a movie or something inside the college, and an actress got poisoned. She's taken a turn for the worse, so all the news crews are here, hoping for a statement."

"What? That's awful!" I stammer, filled with concern for Vivian. Desperate to find out the latest news, I debate wading through the crowd to get to the main entrance, but quickly discard the idea. I hop back onto my bicycle and circle around the block, using my university badge to unlock one of the rear gates.

I make quick work of locking my bike up and jog across the gardens towards the line of trailers, looking for a crew member so I can find out what happened. Sam waves from the Craft Services trailer and I speed his way.

"Morning, Nat. I see you found another entrance to the college this morning. It's an absolute jungle out front," he says as he passes me a latte.

"Is everything okay? I heard something about Vivian..." I trail off.

Sam's friendly face drops, his eyes crinkling with concern. "They've not told us much, but from what I gathered, she had a bad night. The doctors have said that if she doesn't show signs of improvement in the next twenty-four hours, she may not make it. Her body is exhausting itself, trying to fight off the effects of the poison."

I gasp and shudder. "I'm so sorry to hear that, Sam. I barely met her, but you all must know her better. I will send her all the healing vibes I can."

"Yeah, that's about all any of us can do." Sam sends me on my way with a suggestion to avoid the front of the college.

The college grounds are still relatively quiet; filming won't start until later in the morning. I spy familiar faces amongst the crew onsite, but everyone has their heads down, distraught, focused only on completing their tasks. The picnic tables in front of Craft Services sit abandoned.

I am the only one standing around — not a normal position for me. Usually, I'm busy, with one responsibility or another laying claim to my time. There must be something I can do to help. I decide to take up patrol, reasoning that with H off romancing his sweetheart, surely the Eternals can use an extra set of eyes. I clutch my hot coffee cup and stride determinedly towards the nearest entrance to the college buildings, feeling better already.

I'm halfway through a lap around the ground floor when I hear someone calling my name.

"Nat? Is that you? I've been looking everywhere!" Molly's exasperated tone causes me to spin around. She hurries along the hallway, rushing to my side. "Come quick! I've got good news. I found John Wilkins."

❖

Molly doesn't wait for a reply, tucking her arm around my own and tugging me along.

"I had to wrack my brain to come up with a list of places he might be," Molly explains as we hustle through the building. "Then I found him in the second place I looked. Four centuries and that man is still as predictable as he was when he governed the college."

"What did you tell him? Did he say he'd help?" I pause my questions long enough to sidestep a pile of cables someone left in the hallway. "Where is he?"

Molly comes to a halt outside of the hall, hunching her shoulders. "Eh, I didn't know how much you wanted me to tell him, so I kept it simple and said he was needed at the college. As for where he is, well... he caught sight of Gideon Pomerance and was intrigued at the thought of someone playing him in a film." She motions towards the hall door. "I left him in there, watching the film crew."

"Oh boy," I mutter. Even growing up during the age of television and movies, it would still be decidedly odd to see someone pretending to be me. I can't imagine what it must be like for Molly and Wilkins. I peek through the window in the door to make sure the crew isn't in the middle of a scene. When I see them moving around, I know it is safe to open the door and go inside.

Wilkins is standing at the front of the hall, near the high table, staring down at Gideon. Gideon is in full costume, seated at the head of the high table, with one leg crossed over the other as he reads over the script, reviewing his lines.

Wilkins frowns in dismay at his television counterpart, clearly unimpressed with my uncle's casting. Seeing them side-by-side, they don't look much alike. Where Gideon is tanned and fit, Wilkins is florid and overweight. Although they both have salt and pepper hair, Gideon's is darker than the lighter shade of the Eternal Wilkins' hair. I suppose, if I were to squint, I would find more similarities. I decide that with the right light, Gideon might look like a younger, richer, Hollywood version of John Wilkins.

To Ilaria's credit, the wardrobe is identical. The men are wearing the same loose white shirt and tan breeches, with black vests and spectacles. It is the wardrobe which has caught Wilkins' eye. He leans over, rubbing the shirt fabric between his fingers, testing to see if it is as he remembers. Gideon reaches up, brushing Wilkins' hand away as though it were a fly. It probably feels that way to him.

"Warden!" Molly calls out, attracting Wilkins' attention.

Wilkins glances our way. He abandons his assessment of his television counterpart, crossing the room until he ends up before us. "Not here," he says, his voice gruff. He spins around and marches off, confident we'll follow him.

We do, but only because we have little other choice. He travels through the hallway until he reaches the library, where he steps through the closed door. Molly goes right behind him, leaving me to play catch up after I pull the heavy door open. The two are at the far end, near where Mathilde and I sat with Trevor after his own tour of Somerset.

I slide onto the sofa next to Molly, the pair of us seated in front of Wilkins. He leans against a wooden table, standing over us. While I suspect his choice of position lingers from his days of passing judgement over a group of headstrong young men as the college Warden, I wish he'd chosen to sit at our level. But right now, power plays won't do us any favours. I paste a smile across my face and begin my introductions.

"I'm Nat Payne, er, I mean Natalie Payne," I amend when he frowns. "I'm the ceremonial prefect."

"I'm aware of who you are," he replies, arching an eyebrow. "What I don't know is why you sent Molly to call me back to Oxford. Explain."

His stern tone puts me on my back foot. I glance at Molly, but she only nods her head, indicating I should carry on with my explanation.

"There is a problem with the magic of Oxford, sir. Your old nemesis, Thomas Hobbes, along with one of his descendants, is trying to destroy our connection."

Now both of Wilkins' eyebrows shoot up in surprise. He rocks back, ever so slightly, stunned by the news. "That's impossible. I'm sure you must be mistaken."

"I wish I were," I murmur, as I shift uncomfortably. "Perhaps it would help if I started from the beginning."

Wilkins nods his approval, and I launch into my tale. "It all started a year ago, before I came to Oxford..."

I tell Wilkins how the museum and library prefects retired and began their search for their replacements. Kate arrived first, quickly butting heads with one of the museum staff members. Mathilde followed two months later, taking on the role at the Bodleian. Lillian, my predecessor, was left to train the pair. But soon, artefacts and books went missing.

Lillian blamed herself and went to see a doctor, where she was diagnosed with early stage dementia. She decided it would be best if she took her leave, worried she was doing more damage than good. That opened up the opportunity for me to come to Oxford, following in my grandfather Alfred's footsteps.

Wilkins' countenance turns more and more grim as I tell him about the murders at St Margaret and Barnard. He rears back in shock at the news of the discovery of the secret chamber in Barnard's library, only remaining calm when I reassure him we hid away all texts with references to the magic.

"We had barely resolved that situation when someone set fire to the Ashmolean," I explain, caught up in my memories.

"The Ashmolean? Dear god!" he barks.

"Sorry, the Ashmolean archives. Not the museum proper," I hasten to add, but Wilkins doesn't seem convinced that is much better. His disbelief grows as I explain about the false accusation of Francie, the video footage and the eventual discovery of the truth. "And it was around then that we figured out who was behind the problems with the magic. His name is Oswald Beadle, and he is a direct descendant of Thomas Hobbes. He expected to be named Director of the Ashmolean when Kate's predecessor departed, but the magic called Kate instead. He got ahold of Kate's key, unlocked his own connection, and has been working against us since then."

Wilkins waits to see if I have anything else to add, glowering at me. I feel like a primary school child, called before the head teacher for bad behaviour. It takes all my willpower to keep my shoulders from creeping up towards my ears. For his part, Wilkins sits silently, letting the tension build in the room.

Finally, he speaks, his tone incredulous. "Let me see if I have this straight. For more than three hundred years, the magic of Oxford existed without a single problem. But then your friend Kate allows a stranger to find her key and immediately puts everyone and everything in Oxford at risk."

"Well, no, it isn't exactly like that," I interrupt.

Wilkins barrels over my words. "And next you take it upon

yourself to tell an assistant, and then your love interest and now a police officer, someone who isn't even connected with the university, about the magic?" His voice rises, sending goosebumps down my arms. "This is how you have attempted to fix the situation?"

I mentally backpedal, flailing around for a foothold. "We needed their help. We still need it. These are extraordinary times..."

"Extraordinary times? That is the only reasonable comment you've made so far, Miss Payne." He holds up a hand, forestalling any further response. He pushes off from the table and growls, "Of all the incompetence! You asked for help, and help you shall have. As of this moment, I am taking control of this operation."

He turns his gaze to Molly, ordering her, "Molly, round up every Eternal in Oxford and have them meet in the Convocation House at the Bodleian. In the meantime, I will find Wren and the other original members of our group."

Wilkins twists, making to depart. I clench my hands into fists and force myself to speak. "What about me, sir? And the other prefects?"

His eyebrows skyrocket. "You and the other prefects? My word, you have done enough already. Your only task at this point is to stay out of the way."

Chapter Thirteen

Molly and Wilkins disappear, leaving me alone in the library, with dozens of snappy comebacks that are furiously popping into my head now that Wilkins is gone. Kate, Mathilde, and I are far from worthless!

"He has some nerve shoving us aside," I grumble to myself, replaying the exchange in my head.

But a little voice in the back of my mind asks the question. Could he have been right?

I can't blame Kate for keeping her key in her office, or Lillian for leaving as quickly as she did. We've all been doing the best that we can in incredibly difficult circumstances, with little or no guidance.

As much as I dislike being dismissed by such a boorish man, I have to admit that it doesn't look good. If I were him, would I act differently? Probably not.

I abandon any thoughts of chasing after Wilkins and giving him a piece of my mind. There is no need to rush to contact Mathilde, Kate, Edward, or Harry either. They'll all hear soon enough as Molly makes her way around town, alerting all of Oxford's Eternals.

I've let them all down. I can't bear to hear the disappointment in their voices.

Even so, I cannot let go of the thought that there must be something I can do. Wilkins may have warned me off making a move against Hobbes and Beadle, but there is still the film production at risk. With a hoard of paparazzi out front, Uncle Harold must be feeling as though he is living in a vise-grip, the pressure clenching him by the throat. I decide that there must be some stone left unturned, some action I can take to help solve the mystery of who poisoned Vivian and why.

I rise to my feet, ready to set off on my search, but stop before I can get more than a step forward. I've spoken to most of the cast and crew, as have Trevor and his investigative team. If anything were awry here at Somerset, one of the Eternals would have already brought it to my attention. I think back through the pranks prior to Vivian collapsing. The falling lights and the missing scripts — those happened at the Botanic Garden, not at Somerset.

Could there be some clue there? Maybe a gardener spotted something unusual, without realising the significance of it. As far as I can tell, the police seem to be focusing all their attention on interviewing the cast and crew.

There is no harm in me making a trip back to the Garden and asking a few questions, I rationalise. I might jog someone's memories or uncover a fresh angle we can explore.

I dash off a quick text to my uncle, explaining that I'm running an errand and will be back by lunch. With my handbag clutched against my side, I opt for the back hallways, winding through the college buildings until I arrive at the closest exit to where I left my bicycle. The space is empty, no Eternals or crew members within sight.

I take a deep breath, thinking to myself, "Come on, Nat. Stay positive. Focus on what you can do, not what is behind you."

I guide my bicycle out to the road, one more anonymous cyclist among the many. I speed up only to slow down again as I wind through the clusters of tourists who clog the streets. The cobblestones near the Radcliffe Camera are slick with morning dew. My wheels slip and slide until I give up and walk gingerly to where the pavement starts again.

High Street is busy with taxis and double-decker buses. I hold my breath as I jump into the flow of traffic. I don't have far left to go; I can already see Magdalen's tower growing closer. It stands directly across the street from the entrance to the Botanic Garden.

I make a right turn into the small side street which borders the garden, and then a left into the garden proper. Fire, determination, and sheer grit run through my veins as I lock up my bike. Who knows? There could be someone inside holding a clue to the identity of the poisoner. I'm not leaving here until I've exhausted all possibilities.

After waving my university ID at the ticket counter and grabbing a paper map, I power on into the garden. Today, it has none of the buzz and excitement of last week, empty of trailers and busy crew members. Everyone has moved over to Somerset, and life here has returned to normal.

A small child runs past me, chasing after a brightly coloured butterfly; behind him, his mother calls for him to slow down. I give her a smile of understanding as she walks by, reassuring her I'm not bothered by his rambunctiousness.

I follow the map until I reach the garden section where deadly plants can be found. There, amidst a riot of other flowers, I spy the delicate purple blossoms just like the one I found pressed against the side of Vivian's plate. The plants are set back in wide, wooden planters. A slender rope is all there is to block someone passing by from touching them. Small signs warning of the dangers hang from the rope.

I step back to study the scene. If someone were hunting for a potential poison, they wouldn't need to be a botanical expert to find one. The warning signage provides all the information one would need.

"A few sips of a tincture made from monkshood could be enough to prove fatal," I read from a nearby display. I don't have to guess where the poisoner got the idea of slipping the leaf into Vivian's drink.

Getting access to the plant would have required someone to step over the narrow rope and stand in the planter. They also would have needed a glove to protect their hand, and something to fashion as a plant cutter to cut through the stems. If this were a crime of opportunity, it would be likely the poisoner wouldn't have come prepared with the tools needed to cut a sprig. "They must have borrowed them from one of the gardener's sheds," I rationalise, looking around to see if there is one nearby.

Of course, there isn't one. Not here, in the middle of the garden pathways. I consult the map again, spotting a small cluster of huts in the far corner. The lack of labels on the buildings strengthens my suspicions that they are for staff-only. I turn around, identifying the right direction, and set off, keeping on the lookout for any gardeners or other staff who might be able to offer a clue.

"Maybe someone will remember seeing a footprint in the dirt in that flowerbed," I mutter under my breath. The roar of a lawnmower grows louder, giving me hope. I speed up, hoping to catch the person using it, but every turn reveals another trellis of flowers or tall hedge, blocking them from view. I realise they must be mowing the events lawn, which sits in the exact wrong direction.

I stick to my original plan, following the path as it takes me away from the noise of the motor. I pass more families and older couples, all making the most of the dreary summer day. If there isn't rain, locals and tourists alike have to content themselves with whatever weather they find. The vibrant colours of the flowers and burbling of the stone fountains are enough to brighten the day.

I consult the map again, finding I need to pass through the woods to get to the sheds. The old-growth trees remind me of our first day on set. Edward, Harry, H, and I were all so excited and hopeful, no way of knowing the challenges in store for us.

A rustle in the trees catches my attention. I glance upwards to see a squirrel scampering across a branch, observing me from his perch. That thought leads to another, making me wonder whether the garden has any security cameras. If they do, I am sure Trevor will have already requested the footage. But of course, at the time, he wouldn't have known to look out for the impossible. I make a mental note to ask about cameras at the information desk.

Finally, I see the bank of the Cherwell River, the gently lapping water visible between the low hanging tree branches. I quicken my pace, suddenly desperate to get off the tree-covered pathway and out into the muted daylight. This section of the garden feels isolated, almost like it is no-man's-land.

I burst from the trees, stepping into the light, and look up at the sky just in time to see a black shadow soar ominously over my head. The giant bird caws loudly, and then cackles.

The crow!

Before I say a word, I hear a whistle of air and feel a hard whack on the back of my head. I crumble to the ground; the pain overwhelming me. The last thing I feel is two pairs of meaty hands grasping my arms and ankles to carry me off. The world fades to black.

❖

The smell is the first thing I notice. It is dank and loamy, the air heavy with humidity. It smells like freshly turned dirt and enclosed spaces.

I flutter my lashes, struggling to wake up. My clothing feels clammy with sweat. My mouth is dry, the coarse cloth gag cutting into the sides of my mouth. Realising something is wrong, I jerk my head up in shock and nearly pass out from the pain of the rapid movement. Gingerly, I scrunch my eyes shut and clench my teeth, praying for it to pass.

Slowly, the pain recedes enough for me to make sense of things. At least I'm sitting upright, although my shoulders are aching furiously, forcibly pulled backwards with my arms wrapped around the chair back. I tug but can barely move my hands. Coils of garden twine scratch against my wrists and ankles, holding them secure.

Taking care, I ever so slowly turn my head to scan the room. In the gloom, I can barely make out my surroundings. Dark shadows envelop me, and only the faintest hint of moonlight shines through the glass roof overhead, providing a minimum of illumination. Tall green branches block most of my view. I must have been unconscious for hours.

I close my eyes again, letting my other senses take over. Gradually, I hear a drip, drip of water and then a small splash, almost like the one a frog makes when it leaps into a pond. I realise where I must be — tucked away, deep inside one of the Botanic Garden's greenhouses.

This must be the tropical greenhouse I read about in the brochure. I look around again, recalling what I read. Peering carefully, I can make out the edges of palm fronds high above me and smell a faint hint of citrus in the humid air. The brochure mentioned a small pond installed inside one end of the building, and fruit trees growing in pots at the other. I must be sitting in the middle, in the small space between the two sections of the building.

But how did I get here? And why am I tied up? Why am I by myself?

I churn through my memories. I had come to the Botanic Garden, searching for clues of who might be the poisoner. I remember wanting to interview the garden staff and deciding to search for someone near the utility shed. I followed the marked pathway, walking through the small woods. I saw the Cherwell and then... I stepped out of the shadows as something flew overhead. The crow!

Panic crashes over me, the truth of my situation settling in. I screech a muffled cry as terror blocks all rational thought. After nearly choking on the gag, I force myself to take in a few calming breaths. I am uncomfortable, but other than the wound on the back of my head, I don't seem to be injured otherwise.

I tug my arms again, nearly wrenching my shoulder out of the socket in my efforts to break free. Caught by Beadle and his gang of evil henchman! God only knows what they have in store for me. I clamp down, biting back a scream.

The moon is high in the sky, indicating it must be close to midnight. This late at night, gagged and bound, no one will hear me. Besides, the only people around are likely to be my captors. The last thing I want is to let them know I'm awake.

Escape becomes my top priority. I jerk my arms again and nearly topple over, putting paid to any further plans in that direction. I cast my gaze left and right, frantically searching for anything which might help. All I can see are leaves, stalks, and tree trunks. None of which are of any use to me now. Surrounded by so much foliage, I'm probably not even visible from outside the building. I whimper, fearing no one will find me.

My handbag is gone, and with it my phone. Edward and H

must have missed me by now, likely hours ago. As scared as I am, they must be feeling even worse, wondering whether I am even alive. I almost burst into tears at the thought. But no, I have to think positively right now. Fear will not help me get out.

Edward and H won't sit at home, waiting for word. They will be out searching for me, and probably have been for hours. The two can cover much ground, H on high and Edward on foot. Will they recognise my bicycle locked out front? I'm confident they'll eventually discover it and search the confines of the garden, but that could be hours from now. Hours in which Beadle's Eternals could put their years of experience as torture masters to work.

"Think, Nat!" I shout inside my head. I need something more subtle than attempting to drag the chair across the ground hoping to find an abandoned trowel. I twist my hands and feel around on the edge of the wooden chair, nearly sobbing when I find a sharp nail sticking out underneath. Just as I get my hands into position, with the bindings rubbing against the sharp point, I hear a door slam. Low ground lights flicker on, providing a minimum of illumination.

I freeze in place, terror rising again. After a moment of silence, I hear a gruff male voice coming from one end of the greenhouse. I'm not alone inside any longer. I rub the twine against the sharp point as fast as I can, hoping to make some headway while whoever came in the door is still out of sight.

It takes me a moment to work out what the man is saying. His accent is distinctly old-fashioned, making me think of the East End. It isn't a voice I've heard before.

"Guv, we got her like you asked, trussed her up so she ain't goin' nowhere."

"Excellent work, Ike. I knew you were the right Eternal for the task," another man replies. This voice is familiar. Even though I've only heard it once, I'm not likely to forget it. Its distinct nasal tone echoes off the glass walls and ceiling. It can only be Oswald Beadle.

"Let's see if our guest is awake, shall we?" he asks, their footsteps growing louder. Leaves rustle as they wind their way through the greenhouse aisleways.

The sound of wings slicing through the air pulls my attention upwards. A giant shadow swoops over my head, blowing my hair into my face. It is Beadle's crow. The vile bird flares his wings out, slowing his descent until he lands on the branch of a nearby citrus tree.

"Ah, Fenius, there you are," Beadle calls out, earning a caw in response from the crow. "Keep a watch out for Hobbes, please. He should join us shortly."

I track the moving leaves of the greenhouse plants, mentally preparing myself for when Beadle and his henchman will appear. I may be tied up, but I will not let this snivelling excuse of a man defeat me so easily.

Beadle appears first, stepping into the wide aisle where I'm seated. He's wearing the same trousers and hooded sweatshirt he wore on the day he set the Ashmolean archives on fire. I watched that security video so many times; I know them on sight. Up close, he looks utterly ridiculous in the casual clothing, like a grown man playing at being a teenager. He practically rubs his hands together in glee and leers when his eyes land upon me, trussed up like a present on Christmas morning.

I meet his gaze, letting my fury show in my eyes. If only I had a speck of H's fiery magic, I'd set Beadle on fire.

The leaves whisper again and a broader man steps through the foliage. This must be Ike. His shirt hangs loose over his ragged trousers. Bulging biceps threaten to rip through his shirt sleeves. His choppy blond hair is matted to his forehead, his cheeks pockmarked. His pronounced brow turns his eyes into dark shadows.

He doesn't look my way, as all his attention is focused on Beadle. He stares at him in adoration, clearly worshipping the man who brought the magic to the Torture Museum and gave him a second existence. Any hope I had that Ike might be convinced to come to my aid disappears. This Eternal will never betray his master.

"Hullo, Natalie. Fancy meeting you here," Beadle drawls, chuckling at his own cleverness. "I must thank you for that. Here we were, wondering how we were going to capture you, Kate, and Mathilde, with no one noticing. Then you so generously wandered off on your own, practically begging us to grab you."

Unable to speak, I growl in reply, making Beadle laugh again. He elbows Ike and points him my way. "Remove her gag, Ike. I have questions for Miss Payne here, and she can't answer them with your old handkerchief stuffed in her cheeks."

Ike leaps to do Beadle's bidding, circling around behind me. His clumsy, fat fingers take ages to undo the knot. When he finally pulls the cloth away, I turn my head to the side and spit the taste from my mouth.

Glowering, I bite the words out, "I don't suppose you'd be willing to untie my hands as well?"

Beadle smirks as he shakes his head. "I'd get used to the discomfort if I were you. Ike here is an expert at inflicting pain, but I insisted he hold back until we give you a chance to tell me what I need to know." He stops, his expression hardening. "After all, there's no reason to make the last moments of your life miserable."

Ike barks a laugh and Fenius the crow cackles, but I don't think Beadle means his threat as a joke. I slump in my chair, as though in defeat, but really I'm shifting so I have better access to the sharp point under the seat. If there is a time clock ticking away the minutes of my life, I don't intend to spend them sitting here, waiting to be rescued.

My mission is clear: keep Beadle talking long enough for me to break through the twine around my hands, and then hope like hell I can find a way out of here before Ike gets his meaty hands on me again.

Chapter Fourteen

Sweat rolls across my brow as I wiggle my wrists, scraping the twine against the sharp point of the nail. I move my hands up and down as quickly as I dare, but still frustratingly slow. I cannot afford to let Beadle or Ike figure out what I am doing.

Now to get Beadle talking. My mind races through everything I know about him. He's pompous and egotistical and has spent most of his life relegated to standing in someone else's shadow. I don't need three guesses to figure out what his favourite topic must be. Given half a chance, I'm sure he'll jump at the chance to lord his superiority over me, particularly now that he has me at a distinct disadvantage.

I pick up and discard any thoughts of playing the simpering female. It's too cliché; there is no way he will buy it. Plus, there is no chance I could stomach it for long enough to get him talking. I decide to pull an idea from Kate's playbook. With as much condescension as I can muster, he should rise to the bait and rattle on about himself.

"Do you need to wait for Hobbes before asking your questions, Beadle?" I drawl. "I presume he is the brains behind your organisation."

Beadle splutters, his neck flushing red. "Hobbes is dependent on me, not the other way around."

I arch my eyebrow and cock my head to the side. "Really? Are you sure about that? Without Hobbes and his knowledge of the magic, where would you be?"

"Where would I be?" he echoes, and then laughs. "Hobbes spent nearly four centuries languishing in the basement of the Ashmolean. He didn't dare risk showing his face. He had to bide his time, hoping one of his descendants would eventually discover the magic. He could never have dreamt up this plan."

Still sawing furiously away on my bindings, I retort, "What plan? Steal a bunch of random items from the colleges? Rob the Ashmolean archives? Betray your conspirator at the last moment? And now kidnapping? Sounds more like the efforts of an amateur, if you ask me."

Oswald Beadle puffs up his chest, stomps over, and slaps me hard across the face. My cheek burns, and the pain in the back of my head flares up. For a split second, I fear I've gone too far. He rears back, as if to hit me again, but settles for wagging his finger in my face.

"How dare you speak to me that way," he growls, his voice growing louder. "You and Kate and the others... you all think you are so superior because of your magical bloodline. What have you done with the magic? Nothing!"

He spins around, walking back to Ike, his shoulders shaking with fury. He shudders, forcefully regaining his control. When he turns back my way, his eyes glower with hatred. I twist my wrists faster, scraping harder against the nail, even though sliding the twine up and down is rubbing my arms raw.

I steel my gaze, looking him straight in the eye. "So, tell me then, Beadle, about this great plan of yours. What have *you* actually accomplished here?"

I add a hint of disdain to my expression, goading him further.

My challenge is unspoken, but clear. If he wants me to believe he is truly an evil genius, he'll have to offer some proof to back up his words. By accusing him of being a fraud, I can tell I'm getting to him.

Ike might be a thick-headed henchman, but even he has figured out I'm insulting his boss. He flexes his arms and steps my way. "We've had enough of your mouth, wench," he grunts, punching his fist against his other hand menacingly. He glances back at Beadle. "Want me to make her sing for you, guv?"

I can feel the cold drip of sweat running down my back as Beadle contemplates the offer. His wicked grin indicates he is thinking about letting Ike hurt me. The crow adds his gleeful agreement, cawing words of encouragement from above. I move my hands even faster, my arms rigid to disguise my motions. My hands grow slick, a sure sign my wrists are now bleeding.

Finally, Beadle reaches out a hand and rests it on Ike's bulging bicep, stopping him from getting any closer. "There's time enough yet, Ike. If you hurt her too quickly, she won't tell us how we can capture Kate and Mathilde, or who else knows about Oxford's magic. Perhaps if she knows who she's up against, she'll abandon any plans to hold out on us."

I nearly faint in relief, but Ike looks crestfallen. Beadle pats him on the arm and adds, "Don't worry, Ike. I'll let you rough her up either way. You'll get your fun."

Ike smiles cruelly and my cold sweats redouble.

"Now, where were we?" Beadle asks, pretending to think for a moment. "Ah yes. Since you asked so nicely, Nat, I will tell you how we've arrived at this point. Unlike you and your lot of friends, we haven't bumbled our way here. Step by step and piece by piece, I have single-handedly created my own connection to the magic. Do you think I've chosen the items I acquired at random? Ha!" he barks. His stare makes my skin crawl.

He curls his lip up, smirking at me. "That shows what fools

you are! You wouldn't even know where to start, not like I did. After years at the Ashmolean, I knew the location of every single artefact in Oxford. I handpicked items which I knew were likely to be connected to the magic but stayed away from anything which might try to stand in our way... like your portrait of Catherine Morgan at St Margaret. I knew she'd never help."

I must admit, I'm impressed. None of us had a clue why Beadle was stealing the items he did. I let some of my surprise show. "So why did you take the portrait from Iffley College? How did you know the person in it wouldn't react with the same scorn as Catherine?"

"The portrait of Iffley College's Hobbesian professor? He worshipped the ground Hobbes walked on. I let Hobbes do all the talking, and he was more than happy to lend his expertise."

A shiver of fear runs up my spine as I have my first doubt about my ability to get free and to best Beadle. Even after we learned of his connection to Hobbes, we still didn't put all the pieces together — not Kate, our art expert; Mathilde, our historian; or even Edward, our criminal psychologist.

Ikc, sensing my moment of weakness, punches his fist into his hand again. I flinch, jerking upright in reflex to the pounding thud. My movement comes as a blessing. A few strands of the weakened twine bindings break apart, reviving my hope of escape.

"So, Natalie, as you can see, I have taken my time plotting every step of the way. And when I needed more information on how the magic works, Wren himself stepped in."

I can't stop the look of shocked horror which crosses my face.

"Not that he knew he was helping," Beadle adds, oblivious to my reaction, too caught up in his story. "Hobbes had heard rumours of a secret chamber in Barnard College, shortly before his death. It was easy enough to find once we knew where to look. We took the papers which talked about how the magic works and left the rest behind."

I feel another strand in the twine give. I'm getting closer to freedom, but I still need to buy more time. "What about Andrei Radu, the guard at the Ashmolean? If you were so clever at getting in and out, why did you need to involve him?"

Beadle huffs and rolls his eyes. "Ah, Natalie, as you surely must know, there are limits to what the magic can do. I know the security system at the Ashmolean inside and out, so I was all too aware of the challenge it would pose. Finding someone on the inside, someone as disenchanted as I am, wasn't hard."

"And what? You murdered him as soon as he stopped being useful?" I frown in disappointment. "You've become rather bloodthirsty, Beadle."

Ike perks up at my words, swaggering close and leering at me, sending me slumping sideways to get away from him. Beadle laughs at the sight of my fear, further cementing my previous statement.

Losing his job at the Ashmolean to Kate clearly unhinged something in Oswald, turning him from a mild-mannered art historian into a cut-throat criminal. If I hadn't seen it with my own eyes, I would find it impossible to believe. He is intoxicated by his newfound power and his ability to run roughshod over us prefects. Two years ago, I suspect he would have flinched at the sight of blood. Now watching me tremble in fear gives him a rush.

My hand slips sideways, the sharp point of the nail slicing across the pad of my hand. I nearly shriek in pain but swallow it down. I can't stop the tears from filling my eyes, though.

Oswald notes them but takes them to mean something else. "Look, Ike. The poor girl is crying. Do you think she's finally realised she is beaten and that no one is going to rescue her?"

"Is it time, guv? I've been wanting to show her what a broken rib feels like ever since she walked into our Torture Museum. I thought I'd start with the pliers, eh? She'll sing for you, she will. I give you my promise."

I pipe up before Beadle can respond. "Wait, I still have another question." The men stop their discussion and turn to look my way. "Why do you have to kill us? I know you want to rip away Oxford's connection to the magic, to make Kate pay for how she treated you, but why me? Why Mathilde?"

An older man, dressed in a voluminous black cloak and a broad-collared white shirt, steps out from the next aisle.

"I can answer that question, Miss Payne."

The man needs no introduction. It is Thomas Hobbes, looking the same as he does in his portrait, sitting in the basement at the Ashmolean. Painted at the height of his popularity, he looks every inch the distinguished scholar. The crown of his head is bald, shining in the pale moonlight. Thick, white hair circles his head and tumbles down to his shoulder. A matching moustache and narrow beard complete his look.

His eyes are feverishly bright, hinting at the madness brought on by spending an eternity burning in a jealous rage. He sweeps across the floor, coming to a stop halfway between my chair and where Beadle and his henchman, Ike, are standing. He crooks a finger up at the tree and holds out his arm. The crow glides down and lands on Hobbes's outstretched arm.

"Fenius, that dreadful wyvern creature has been circling over the garden. Be a good lad, will you, and chase him off for us? He's no match for your cleverness," Hobbes instructs him.

Fenius preens under Hobbes' gaze, bobbing his head in agreement. His screeching voice echoes off the glass walls and ceiling, promising, "I'll lead that sad excuse of a lizard on a merry chase, and pick over his bones when he tires out. You needn't worry, he won't bother you."

Hobbes uses his free hand to reach into a pocket in his robe, pulling out a grizzled piece of meat. Fenius plucks it out of his hand and then flies off. The scraping sound of a window opening signals the bird's departure from the greenhouse.

Hobbes steeples his hands together, peering over the top of them. His stare makes my skin crawl. There is so much evil in his gaze that I decide slicing my hand again will be a small price to pay for getting out of here. I line up the twine against the sharp point, furiously working on remaining strands.

"Oxford University has been a juggernaut for too long, Miss Payne," Hobbes begins, twisting to pace in front of me. "Its leaders refused to acknowledge my brilliance while I was alive. I clung to Eternal life, determined to bring them and their beloved colleges down. With your help, I will finally see the situation remedied."

"My help?" I squeak, my voice heavy with concern and a healthy tinge of fear.

Hobbes turns, pacing the other way. "I have studied the magic for centuries, seeking to understand its secrets. Wilkins, Wren, and their group of mad philosophers have kept some things from me, but not all. I know now what it takes to keep the magic stable."

He pauses directly in front of me. "The magical connection requires two things — the copper rods, endowed with an as-of-yet unknown property, and a prefect." He leans over, sneering in my face. "That's you, my dear."

Beadle coughs, making a valiant effort to regain control of the situation. "At first, we thought stretching the magic to London would be enough to destabilise it. When that failed to rip the magic away, we began stealing some of the magical items."

"I still believe that approach would work, boy," Hobbes interrupts, glaring Beadle back into his place. "But it is taking too long. I have eternity, but my many-great-grandson does not. So unfortunately for you, this leaves us with only one option remaining."

"To torture her," Ike jeers. "Is it my turn to have a go at her yet? I'll get you the information you need."

"Almost," Hobbes calls out, smiling generously at the muscle-bound Eternal standing behind him. "I am sorry for you, Miss Payne. You and your friends are innocent, bound up in this system through no fault of your own. But we are not inclined to pardon you. As long as you and the other prefects live, and any person aware of your connection, so too lives the magic of Oxford."

Having completed his speech, Hobbes waves Beadle to the front and turns over the proverbial reins. Beadle nods at Hobbes and circles around me. I take great care to keep him from realising how close I am to loosening the twine around my wrists.

I can hear the glee in his voice when he returns to his place beside Ike. "Nat, you will tell us who knows about the magic of Oxford. I have my suspicions that it goes beyond you, Kate, and Mathilde. We can do this the easy way, or the hard way. I will say that the choice is yours, but perhaps it will help you decide quicker if you get a taste of the hard option first."

My eyes grow wide as he rests his hand on Ike's back and says, "Break her nose, Ike."

Ike flexes his muscles in delight. His smile is warped and monstrous as he swaggers across the small clearing. With my hands and feet tied, there is nowhere I can go and nothing I can do to escape the blow which is about to come my way. Ike knows this. The vein in his forehead pulses in a frenzied glee.

He straightens up, pumping his arm forward to check his aim. My face drains of colour and adrenaline races through my body, begging me to do something, anything to avoid the pain which is coming. Satisfied that everything is as he likes, Ike casts one last glance at Hobbes and Beadle, making sure there is to be no last-minute reprieve.

The two men limit themselves to a single nod of the head, dooming me without saying a word.

Ike holds his hand in front of my face, folding his fingers over, one by one, into a fist. I cower. He gives me a toothy grin, satisfied by my fright.

Three things happen simultaneously.

Ike pulls his arm back.

Glass shatters, raining from the ceiling.

I throw myself sideways, toppling over in the chair and ripping my hands apart with the force.

Ike's fist misses its target, grazing the side of my head as he twists upward in shock at the crash of breaking glass. Unable to get free completely, I stick my hands out and cushion my fall as the chair tumbles sideways. Before I can do anything else, a sleek black body bullets past me, sending a stream of flames at my feet. I kick the rope from my ankles as it burns with small flames. I have to rush to get loose of them before the magic repairs the damage H has done.

"H, you found me!" I cry, nearly weeping with joy at the sight of my best friend somersaulting above the citrus trees in the greenhouse, the crow fast on his heels. Beadle and Hobbes stare up in shock at the sight of the two winged creatures chasing each other furiously. Ike, instead, is dumbfounded, unable to process the sudden change in the situation.

I take advantage of the momentary distraction and dart off into the depths of the greenhouse. With any luck, I'll find a doorway and escape into the garden. Ike's roar of frustration fills the air as he smashes his way into the narrow path, shoving potted trees out of his way. I scurry in and out of the small openings, rethinking my plan to dash for the door. Ike is too close behind; I'll need to outsmart him if I hope to escape.

Hobbes recovers from his surprise and begins issuing orders. "Ike, don't let her out of here. Kill her if you must. Oswald, check all the doors and make sure they are locked. If the lizard found us, her friends won't be too far behind."

Moving as quickly as I dare, I hunt for a hiding space. There are plenty of pools of shadows, but all of them are too exposed for me to feel safe. Finally, I spot a cluster of shrubs sitting close together. Heedless of their sharp-edged leaves, I drop to my knees and crawl in between them. I scrounge around in one of the pots until I find a small stone, daring to reach out an arm to toss it as far as I can to redirect him away from me. Amazingly, it works. Ike pauses at the sound and turns to follow it, moving away from me.

I take a moment to catch my breath and examine my wrists and hands. They are red with blood, rubbed raw from the twine and further slicked from the cut in my palm. My ankles are tender from where H's flames licked across them, but I'm amazed they aren't worse. How he aimed his flames and severed the ropes without hurting me more, I will never know. I forcefully stave off the mental breakdown I can feel looming over me. Now isn't the time to fall to pieces. I can do that when H and I are safe. I gulp back a sob and take a few steadying breaths.

The sound of more shattering glass pulls my attention upwards. H is crashing in and out of the roof, barely staying ahead of Fenius. It takes me a moment to figure out what he is doing. "Of course! He must be signalling to the others where we are," I whisper. Indeed, each time he soars into the sky, he shoots a jet of flame and a shout for help.

As Eternals, Hobbes and Ike don't have to worry about the falling glass, but Beadle and I don't have the same luxury. I pull my knees tight and tuck my chin against my chest, burrowing deeper into the shrubs. Beadle shouts for assistance at the other end of the greenhouse, urging Fenius to stop playing with his prey and finish H.

How long can H hold his lead? Where is Edward? Why aren't

the other Eternals here yet? My mind overflows with questions, nearly pushing me into a panic. One thing is clear — I can't stay hidden here forever. I need to get out of this greenhouse and into the open, where Edward and the Eternals can more easily lend a hand.

In the cacophony of breaking glass and men's shouts, I have to fight past my fear and lift my head up for a look around. I strain my eyes, searching for any hint of a doorway. Leafy fruit trees sit in carefully tended rows, blocking my view. My throat closes, terror rising as my aches and pains clamour for attention. I need to move now.

Ike is nowhere in sight. I shift until my feet are underneath me. It takes all my strength and willpower to raise my head above the shrubs and glance around. I scan the space, desperate for a clue. My gaze snags on the metal joints crisscrossing the roof. I trace one of them until it slopes downward. That must be the wall, and it isn't far away. There can't be more than two rows of trees separating me from it.

The way still clear, I drop and crawl out of my hideaway. Staying bent over, making use of the shadows, I skitter sideways into the nearby row of trees. Creeping slowly, careful not to touch a single branch which might giveaway my movements, I slink forward. My eyes land on the doorframe and Ike at the same time. He must have cottoned onto my plan and decided, why hunt your prey if you know it will eventually come to you? He has taken up guard in front of the doorway instead of trying to flush me out of my hiding space.

He stands in a circle of moonlight, his muscles etched in silver, his stance menacing. I tuck deeper into the shadows, sizing up my chances for escape. There is no way I can get past him, not without help. Nor can anyone hope to get inside to help me, not with Ike blocking the way.

There is only one Eternal who stands of chance of sending Ike running for cover: my wyvern, H. H's flames don't have any effect on Bartie and my grandfather, but they do on creatures like the crow. Will Ike, a newly created Eternal, know that he is safe from the flames, or will the threat of fire be enough to scare him away from his post? There's only one way to find out.

I cup my hands around my mouth and shout into the air. "Aiitchh! The doorway! Come burn us a way out of here!"

❖

H wrests his upward trajectory and arcs downward, hurtling straight at Ike. This is the make-or-break moment in my hastily assembled plan. Will Ike stand his ground in the face of a fiery cannonball?

I move one leg back, readying myself to sprint for the door as soon as the way is clear.

H whizzes lower and lower, spewing flames left and right, setting all the fruit trees inside the greenhouse on fire. The warning is clear. Ike is his next target.

Ike stands tall, his chest puffed out, seemingly invincible, but minor tremors betray his fear. I am almost convinced that our plan is doomed to fail when an unlikely source comes to our aid.

"Move, man!" Fenius shouts at Ike. "He'll burn you to a crisp!"

That's all the encouragement Ike needs. He throws himself out of H's way just in time. H doesn't slow his pace. He lets his momentum propel him through the doorway, banging it open so hard that the glass shatters and the frame pops loose. I am a half step behind him, gulping in the fresh night air as I sprint onto the riverside path outside.

"Nat!" Edward shouts from ahead, his voice ragged with emotion. He steps out from the shadows, his arms open wide. I throw myself into them, sobbing in relief. He clings to me just as tightly, both of us elated to find one another, safe and whole.

H circles around us, skidding to a stop between us and the greenhouse. He gives a quick glance, checking we are okay, before returning his attention to our advancing enemy.

The crow bursts from the open doorway, his ear-piercing caws sending shivers down my spine as he flies out of the greenhouse. Fenius shifts his body, expanding his wings and pumping them backwards, slowing to hover a few metres in front of H.

Fenius cackles. In the moonlight, he looks like a creature straight out of hell, his black eyes ablaze with warning, threatening agony for all around him.

"Look at you three, gasping for breath. Pathetic!" Fenius cackles. "You've gotten free of the greenhouse, but where will you go? Our Eternals will soon fill the garden."

H glares at Fenius but remains silent.

"Cat got your tongue?" Fenius taunts H. "Or have you finally reached the end of your energy stores, old man?"

H gives us one more quick look over his shoulder. Edward clutches me tighter, pulling us back a few steps.

Smoke curls from H's nostrils, twirling in the air. He takes in a deep breath, flares his wings out and roars. His thunderous roar booms louder and louder, his chest expanding, his wingspan doubling and tripling. In seconds, H transforms from a cat-sized wyvern into an enormous, fire-breathing beast. His spiky tail smashes into the ground, sending dirt and stones flying into the air. He towers over us, standing twice our height. His eyes glow bright yellow, shining brighter than the streetlights. His teeth are sharp daggers, and his talons are larger than my hand. He is a creature of nightmares.

His transformation happens so fast, none of us have time to react. Edward and I are frozen in H's long shadow, staring agape. Fenius squawks in shock at the sudden loss of his advantage.

H, now a gargantuan winged daemon, throws his head in the air, shooting a jet of flames into the sky, lighting up the garden as bright as day. Then he tosses his head in the other direction, his jaws open wide, and he snaps his mouth shut over Fenius so quickly that a muffled caw is our only hint of what has happened to him.

H swallows, burps a cloud of black smoke, sneezes and shrinks back to his normal size.

Edward and I look at one another, disbelief written across our faces, desperate to know whether we imagined the last few moments or if they actually happened.

H coughs, attracting our attention. He spits out a single black feather, sending it sailing into the air, and then wipes his mouth with the back of his scaly hand.

"Lor luv a duck, mates. I 'ate it when I 'ave to eat one of them feathered fiends. Birds always give me 'eartburn."

Chapter Fifteen

I am full of questions for H, but I shove them aside when Beadle, Hobbes, and their henchman emerge from the greenhouse, spreading out as they close in on Edward and I. Hobbes takes up position on the far right, sneering cruelly. Beadle stands in the middle with his hands on his hips, his face red with anger. Ike is on the far left, grinning eagerly at us as he swings a giant club in his hand, anticipating violence.

Beadle alone looks upwards, searching the skies for a sign of Fenius.

I slip from Edward's embrace, twisting around to stand at his side, but letting my hand trail down his arm until I reach his hand. Sliding my fingers through his, I stare stoically at the trio who are determined to kill us all. Not one to be overlooked, H leaps into the air and flies up to hover next to me, evening the odds. Three against three. I think we can take them.

Hobbes must read the confidence in my face. He booms out a mocking laugh, waving his arm at us. "Look at the three of them, men. They actually think they still have a chance of escaping us. Ha!"

I square my shoulders, unfazed by Hobbes' taunt. My head

may be pounding, my wrists slick with blood, but I am far from ready to fall at his feet and beg him to let us live. Seeing H transform into a nightmarish creature from the pages of a fairy tale has reminded me of one fact — we all have our secret strengths and powers.

Edward squeezes my hand, letting me know he is beside me. H never shifts his gaze from our enemies, as black smoke spirals from his nostrils.

Tossing my hair over my shoulder, I meet Hobbes's gaze. "I'll admit that Ike is fearsome, but you other two? A snivelling rat and a doddering old fool? Now that you've lost your advantage, you might as well pack it in."

Hobbes winks out. For a moment, hope rises in my chest; perhaps he has taken my words to heart and has run for the hills. But he reappears seconds later, joined by another man. My eyes grow wide as I recognise the bald medieval man H and I chased through the Covered Market. Then another cloaked man appears, armed with a fiery torch.

By the time two more Eternals join them — a haggard old crone and a masked executioner — I realise our odds are no longer so even. These are all characters from the Torture Museum, plucked from their displays to stand against me and my friends. They cackle and crow, rubbing their hands together in excitement or brandishing their weapons menacingly.

I do my best to hide the wave of fear that rushes over me, but my legs and arms tremble ever so slightly, begging me to take flight while I still can.

I glance first at H. He seems undaunted. His wings flap gently, hovering in place, and he huffs a small flame, almost as though he is laughing back. From where I'm standing, however, it is impossible to tell whether it is pure bravado or if H has another trick up his sleeve.

Edward's squeeze of my hand pulls my attention away from H.

He meets my eyes, his gaze silently urging me to stay strong. I quirk an eyebrow up. But he gives a tiny shake of his head, refusing to explain the source of his confidence.

It is a make-or-break moment. Do I trust this man and this creature to keep me alive? I roll my shoulders back, tightening my muscles to cease the trembling.

Beadle opens his mouth, undoubtedly preparing another taunt, and Hobbes raises a hand to silence him. Of the three, Hobbes seems to be the one to realise something is off. He stares at us, his narrowed gaze hunting for an explanation as to why we are still standing there instead of cowering.

Beadle, however, refuses to be quiet. He paces forward two steps, and sneers. "Still here, Natalie? I assume by his absence that you must have defeated Fenius, but don't let that go to your head. You don't have a hope against my army of Eternals." He spreads his arms wide. "Look at them, Natalie. Each one more bloodthirsty than the next. They live for pain and suffering... your pain and suffering."

I tighten my grip on Edward's hand, unable to stop a hint of fear from creeping across my face.

Beadle spins around, addressing his crew. "What say you, Eternals? Shall we give Natalie a head start? Seems only fair, seeing as no one else is coming to save her and her friends."

"I wouldn't bet on that, Beadle!" Kate shouts, her voice hoarse with anger as she steps out from behind a nearby garden shed with Bartie at her side.

"How delightful!" Beadle jeers, unfazed. "So pleased you could join us, Kate. This will certainly make things easier for us. Here I was, worried how we'd get you alone, and you've presented yourself practically on a platter." He turns, nodding at his old crone. "Griselda, make her suffer before you kill her." The old crone smiles, flashing fanged teeth.

"She hasn't come alone," a voice calls from the river.

Mathilde floats up in a rowboat, Trevor seated beside her. Trevor stands up and leaps onto the riverbank, pulling the boat close and helping Mathilde step out. I stare, unable to believe they are here. Somehow Mathilde has not only convinced Trevor that magic is real, she's also brought him here to stand at our side.

A spark of hope flickers in my chest. With Kate, Bartie, Mathilde, and Trevor here, we are evenly matched. That spark bursts into a flame of confidence when my grandfather appears at my side. He pats my arm, but never shifts his gaze from Hobbes.

"You're outnumbered, Beadle," Trevor calls out in a mocking tone. "We've got prefects, Eternals and even the police represented here. Seeing as you are the only one who will end up in jail, if you give up now and turn yourself in, you'll have a much better chance of negotiating a plea."

I hold my breath, waiting to see how Beadle will react. I don't have to wait long. He stares at Trevor, his face growing more and more red until his veins stand out on his forehead. "Give up? I will never give up!" he shouts. "Look at me! Look at my army! They will eat you weaklings alive!" He growls, shaking his finger at Trevor. "I am connected to the magic now. There is no way you can hold me. My Eternals will free me." Beadle widens his stance and raises his hands above his head. "No one can stop me from ripping the magic away from Oxford!"

His words echo across the garden, his intent clear. There is no chance he will see reason. If we want to take him down, we will have to fight. I glance down at my bloody hands, my head still pounding. How much worse will I be in the end? How will my friends fare? This isn't what we wanted or intended! How did things go so wrong?

Daring to look at my friends, I notice that strangely, none of them exhibit any signs of worry or anxiety. They are all looking straight forward, unbowed by Beadle's threats. I choke back my fear and frustration, forcing myself to stand tall against the pain. Clearly, my side has one final card to play.

Beadle's army of torturers sink into fighting stances, preparing to launch themselves against us as soon as Beadle gives the command. They jeer and chant, hurling threats at us. Beadle basks in front, letting the sounds of his Eternals fill him with strength and determination. He opens his hands wide, preparing to call his troops forward, when suddenly, two men appear in front of him.

I recognise Wilkins right away, having made his acquaintance mere hours ago — was it only this morning that Molly found him? At his side stands none other than Sir Christopher Wren. With his Roman nose and cleft chin, and his dark hair pulled back in a style identical to the one Caleb Farrow has been sporting on set, he looks practically regal.

Wilkins and Wren stand shoulder to shoulder, looming over Beadle. Beadle splutters, unsure of the identity of these new arrivals or the threat they might pose.

Hobbes doesn't have the same problem. He shoves the henchmen aside, stepping through the group to join Beadle out front. "Wilkins and Wren," he hisses. "Just in time to witness your downfall!"

Wilkins glowers, leaving Wren to respond.

"No, Hobbes..." Wren lets his voice trail off, gathering his words. "What happened to you, man? You had an incredible mind once. But you couldn't stand to be questioned and could not admit your mistakes. You were only ever interested in proclaiming your genius, not in contributing to the greater good."

Wilkins picks up the thread. "Look at what you've become, Hobbes. Bloodthirsty, cruel, and insensitive. Four centuries of eternity have wrought a terrible change, the worst of aspects of your personality twisting a once great philosopher into a story book villain."

Beadle shifts uncertainly, unable to understand what is happening. "Get rid of them, Hobbes!" he shouts.

Wilkins exchanges looks with Wren, the two men in silent communication. They must reach some decision because they turn their attention back to Hobbes.

Wilkins' voice booms over the garden. "Thomas Hobbes, tonight we called together the Eternals within the Convocation House. They have heard our case, and you have been judged. You have sought to twist the magic, causing damage and injury to others... and even death. We Eternals have found you guilty. The punishment is ultimate death."

Without another word, Wren pulls a copper knife from his hip and stabs Hobbes in the heart. What happens next is obscured by a brilliant flash of light. When I can see again, Hobbes and all the Torture Museum Eternals have disappeared. Only Beadle is left standing alone.

"Where are they?" Beadle asks, looking around with confusion. "What have you done with Hobbes and the others? When did the wyvern turn into a cat?"

I blink rapidly, unable to comprehend his words. I turn to Edward for an explanation, but all he offers is a grim smile as he squeezes my hand.

Trevor marches forward and grabs Beadles' arms, forcing them behind his back. He reads off the caution as he locks handcuffs around Beadles' wrists.

When he finishes, Wren stares at Beadle with profound sadness in his eyes. "Oswald Beadle, with the ultimate death of your ancestor, your connection to the magic of Oxford has been severed. You can see me now only because I choose to make myself visible. Any magic you attempted to stretch to London is gone as well. The magical borders are now back as they should be."

"You will face a trial by your own peers, Beadle," Trevor assures him, as he hauls him up straight. "We have more than enough evidence to convict you of kidnapping and attempted murder of Natalie Payne. I suspect we can add theft, arson, and Andrei Radu's murder to the matter after we search your museum in London."

As Trevor calls in for a team of investigators and paramedics, Mathilde and Kate dash over and throw their arms around me, enveloping me in a giant three-way hug. I let myself burst into tears, overcome with emotion.

"You all came!" I finally choke out, still hugging my friends tight.

"Of course, we came!" Mathilde replies. "When Edward phoned to say you were missing, we were terrified, Nat. You should have seen H. I had no idea he could fly that fast."

"Oh my goodness, H!" I extricate myself and scan frantically around me, looking for the hero of the day. "Aaitchhh!"

"'Ere I am, Nat!" he shouts back, winding his way through Edward's and Bartie's legs. He scampers across the ground and leaps into my arms. On any other day, he'd grumble at my attempts to give him a hug. But not today. After the last hour of our lives, there is nothing we need more than to reassure one another that we are alive and in one piece.

"How did you do it, H? One moment you were your normal self, and then a second later, you were towering over us. Was it some kind of one-off trick the magic allowed you to do to protect us?"

"Err," H replies, shrugging his shoulders. "That was my real size, Nat. Wyverns are 'uge, don't you know? The only reason I can stay this size is because 'umans think I'm a cat."

"What?" I exclaim, stunned by his reply.

"You can 'ardly blame me, Nat. In my natural size, I can't fit through the doorways and I was forever crashing my loaf against the ceiling. I got into the 'abit of staying small and almost forgot myself that I 'ad an alternative."

I press a quick kiss of thanks against his snout before he can stop me. "I'm glad you remembered. And I'm sorry you had to choke down that old crow to save us. I foresee a lifetime supply of Lincolnshire Poacher in your future, H."

"What about some Stout to wash it down?" H asks, wiggling his eyebrows.

"The first round will be on me," Edward offers, coming up behind me and wrapping an arm around my waist. "I'm sorry to interrupt your reunion, but the paramedics are here and they need to check you over, Nat."

I submit after glancing at my wrists, horrified to see how bad they are. The excitement and fear of the moment had helped me hold pain at bay, but it all comes crashing back when the paramedic cleans my cuts. Edward stays at my side the entire time and H and my grandfather take up posts nearby, neither of them willing to let me out of their sight.

Seeing them there, I understand how scary the evening was for them. I might have been the one tied to a chair and threatened with physical harm, but they were dealing with the unknown. They would have torn Oxford apart at the seams to find me, and I have never felt so loved and treasured.

After wrapping my wrists, the paramedic convinces me to come to the hospital to have my head wound checked. They offer Edward the chance to accompany me in the ambulance, and of course, H and my grandfather pile in as well. The ride is tense; I have a million and one questions for them, and I'm sure they do for me. I'm desperate to know how Mathilde convinced Trevor to join in, and how they organised everyone's arrival. It's frustrating

to hold questions back until I'm in a private room in the A&E to
wait for a doctor.

My grandfather and Edward refuse to tell me anything until I
recount my own adventures, so I hurriedly share my tale, starting
with my run-in with Wilkins and my decision to visit the Botanic
Garden. My grandfather looks fit to be tied, mostly with Wilkins.
"He should never have dismissed you like that, Nat. You are the
prefect. You deserve a minimum of respect!"

I shush him before he can carry on too much, wanting to
finish my explanation. I fast-forward to when I woke up, bound
and gagged, my discovery of the sharp nail under the chair, and my
attempts to keep Oswald Beadle talking long enough to give me a
chance at getting free. "He wasn't terribly bright," I mention, to
nods of agreement. They are all suitably impressed with my ability
to keep a clear head under incredibly trying circumstances.

My grandfather caresses my cheek and then bends over and
gently kisses my forehead. When he straightens up, he has a
strange gleam in his eye.

"Did you know your father was born in this very hospital?" he
asks. I shake my head. "Back in those days, men weren't allowed
in the delivery room. I must have worn a hole in my shoes, pacing
up and down the hallway while I waited for news. I was terrified
that something would happen to your grandmother or to the
baby. As scary as that day was, it pales compared to when I found
out you had gone missing."

"I was scared too, Grandfather. But I knew I had to get free of
that chair and stay alive long enough for you all to figure out
where they were hiding me. I never doubted you would get there
in time to save me."

"You did a lot of the work to free yourself, Nat. I'm just glad
we got there in time to stop them from doing anything worse."
Edward chimes in from my other side.

H had been the first to notice my absence when he came to Somerset College to find me for lunch. One of Somerset's Eternals remembered seeing me leave, but no one knew where I had gone. H then alerted Edward, who rang my mobile, and when an hour went by without a response, they called in the troops. Kate, Mathilde, Bartie, and every Eternal in Oxford were pressed into action to help with the search.

"Mathilde thought of tracking the location of your mobile phone. She set off to find Trevor, determined to get him to listen to reason and help. Luckily, she did. He was able to narrow the search area to the Botanic Garden, but we didn't get the information until well near midnight," Edward explains.

"Edward and I 'eaded straight to the garden to find you, and the others were due to follow behind," H adds, lifting his head up from where he is curled near my feet.

"Did you know what Wilkins and Wren had planned for Hobbes and Beadle?" I ask when they finish. "I didn't know it was possible to sever someone's connection to the magic."

My grandfather frowns, his forehead creasing. "Wilkins and Wren were the only Eternals who knew that secret, and they didn't share the full plan with any of us. I knew they were up to something when they called an emergency convocation of the Heads of Eternal Affairs. Together, with Bartie's help, they presented their case. The verdict was unanimous. It was a harsh punishment, but I cannot deny that it fit the crime. It was the only way Wilkins and Wren could ensure Beadle would be stopped."

"What will happen to Beadle now? Will I need to provide a statement? Or testify in a trial?" I shiver at the thought of standing before a judge and trying to explain what happened without referring to the magic of Oxford.

"One step at a time, Nat," Edward reassures me. "Right now, the only thing you need to worry about is recuperating. Trevor sent me a message letting me know his team will search the Torture Museum tomorrow morning. They should find enough there to remand Beadle to prison without needing your statement."

Before I can ask any other questions, the doctor shows up, putting a stop to any further discussion. I get wheeled off for more rounds of tests and scans until finally I am cleared to go home. "Your head wound looks worse than it is, and your blood work all came back fine," the doctor explains. "I suspect you were drugged after they knocked you out, and that was what accounted for the extended period of unconsciousness. Stick to paracetamol or ibuprofen to manage the pain, and you are under strict orders to rest for at least twenty-four hours."

Edward knows where I want to go without even asking. He calls a taxi to take us to my house rather than to his flat at St Margaret. After tucking me under the covers, he curls up beside me, taking great care not to jostle my bandaged head or wrists.

Safe and sound, wrapped in Edward's arms, I fall into a restorative, deep sleep.

Chapter Sixteen

On Thursday, I follow the doctor's orders, passing the day by lying on my sofa. Edward and H keep me company, plying me with comfort food and an endless amount of my favourite reality television shows.

Late in the afternoon, I look around the room. Edward sits at the far end of the sofa, my feet propped in his lap as he gently massages my arches. H is sprawled across an armchair with a dish of cracker and cheese crumbs at his side, his clawed hand laying on his full belly. If anyone had told me a year ago that I'd be playing house with an Oxford professor and a wyvern, I'd have taken them straight over to have their head examined. Yet here I am, living my very own picture of domestic bliss. I wouldn't trade it for anything.

Friday morning, I rise bright and early, feeling much closer to my normal self. The gash on my hand is still an angry red, but my wrists are looking much better. I take extra care when brushing my hair, avoiding the still-sensitive lump. I was lucky not to need stitches. The mirror reflects a confident twenty-something professional woman — a little worse for wear, but not too bad, all things considered. I give her a wink before sashaying out of the bathroom.

From the foot of the stairs, I can hear Edward and H chatting away, their spoons scraping in their cereal bowls. I take a moment to steady myself before rolling my shoulders back and marching into the kitchen.

"I'm going to Somerset today. There are only two days left of filming here in Oxford and we still haven't identified the person who poisoned Vivian. I'm feeling much improved this morning, and I've made my decision. I don't want to discuss it further." I level a hard stare at Edward and H, daring them to question my plan.

"Of course you are," Edward replies and then flips over the page of his newspaper. He doesn't even bother to look up at me.

"I'm ready to go when you are, Nat," H adds, flying his empty bowl to the sink.

"Huh." I scrunch my forehead, trying to figure out their angle. After hovering over me yesterday, barely letting me off the sofa, today they seem remarkably nonchalant.

Edward folds his newspaper shut and rises from the table, crossing the room to kiss my cheek. "I figured we'd have to force you to stay home yesterday, so you've already done better than I expected. Harold has promised to have the crew keep an eye on you and send you home if you look tired. Molly and Alfred will also be there in case you get any other ideas about wandering off on your own again..."

I pull Edward close and plant a heartfelt kiss on his lips. "Thanks for having my back, babe, and not standing in my way."

"Always," he replies, stealing another kiss. "Now you'd better hurry and eat a slice a toast. Harold is sending a hire car to pick you and H up. It should be here in about ten minutes."

At Somerset, Molly and my grandfather are waiting at the

front entrance. Molly hugs me tight, her eyes bright with tears. "You done good, Nat Payne," she whispers in my ear.

"We couldn't have managed it without your help, Molly," I whisper back. "If you hadn't found Wilkins and Wren..."

She steps back, reaching up to cup my face. She examines me with a critical eye, checking for herself that I am really doing okay. Finally, her mouth twists into a beaming smile. "If I hadn't found those two, you'd have come up with another plan, Nat. Don't sell yourself or your friends short, dear."

I hug her again, unable to help myself. It's no wonder the young college boys turned to her when they ran into trouble. Molly offers that perfect balance of loving care and support, leaving you feeling much better and convinced that you can get yourself through whatever it is if it happens again.

When our greetings are behind us, I ask the pair what I should expect upstairs. "I chose a long-sleeved shirt for today so that it would hide my bandages. Do you have any idea what Harold knows? Or what he told the rest of the crew?"

"Don't worry, Nat," my grandfather replies. "Harold told everyone you were under the weather yesterday, including Will and Jill, when they showed up to begin set-up for the wrap party. Tell everyone you're feeling better and that should cover it."

"Right, then." I make a last check to ensure my bandages are tucked away. "We've got a poisoner to catch. H, lead the way. Where do you suggest we begin?"

"Where else?" H replies, flapping towards the courtyard. "Let's check out the situation at the Craft Services trailer!"

I give a knowing shake of my head and roll my eyes, making Molly and my grandfather laugh. As we move through the courtyard and under the archway to the back garden, I get plenty of calls of hello and welcome back. I was only gone for two days, the first spent unconscious at the Botanic Garden and the second at home, but somehow it feels like ages. In the close-knit environment of a film set, friendships are forged fast and strong. Any unexplained absence is bound to catch people's attention.

Sam smiles from the Craft Services trailer, beckoning me over. "Have you heard the news?" he asks, passing me a fresh latte smothered in whip creme and chocolate sauce.

"No, what's up?"

"It's Vivian! She turned the corner and is on the mend," he explains. "We got the word yesterday morning, and I thought you might not have heard."

"That's fab news, Sam! Thanks so much for letting me know. Has she been released from the hospital yet?"

"Hopefully today or tomorrow. It almost seems like a miracle, given how dire the situation was a couple of days ago. It's done wonders for everyone's mood here on set, as I'm sure you can imagine."

We chat some more, catching up on the rest of the production gossip. The takes have gone well, and the crew is feeling confident they can wrap everything up by tomorrow afternoon as planned. My phone buzzes with a text from Uncle Harold, wanting to know where I've got off to. I say goodbye to Sam, thanking him again for the food and drink which has kept me fuelled during the last two weeks.

Molly and my grandfather take their leave as well, saying they have a few tasks of their own to attend to while I'm watching the day's scenes. H steps forward, ready to keep me company as I make my way to the room where they are filming today.

"Sam wasn't joking around," H notes, flying up to head height so we can chat more easily. "Everyone is smilin' from ear to ear today."

"It's great news about Vivian..." I pause, thinking through my last statement. "Great news for everyone except her poisoner. That gives me an idea, H. Can you help me keep an eye out as we walk around and observe the filming? Maybe we'll spot someone who seems less enthusiastic than the others."

"Not a bad idea, Nat," H admits, nodding his head to show he's impressed with my thinking. "Let's 'urry up and get inside."

We high tail it across the courtyard, back into the main building and up the stairs. Following the sounds of people chattering, we eventually find the crew setting up in the dining hall. Gideon Pomerance and Caleb Farrow are at their places at the high table, while a rowdy crowd of young men are seated at the longer trestle tables in the main section of the room. A large poster taped to the back of the door lists the day's shots. First up is a dining hall scene, including a group of extras playing the role of Somerset students. That explains the unknown faces.

With all the extra people on set, H and I end up tucked away near the door. I have to stand on my tiptoes to see over the various assistants and techs filling the space. H opts to fly up high, perching on a window ledge. As hard as I try, it is practically impossible to judge anyone's feelings. The crew is too busy struggling to keep the kids in line and stick to the schedule. Everyone looks ready to pull their hair out.

I'm determined to stick it out.

Half an hour goes by with me shifting sideways, trying to get a clear view, when I feel someone tap me on my shoulder. I glance over to find Trevor Robinson standing beside me, looking very official in his suit and tie. He gives me a warm smile and nods his head towards the door, inviting me to follow. I wave at H before I leave, so he doesn't worry if I go missing for a few minutes.

"Hi Nat, how are you recovering? You went through a lot the other day. I was surprised to hear you were already back at work." Trevor says once we are in the corridor.

"I'm much better, thanks. I spent yesterday on the sofa, barely lifting a finger. My wounds are healing well and the red mark on my cheek where Beadle slapped me completely disappeared."

Trevor flinches at my last comment. "I'm glad you're feeling better, but don't overdo it, okay? You might be a prefect, but you aren't invincible. Make sure you're taking good care of yourself."

I nod. "Don't worry, between the Eternals and my Uncle Harold, there is no chance I'll stay here longer than I should today. They've all got an eye on me and will send me home if it looks at all like I'm reaching my limit."

Reassured that I am okay, Trevor moves on to his reason for his visit. "I hope you don't mind me tracking you down here. I need to get your statement and Edward told me you plan to spend the day on set."

"Not at all, Trevor. In fact, I'm glad you're here. Thank you again for showing up the other night and helping us stop Beadle."

Trevor brushes off my comment. "I should be the one thanking you. I shouldn't have reacted so badly when you told me about the magic. I'm glad Mathilde could convince me to see reason so I could be there to haul Beadle off to jail. You were right to bring me in on the secret. I never would have solved the crimes without knowing the bigger picture."

I hold up my hand, stopping him there. "Don't apologise. If anyone is to blame, it is me. I should have waited and let Edward tell you. Instead, I caused both you and Mathilde to suffer. I am genuinely sorry about how I handled it."

"I don't think there is a right way to tell someone magic exists. No matter how I found out, it was bound to upend my life. The important thing is we got to the right place in the end, and Mathilde and I have a second chance. She's an incredible woman. I'm looking forward to seeing where our relationship takes us. As they say, all's well that ends well," Trevor quips, making us both chuckle.

When our chuckles subside, Trevor continues, "Speaking of ending well, we searched the Torture Museum yesterday and found all the missing items from the colleges and from the Ashmolean

Archives. If there was any doubt remaining about Beadle's guilt, it has been eliminated. However, I still want to get your statement to add to the complaint. I don't want to give the judge any excuse to offer him a lesser sentence than what he deserves."

I motion ahead, suggesting, "We can use one of the conference rooms on this floor."

We settle into the room and Trevor pulls a notepad and pen from his coat pocket. Carefully, I recount all the details I can remember, the two of us working together to produce a magic-free account of my kidnapping and bid for freedom. When Trevor is satisfied he has enough, we switch the conversation to our other pressing matter — the poisoner.

"There's one thing I still don't get, Trevor," I say as I lean forward to prop my elbows on the table. "Why were you so quick to dismiss the notion of Caleb and Vivian having an affair?"

Trevor shifts in his seat, getting more comfortable. "Caleb and Vivian? I had already spent a day chasing down rumours of another alleged affair. I figured it was nothing more than gossip."

"Another affair?" I arch an eyebrow, intrigued. "What did you hear?"

"My source pointed me towards Vivian and Gideon Pomerance," he answers. "So, you can see why I wouldn't put much weight against a similar rumour about her and another leading man."

"Vivian and Gideon?" I shake my head. "No way! He is her godfather. Did you know that?"

"Now I do, but I had to chase down Gideon to find out the truth. Plus, Caleb had a reasonable enough excuse for being in Vivian's trailer that morning you caught him inside. There was nothing to suggest he has anything other than a professional relationship with her."

"Hmmm." A thought tickles the back of my mind. I grow

silent, waiting for it to become clear. "Trevor... who told you the rumour about Vivian and Gideon?"

"It was one of your uncle's assistants. Joyce? I think that was her name. I'd have to review my notes to be sure."

"Joyce? Joyce told you?"

Trevor raises his brows, wondering why I look so surprised by his answer.

"Joyce is the one who told me Vivian was having an affair with Caleb. She was pretty clear about it; there is no way I misunderstood her."

Trevor pulls his notepad back out of his pocket and flips through the pages until he finds the one he wants. His finger skims across the lines of scribbles, his mouth moving as he silently rereads his notes.

"It was Joyce, and as you said, she didn't mince words when she described them together." He places the notepad on the table and taps his chin. "Why would she tell you one thing, and me another?"

I push my chair away from the table and rise to my feet. "Why don't we ask her?"

Trevor, however, doesn't follow my lead. "Hold on a second, Nat. If Joyce is our poisoner, we need to plan our next move carefully."

He stands up and circles around the conference room, scanning the space. On one wall there is a large whiteboard, wiped clean and ready for someone to take notes. The middle of the room is occupied with the table and chairs. The opposite wall is filled with an accordion-fold door. Trevor finds the latch and gives the accordion a tug, revealing another empty conference room on the other side. I can practically see the wheels turning in his head.

"How well do you know Joyce?" he asks.

"So-so, I guess," I reply, shrugging my shoulders. "Uncle Harold assigned her as my point person on the crew. She toured me around, introduced me to everyone, and we've had lunch together a couple of times."

"Okay, I want you to think back on all of your interactions with her. Has she ever shown any sign of disliking Vivian?"

I lean against the wall, considering his question. "Nothing overt, but..."

"Go on," he prompts.

"Well, it was the first time we met, actually. I had shown up early at the Botanic Garden on the morning after the lighting rig fell. Joyce met me outside, explaining that my uncle had asked her to introduce me around. When we talked about the incident, she got this funny look on her face, almost as though she was mad when I expressed my concern for Vivian."

Trevor frowns. "Why didn't you mention this before?"

I raise my hands up and wince. "I thought it was odd, but Joyce explained that she'd ended up facedown in the dirt, and then Ilaria, the costume designer, made a similar comment later... I wrote it off as petty jealousy. But maybe it is more than that?"

"Jealousy is one of the most common motives," Trevor points out. "Why would Joyce be jealous of Vivian? What would Vivian have that Joyce would kill to get?"

"Fame? Fortune? I rarely saw them together. Joyce was always busy with something else, even on the day she was tasked with introducing me. She half abandoned me outside of the costume trailer, offering an excuse about needing to do something else. But they must have interacted on set, right? I remember seeing Joyce in the footage of the moments before Vivian was poisoned." I jog my memory, but I can't remember exactly what Joyce was doing at the table. "You don't have the footage with you, by any chance?"

Trevor nods, smiling at me. "I should have it in my email on my phone. Give me a second to find it." He flips through screens, his fingers scrolling through his inbox, until he finds the right message. With a few clicks, he has the video playing on the small screen.

"See, there she is," I comment, pointing Joyce out. "She has her back to us, but look how much she is moving her hands around, fiddling with items on the table. She could have had the Monkshood tucked away in her sleeve and dropped it into the cup, and no one would have noticed."

We pause the video and replay those few seconds again and again. Joyce's arm crosses over Vivian's cup multiple times, but the shot isn't clear enough for us to see clear evidence of her dropping anything into the glass.

"What do you think, Trevor? Do you want to take her down to the station for questioning?"

Trevor considers the idea, but quickly sets it aside. "This is all very circumstantial. Even if we are right to suspect her, if I push her too hard, she could ask for a lawyer. Then we won't get anything out of her. What we need is more information, because my research team hasn't turned up any connection between the two women."

Trevor raises his gaze, assessing me. "How do you feel about helping me with an informal approach?"

He doesn't have to ask me twice. After investing so much of my time and energy into solving this mystery, there is no way I want to miss out on any step in the process.

I give Trevor a sly smile. "What do you have in mind?"

We knock around a few ideas before finally landing on one we think will work. Trevor will step into the next-door room, staying out of sight but not out of earshot. With the accordion door cracked open, he can record our conversation without Joyce having a clue. It falls to me to coax her into implicating herself. All we need is for her to give us a motive or, even better, to let slip one of the details the police have kept hidden from the crew — namely, that Vivian's wine was poisoned, and that the poison was Monkshood.

A nearby cupboard provides me with some paper and a pen, which I arrange at the end of the conference table, closest to where Trevor will be positioned. When we're all set, I slip out of the conference room and down the corridor into the dining hall. I quickly find Joyce standing towards the back of the crowd, her attention focussed on her mobile.

H sails down, landing beside me. "Everything okay, Nat?"

"Yes," I whisper, bending over to stroke his back, taking me out of earshot of anyone else. I pitch my voice low and explain, "Trevor and I have been comparing notes. It seems Joyce has had us running in opposite directions. We've set up one of the conference rooms to question her. Stay close. You can come with me."

H waits at the dining hall door as I pick my way across the room. When I get close, I tug on Joyce's shirt to get her attention. "Hi, Joyce. Would you have a few minutes to chat? I've got some paperwork to complete for the college before filming wraps up."

"Sure," she says, buying my explanation. She shoves her mobile into her pocket and follows me to the door, tucking her mop of brown hair behind her ear. Her face is half-hidden by her long fringe.

In the hallway, I explain that I've booked one of the conference rooms for our use.

H darts through the door as soon as I open it, scampering under the table, just like a cat would do. I take my seat in front of my stack of papers and motion Joyce to sit beside me.

I tidy up the stack of papers and jot Joyce's name across the top sheet, pretending to take notes. "Thanks for making time, Joyce. The college asked me to check in with all the crew members to gather feedback on your experience here — nothing arduous, they just want to know if the rooms and services were up to snuff. You know how it is."

Joyce laughs, nodding her head. "Sure, Nat. No problem."

I poise my hand with the pen over the page, and then stop and look up at her. "I just realised this is the first time I've seen you since we got the good news about Vivian's recovery. You must be feeling relieved."

"Err, yeah," she says, freezing in her chair.

I blather on, acting as though I don't notice her awkwardness. "You can tell we were all worried sick about her. Everyone is walking around on cloud nine now. I just can't get over it."

"Um hmm," Joyce replies, evading the discussion.

I scoot my chair closer to the table, hunching closer. "Has Harold told you about his plans for Vivian?"

This catches Joyce's attention. Her head snaps up. "What plans?"

I pause for a second, pretending to contemplate whether I should tell her. "I'm sure he'll tell you as soon as the shoot wraps... he has been so impressed by Vivian that he is considering making her role permanent if the show gets picked up for another round of episodes."

Joyce's eyes spring open in shock. "Permanent? He's going to add her to the cast?"

"That's what he said. It's all hush-hush, so don't say anything until he tells you, okay?" I mime zipping my lips shut. Joyce is still flummoxed — too flummoxed. Maybe Trevor is right about Joyce resenting Vivian.

I decide to probe a little deeper. "You were the one to

recommend her for the role, right? I thought that was what I heard."

Joyce gives a furious shake of her head, sending her brown fringe flying. Her cheeks blush pink as she replies vehemently, "Absolutely not! I told Harold he should have a small casting call and find an unknown for the role. He's already got two major stars in the show in Caleb and Gideon; he didn't need a famous actress."

I pull my head back, acting confused. "An unknown? Really? On a show this big?"

"Why not?" she retorts, growing even more heated. "Harold could have given someone their big break. But no, he has to take the easy way out and hire the first person who came to Caleb's mind." She grits her teeth to stop herself from saying anything more.

This is way more than petty jealousy. Based on Joyce's reactions, I'm thinking I'm on the right track. However, if I push too hard, I'm likely to send her running. The best approach is to continue playing the role of a confidante, encouraging her to talk without overthinking about her word choice.

"Vivian's dad was a cameraman. Did you know that? And Gideon is actually her godfather!"

"See!" Joyce waves her arms around, making her point. "That's exactly what I'm talking about. There are tons of actors and actresses who would do anything to get a break, and people like Vivian stand in their way."

I shake my head, commiserating with her. "You're right, it is so unfair. I'll have to bring this up with Uncle Harold. Maybe it isn't too late to make a change. You know, if he hasn't offered Vivian a contract."

Joyce reaches over and grabs my hand, giving it a squeeze. Her eyes shine brightly as she thanks me for trying.

I glance down, looking morose, but really needing a moment

to plan my next move. Something tells me Joyce had a particular person in mind for the role. Did Vivian unknowingly steal Joyce's chance of discovery?

Sure, Joyce has plenty of industry contacts, but who would think of hiring their production assistant to be their supporting actress? However, with the right hair and make-up, and knowledge of an unplanned, secret casting call, could someone like Joyce shine? How far would Joyce be willing to go to get her big break?

I lift my head back up and sigh. "To think, I was actually excited for Vivian, but now... well... I sort of wish she'd have dropped out early on and forced Harold to go for your option."

Joyce blows her fringe off her forehead, huffing in frustration. "I thought she would get the hint when we started having all the problems on the set. Her costume went missing, as did her scripts. Even her footage was lost, but no, she gamely stepped up and offered to reshoot all the scenes. Even calling it a curse had no effect! Actors are known for being superstitious."

"She must have really wanted this role," I quip, to keep Joyce on her roll.

"After the lighting rig collapsed, she had to know she was the target. It practically fell on her head."

"On both of your heads," I correct Joyce.

Joyce waves off my remark. "Hardly. I was completely out of the way, or so I thought. Then Vivian had to turn hero and shove me into the flower bed as she leapt aside."

Completely out of the way? Joyce seems a little too confident at that point. I almost stop and call Trevor in, but something tells me to keep going.

"You must have been livid. There you were, covered in dirt, and everyone rushed to fawn over Vivian."

"I might as well have been invisible," Joyce grunts, her neck and cheeks flushing red again. "Poor Vivian," she mimics in a high-pitched tone. "You could have been hurt, Vivian."

"I bet no one bothered to help you up," I chime in.

"As if. I was furious, and justifiably so. I had to take a walk around the garden to calm down." Joyce frowns, reliving her memories of that day. "Do you know what plants they have in the garden? I found an entire section filled with deadly plants. If I'd face-planted in the monkshood, that would have been the end of me."

"Monkshood? I've never heard of it." I ask, playing dumb.

Joyce gets a faraway look in her eyes, her mind clearly still fixated on the Botanic Garden. "My grandmother had it in her garden in Slovenia. She made medicine out of its roots. She always warned me against touching the flowers. They are highly poisonous, particularly if distilled in any sort of liquid."

I keep my voice low, my tone gentle, probing without pulling Joyce's attention back to the present. "I bet Vivian didn't even recognise it after you dropped it in her cup."

"She fished it out and wiped it on the tablecloth, can you believe it?" Joyce replies before halting herself. Her head jerks towards mine, her mouth hanging open. "Wait, what? What did you say?"

I look her straight in the eye. "I said you dropped the monkshood in Vivian's cup during her scene in the dining hall. Just like you somehow arranged for the lighting rig to collapse, and pulled numerous pranks on set, attempting to run her off."

Joyce stares daggers at me, now livid. "All that effort, and for what? Nothing! All she had to do was resign her role and move onto another one of her dozens of offers. It wouldn't have cost her anything! But she was too stupid, or too stubborn." Joyce bursts into tears, hiding her face behind her hands. "It should have been my role. Not hers. I would have shined in an audition, but I never got a chance. Women like Vivian get everything."

The rest of her words are lost in her sobs as they wrack her body. For the first time, solving a crime doesn't bring me any sort of satisfaction.

Trevor must feel the same. He pushes open the accordion door and steps into the room, his expression filled with regret. This poor girl nearly killed someone, and most certainly ruined her own life, all because she built up a fantasy in her own mind. When Trevor reads the police caution to her, H and I exit the room, both of us utterly downcast.

Worst of all, now I have to find Harold and break the news to him. I know this will shatter him. If he'd had any clue of Joyce's dream, he'd have given her a try-out, no questions asked. That is the type of man he is, but somehow Joyce didn't see that.

H flaps his wings, calling my attention. "Your lucky, Nat. It could 'ave been you lying in the 'ospital bed, you know. I wonder why she didn't get mad about 'Arold adding you to the cast."

"Joyce dreamed of the spotlight, H, not a two-bit part playing a middle-aged laundress," I remind him. "Will you come with me when I tell Harold? I think we'll both need some comforting after he hears the news."

"Course, I will, Nat." H reaches an arm over and pats my leg. "I'll always be 'ere for you, anytime you need me."

Chapter Seventeen

Uncle Harold calls production to an early stop after I give him the news about Joyce. As expected, he is devastated, but he pulls himself together enough to address the cast and crew.

Based on the chorus of gasps and horrified expressions, everyone is as surprised to discover Joyce has been the one behind the production problems this whole time. I overhear people murmuring around me, saying things like, "But I've known her for years!" and "How could she do something so evil?"

Uncle Harold whistles between two fingers, calling for quiet. He holds his arms out wide, waiting for calm to spread through the room. When all is silent, he scans the crowd, meeting everyone's gaze.

Finally, he speaks. "Look around the room at one another. The people gathered here are more than your coworkers. We are a family. We have one shared goal, which is to create an environment where each and every one of us can perform at our best. This is why the news of Joyce has hit us so hard. I imagine that many of you are feeling the same way as I do now — a sense of betrayal and a deep welling of sadness rising from the discovery that one of our family members was working against us."

Harold chokes up, causing me to step forward and wrap an arm around his waist, lending him my strength. When he regains control, he wipes his eyes and forces a smile on his face. "I am calling an early stop today. Like any other family, we need time to come together, to process this, but also to remind ourselves of what we have. I invite you all to join me in Somerset's Junior Common Room for pizza and drinks. We will pick back up with our final scenes tomorrow morning."

Uncle Harold invites me to come along, but I beg off. As nice as his invitation is, I can feel myself flagging. "I'd rather take it easy tonight and make sure I'm back in form tomorrow for the wrap party." Harold nods his understanding and I say a few quick goodbyes before H and I head home.

Another evening and night of rest does me a world of good. Edward kisses me goodbye in the morning, promising to send H over to Somerset as soon as he returns from his night out with Princess Fluffy.

Sunshine warms my shoulders during my walk to Somerset for the final day of filming. The day promises to be clear and sunny, which bodes well for our wrap party later on. There is a spring in my step, no doubt about it.

As Edward reminded me last night, there is so much to celebrate today. We stopped Beadle and Hobbes. The magic of Oxford is newly repaired and once again strong. Vivian has made a remarkable recovery, and Trevor has taken Joyce to stand trial for her crimes. Last, but certainly not least, my friends and I have all made it safely to the other side.

Will and Jill are already hard at work when I arrive at the college, making the last-minute arrangements for the wrap party scheduled for the evening.

"I'm here to help! Put me to work wherever you need me," I call over, as soon as I spot Jill sitting at one of the picnic tables in the garden, surrounded by paperwork.

"Thanks, Nat," Jill replies with a smile. "But honestly, we're doing pretty well here. Harold assigned some of the crew to help us out today. Plus, the caterers are bringing a few extra hands, as well as the furniture rental company..." She shrugs, unable to offer any explanation.

After mulling for a moment, I hazard a guess. "Everyone wants a chance to see the famous people?"

"That's what I suspect," Will responds, walking over to join us. "We tried to keep the reason for the event a secret, but once word got out about Vivian's poisoning, all our vendors rang up, asking if the film production and the party were connected."

"They were all bound to find out, sooner or later. If it means we get extra staff for the same price, I won't complain. We are expecting around sixty people, last I checked." I stop, struck by a thought. "We should do something nice for the vendor teams. Maybe I can ask Caleb and Gideon to autograph a stack of headshots? Would that work?"

"That would be great, Nat!" Jill agrees. "Will and I were about to review the plan for the evening one last time. Would you like to join us? Make sure we haven't missed anything?"

"I am confident you two haven't missed anything, but I'd love to sit in on your chat if you'll have me. I am really looking forward to seeing what you have put together for tonight. I am sure it will be fantastic."

As expected, Will and Jill have the situation well in hand. The wrap party is scheduled to run from nine until midnight, the late start allowing the crew time to clear out the last of their gear from Somerset once filming finishes. The trailers will be shifted around to create a large clearing in the middle of the rear garden. My assistants show me the space plans, highlighting where the dance floor will be and where the band will sit. Food and drinks will be served buffet style, with plenty of things to nibble upon as the night progresses.

Jill passes me the menu, explaining, "We asked Sam in Craft Services to help us make the final decision on the caterer. After tasting his amazing creations, we didn't want to take a chance on the food not being up to snuff."

"This all looks incredible, mates," I say, glowing with pride. "I have attended a few of Harold's wrap parties over the years, so I can say with confidence that this is going to be his best one yet. You two have organised an incredible event and accounted for every contingency."

Both Will and Jill blush, but they can't hide their pleasure at my words.

"But tell me, how do you feel about tonight? You've done nearly all the planning on your own. Have you enjoyed the challenge? Be honest with me."

They nearly trip over one another in their rush to tell me how great the experience has been. They saw the opportunity for what it was — a chance to showcase their skills and prove they are ready to take on more responsibility.

I grin from ear to ear, pleased to see how well my plan to let them test their proverbial wings has worked. "You've got two weeks of annual leave coming up, and I want you to relax and enjoy a well-deserved rest. When you get back, we can start working on a proposal to the university to grow our team and take on more events each term. Sound good?"

"Absolutely," Will and Jill reply in unison before breaking into laughter.

As I extricate myself from the picnic bench, Jill gives me a clear set of instructions. "Will and I would like you to attend the party tonight as a guest, Nat. We both want you to get the full experience, and let us show you what we can do. So don't worry about coming early or helping with the final arrangements."

I narrow my eyes and tilt my head. "Are you sure? You know I don't mind helping. I even brought my dress with me, so I can get changed here without needing to go back home."

Will and Jill exchange a look, nodding at one another.

"We're sure, Nat." Will insists, leaving me no room for any further discussion.

That settled, I leave them to their work while I track down the film crew. I find them filming in the old library, the old-fashioned, leather-bound books providing the perfect backdrop for the last few scenes.

Between lighting and sound techs, the camera crew, Uncle Harold and his assistants, and the cast, the room is nearly at capacity. I skirt around the back of the crowd, making my way over to the vacant information desk which has been pushed aside. I hop up onto it, taking care not to bang my feet against the wooden front. From here, I've got an unobstructed view of the door and the cast filming deeper inside the room.

There is something different about the cast and crew, but it takes me a few minutes to figure out what it is. They are more light-hearted, almost carefree. For a moment, I attribute the change to it being the last day of filming. But soon enough, I realise it is more than that. There was a tension there that is now gone.

Crew members smile more, particularly at one another. Harold cracks jokes in between takes. Even Caleb lets his professional veneer slip, revealing his true personality. Whether the crew knew it or not, they've all had a protective shield up since they arrived at Oxford. The pranks and incidents, growing ever more serious, had them all eyeing one another with suspicion. Discovering the identity of the rogue crew member has allowed them to relax.

I can't stop my mouth from turning up in a smile. By putting our heads together, Trevor and I solved the mystery of who was trying to sabotage the production. Yesterday was a hard day for all of us, but today's joy makes it all worthwhile.

I keep an eye on the door, turning my head every time I hear it open, thinking it might be H arriving. The first few times it is one crew member or another. Then Donald, the security guard, cracks the door open and pokes his head inside. He watches silently, motioning for someone in the corridor to wait. I spot a familiar scaly little beast slide through the opening and I wave for H to come and join me.

"Your not goin' to believe who is outside, Nat!" H whispers after he lands beside me.

"Who?" I ask, but H refuses to answer. My curiosity grows as I wait for the cast to finish filming their scene. When Uncle Harold yells cut, my eyes go straight to the door.

Donald pushes it open wide and then steps aside. An older woman enters, pushing a younger woman in a wheelchair. The younger woman is thin and pale, but her face is recognisable.

"Vivian!" One of the crew members squeals, rushing over to greet the actress. Within seconds, I lose sight of Vivian. Well-wishers and friends mob her, excited to welcome her back to the group. H and I sit tucked away on the far side of the room, marvelling at the change in the mood on set. We can almost feel the elation as the final worries disappear.

I'm lost in thought when H prods me with a talon, recalling my attention in time to hear my uncle calling my name.

"Nat? Can you come here for a second?" He motions for the team to clear space for me to get through. "Here she is, Vivian," he says when I reach his side.

Vivian offers me her hand, which I take without thinking about it. She clasps my hand tight and pulls me close for a hug.

"Thank you so much, Nat. I hear I have you to thank for figuring out who was behind my near-death experience."

"It was as much DCI Robinson as it was me," I demure as I

stand back upright. Vivian keeps hold of my hand, not yet ready to let me go.

"I've thanked him as well," she assures me. "He told me what Joyce said, that she didn't have anything against me. She only wanted my role. But when you're lying in the hospital, wondering if you will see another day, it is hard not to take things personally."

"I, um," I stammer, with no clue what to say.

"I've spoken with your uncle and accepted his offer to extend my role on one condition."

I raise an eyebrow, glancing between Vivian and Harold.

"I've made him promise he will create an opportunity for at least two unknown actors - one male and one female - to join the cast as well. I don't agree at all with Joyce's methods, but her message was an important one. Those of us in power need to lift the people below us."

I squeeze Vivian's hand and then let go, overwhelmed by my own emotions. Now it is Harold's turn to throw an arm around my waist.

"I take it the doctors expect you to make a full recovery?" I ask once I can speak again.

"Yes," Vivian assures me. "Although I've been instructed to take it easy. I had to strong arm my mum to bring me here this morning. I wasn't sure if you were planning to attend the wrap party, since I heard you had also been ill. I wanted to make sure I gave you my thanks."

"And on that note, we need to get you home to rest if you want to come back later," Vivian's mum says, her tone firm.

"And we'd better get back to work," Harold adds, calling the cast and crew back to their spaces. "Enough goofing off for you lot," he says with a smirk. "We've got three scenes left to get in the can before we lose the light. Places, everyone!"

I return to my seat on top of the desk, but not before

grabbing a packet of biscuits off the snack table to share with my best friend, H.

When filming finally wraps late in the day, Ilaria shouts my name across the courtyard. H and I stop in our tracks, waiting for the costume designer to catch up.

She steps close, air kissing my cheeks. "Ciao, bella. I've been looking for you. Are you done for the day?"

"Yes, I was about to head home to meet Edward and get ready for the party."

"Text that handsome boyfriend of yours and tell him to meet you here instead. We've arranged a pampering session as a surprise for you. A small thank you for solving our crime." She holds up a hand, forestalling any further questions.

I take a quick glance at H to see what he thinks. He gives me a toothy smile and a thumbs up while saying, "Go on, Nat. I'll let Edward know where you are." Then he flaps his wings and flies off. As always, the magic steps in and Ilaria doesn't notice my cat flying away.

I feel a tingle of excitement, wondering what Ilaria could have in store for me. "Okay, I'm in. Where to now? Your trailer?"

"First, a shower. You can use Vivian's trailer. It's empty, and she left the key for you. Take your time. Joe will be ready for you in hair and make-up an hour from now." Ilaria passes me a key and sends me on my way.

It feels strange to be back in Vivian's trailer. I lock and latch the door behind me once I go inside. Hopefully Caleb has somewhere else to shower today, because he is not getting in here. A glass of cold juice and a plate of cucumber sandwiches sit waiting on the table, next to a little card with my name on it.

I carry the snack into the small living room, relaxing on the sofa while I enjoy the thoughtful food and drink. On the night of a big event, I'd normally be running left and right, hopping from one fire to the next to make sure the event went off without a hitch. It feels absolutely luxurious to be sitting alone, in a peaceful space without a care in the world. I let my head fall back against the sofa, close my eyes, and soak it all in.

Soon enough, it is time for me to get moving. In the bedroom, I find a fluffy robe, fresh towel, and tiny bottles of fancy toiletries. Once I'm clean and dry, I wrap up in the robe and make my way a few doors down to hair and make-up.

As promised, Joe is waiting inside. He is a man of few words. He bids me to take a seat in his chair and steps back to assess. "I'm thinking... glowing, fresh, natural with a tiny hint of glamour. Does that work for you?"

"Perfect!" I reply with a broad smile. Joe leaps into action, first applying flawless make-up in subtle shades. Next, he moves on to my hair, blowing it straight and then curling it into bouncy ringlets. I'd never have the patience to go through all the steps he does. I usually rely on my natural curls to cover-up my hurried morning preparations.

When he spins me around to look at the result, I am stunned. He has worked his own version of magic, accentuating my best features and tidying my normal riot of curls into perfect order. I gush my thanks, but he waves me on to Ilaria for the final step in the process.

"Now, cara, let's see about a dress for you." Ilaria leads me through the maze of tightly packed clothing racks until we emerge at her changing rooms. Hanging on the door is the most gorgeous dress I've ever seen. I reach out to touch it, but remember to stop myself and ask permission first.

"The dress is yours, cara. I tailored it to your measurements, custom-made by my best seamstress."

I sigh blissfully as I stroke the sheer, pale gold sleeves. "It's too much, Ilaria. You've already tailored one of my dresses. I love it, but I can't accept it for free."

"Nonsense!" she remarks, scowling at me. "You've been here on set nearly every day, answering questions and offering advice on how to make the sets and scenes as authentic as possible. If that isn't enough, you also stepped in front of the camera, and refuse to take any credit for it. Plus, you worked tirelessly to figure out Joyce was behind the efforts to sabotage the production. A dress, even one of my bespoke designs, is the least we can do for you."

I am overwhelmed by her generosity, tears threatening to come to my eyes. She quickly fans my face, warning me against messing up my make-up.

"None of that now. Take the dress into the changing room and put it on."

I step out, feeling like Cinderella. The champagne dress makes my face glow, perfectly complimenting my blonde curls. The ruffled neck mini dress hits a few centimetres above my knee. The sheer silk fabric glitters in the light, while the ruffles at my wrists hide my narrow bandages. The cream-coloured bustier and skirt underneath the silk hug my curves.

Ilaria adds a pair of cream-coloured wedge sandals to the mix, and my look is complete. I thank her again and again, only stopping when we hear a knock on the door.

"Nat?" Edward calls out from the door near the hair and make-up area. "Are you in here?"

"Coming!" I shout. I give Ilaria a final hug of thanks before she shoos me out of her domain, reminding me she and Marcello still need to get ready.

Edward is staring out at the busy scene in the courtyard when I exit the trailer. Workers scurry around, unfolding chairs and setting tables out onto the temporary floor. The band is warming up and doing sound checks. Right in the middle of it all are Will and Jill, looking remarkably cool-headed in the face of such chaos. Jill must feel my gaze, as she looks around until she spots me. Her mouth drops open, and she pretends to fan herself, before giving my makeover a big thumbs up.

I clear my throat, causing Edward to spin around. He's wearing his garden party attire of trousers and a pale blue button-down shirt. The colour of his shirt brings out the blue in his eyes as they smile out at me. His wavy hair, as always, is winning the battle against all his attempts to gel it in place. All the better for me to run my fingers through it. A shiver of attraction runs down my spine.

"You are worth the wait," Edward murmurs as he holds his hand out to me.

"Am I late?" I ask, confused.

"Tonight? No. But I've been waiting my whole life to have a woman like you on my arm." His eyes glow with love, making my heart skip a beat.

I flounder around for a reply, unprepared to hear such romantic words coming from Edward. He doesn't give me a moment to find my feet, however. He tucks my arm into his and suggests we take a short walk around while they finish the party preparations.

"Have you seen Somerset's Fellows Garden?" he asks once we're away from the noise.

"Fellows Garden? No, I didn't get over to it, what with everything else going on."

"Then let's walk over there, shall we?" He asks about my day, making all the right noises when I tell him about Vivian's visit and her new contract demand to create opportunities for new talent. He keeps me talking as we meander past Molly's vegetable patch. The Fellows Garden sits behind it, blocked off by large stone walls. Much like St Margaret, the entrance is a large wooden gate. Edward produces a key from his pocket and slides it into the lock.

"Where did you get the key?" I ask, once again thrown off balance. He doesn't answer me, smiling as he holds the gate open, ushering me inside.

The paving stone pathway is lined with twinkling white lights. I walk forward, unsteady. We wind between trees and shrubs, the flowers in full bloom, perfuming the air. After a couple of twists, we emerge into a small courtyard with a gazebo sitting in the middle of it.

More white lights outline the openings in the gazebo, glittering against the shadows made by the low evening sun. Inside the gazebo is a small table, with a bucket of champagne on ice and two champagne glasses.

My heart seizes up as the realisation hits me. This isn't a casual walk to kill time. Edward has plotted every minute of this, perhaps even the impromptu make-over. After a beat, my heart races, my palms sweating.

Edward leads me into the gazebo and turns, positioning us so we are facing one another. He looks deep into my eyes, radiating so much love and affection that I can't help but blush.

"One year ago, I thought I had everything I'd ever wanted out of life — tenure at Oxford, a comfortable home, a few friends. Then you showed up at St Margaret. You didn't let anyone stand in your way... least of all me. As I told you before, you upended my quiet existence. What I didn't say is how thankful I am that you did. I cannot imagine my life without you."

Edward lets go of my hands and reaches into his pocket, pulling something out. He drops to one knee and raises his hand, revealing an open ring box. An oval-shaped diamond ring sparkles inside.

His voice is low and deep, full of emotion. He gazes at me, his mouth turned up in a hopeful grin. "Natalie Payne, will you marry me?"

Chapter Eighteen

When I was a child, I often imagined my future marriage proposal. There would be a handsome man whom I adored. He would get down on one knee, his voice trembling with nerves, and he would ask me to spend the rest of my life with him. I would be so overcome with emotion, I would burst into tears. He would grow more tense, wondering what my tears might mean. Eventually I'd choke out a yes and we would kiss.

Sure, my daydreams reflected what I saw in movies and on television, but there was another reason they were fraught with emotion. As a child, I couldn't fathom committing to stay with someone for the rest of my life. As exciting as the notion might seem, it was also terrifying. Of course, my future spouse would sweat nervously. Obviously, I would sob, overcome with emotion. I couldn't imagine any other way it could happen.

Here is what I didn't know when I imagined this moment: when the *right* man asks you to marry him, the only emotion you feel is pure joy.

When Edward holds out the ring box and says those four magical words, I say yes. I practically shout it, I am so excited. He leaps up, pulling me into an embrace, and kisses me so fully my toes curl.

Then he pulls back, looking at me carefully. "Are you sure? I've been planning this for a while now, but I don't want to rush you. If you need more time..."

I kiss him again to shut him up. "I don't need more time, Edward. I love you, and I can't wait to spend the rest of my life with you."

"Maybe you'd like to have the ring," he says, winking at me. He unwraps his arm from around my back to reveal the ring box still in his hand. He holds it out to me, waiting for me to take it.

"It's beautiful, Edward," I say with awe, gazing at the platinum setting and bright jewels. "I've never seen anything like it, and yet, it is perfect."

"More perfect than you know, Nat," he quips back. "The oval diamond in the centre was my grandmother's. The smaller diamonds encircling it come from your grandmother's wedding band. It represents the union of our two families."

Edward takes the ring from the box and slips it onto my finger, giving my hand a gentle squeeze before letting go. It is the exact right size. I can hardly take my eyes off it as I shift my hand to the left and right, watching the diamonds glitter and glow. Edward opens the champagne with a soft pop and pours two glasses.

After we toast, I take a moment to look around again. "I can't believe you came up with all of this, Edward. The fairy lights and champagne, the bespoke ring... are you also responsible for my surprise pampering and new dress?"

Edward rubs his hand on his neck and looks up at me, sheepish. "I had some help... well, a lot of help, if I'm being honest. You nearly caught me a couple of times."

I cock my head to the side and rummage through my memories. I didn't have a clue what Edward was organising, so how could I have come close to catching him in the act? Edward so rarely acts secretively; you'd think those moments would have stood out.

"Wait a minute, were you and H working on this at the dining room table the night you two took on the neighbourhood cats? Now that I think about it, you were quick to gather up the papers on the table."

Edward nods, grinning with pride. "We were working on our battle plan, but before you arrived, we'd been looking at ideas for your ring. H spends so much time with you, I thought he might have some insights into what you like."

I hold up my hand again and point to the ring. "H came up with this?"

"Oh no, he was as lost as I was," Edward admits with a chuckle. "You have Dominic to thank for the result. I remembered his offer to help pick your gifts, and I gave him a buzz. He contacted a jewellery designer he knows, and they whipped up the design and put it through as a rush order."

I sigh with delight as I admire the ring. It is gorgeous and I am not at all surprised to find out Dominic had a hand in its design.

"Okay, that covers the ring. Let me guess, Will and Jill helped you arrange all of this?" I motion to the lights and champagne. "Is that what you three were discussing on the day you came to take me out to lunch?"

"Jill came up with the idea for stringing up the fairy lights. Will and I met here earlier today and hung them all up. But the table, champagne and glasses were all me." Edward points at his chest, clearly proud of himself. He is so boyishly cute at the moment that I have to reward him with a kiss.

"What about Mathilde and Kate? Harry? Oh, my goodness, does Harry know you were planning to propose?"

Edward shakes his head, beaming down at me. "I told as few

people as possible, because I knew you'd want to be with me when we share the news. H, Dominic, your assistants, and Harold are the only people who knew the full plan. I swore your dad and my mum to secrecy when I got the family rings, and I didn't tell them I was going to propose so soon."

He checks his watch. "On that note, shall we take this bottle of champagne to go and join the rest of the party? I imagine there might be a few people there who would be thrilled to see your ring."

We share one more spine-tingling kiss before we leave the privacy of the Fellows Garden.

No surprise, Harold, Dominic, Will, Jill and H are the first people we see. The group is staking out on the edge of the party closest to the Fellows Garden, casting glances over their shoulders as they keep an eye out for us. Our broad smiles and champagne glasses are all the proof they need to know what my answer was.

H spots us walking over, flies ahead, and gives me a big hug, taking care not to jostle the hand holding the champagne. "Were you surprised, Nat? Did it look amazing? It was my job today to keep you from goin' anywhere near the Fellers Garden."

"It was better than anything I could have imagined, H. Thanks for doing your part to make it happen."

Edward gives H a quick scratch between his wings, conveying his gratitude as well. Standing together — our little, magical family — makes my heart sing with joy.

H lands at my feet and walks the rest of the way to the party with us. They sweep Edward and I into embraces and a chorus of congratulations mixed in with requests to see the ring. I kiss Dominic on the cheek, thanking him for his help.

No sooner are we past the welcoming committee than we find out more surprises are in store for us. Although this is the wrap party for the cast and crew, Harold arranged invites for a few extra special guests. Standing together are mine and Edward's parents, all chatting with Harry and her husband, Rob. My grandfather is a step behind them, beaming with pride. Kate, Bartie, Mathilde, and Trevor are spinning around on the dance floor. Edward wasn't kidding that day when he said this would be an event I wouldn't soon forget.

The first hour of the party speeds past as Edward and I work our way from one group to another, sharing our news and showing off the ring. My mum raps my father on the arm for keeping the ring a secret, making us all laugh.

Mathilde and Kate sweep me into a double hug, practically jumping up and down with excitement.

"You'll let us help you plan the wedding, right?" Mathilde asks, rubbing her hands together.

"Better than that," I assure her. "I'd like you and Kate to both be bridesmaids, and Harry to be my matron of honour."

Kate rushes off to grab Harry, pulling her into our fold so I can make my request. Harry tears up, smiling from ear to ear.

"I had a feeling something would spark between you two. That's why I assigned you the flat in Edward's building," Harry proclaims.

I roll my eyes and laugh as I reply, "You assigned me the flat before you even met me. How could you possibly have known that Edward and I would be a fit?"

Harry quirks up an eyebrow and gives me a long look. "Magic, my dear."

That shuts me up.

Finally, Edward and I extricate ourselves long enough to get a plate of food, retreating to the tables for a quick bite. Although it hasn't even been two hours since Edward proposed, I'm already bubbling over with ideas for the ceremony and reception. "Obviously, we'll need to have the wedding here in Oxford, so Bartie and H and my grandfather can attend. Maybe we could rent the Convocation House at the Bodleian?"

Chuckling, Edward holds up a hand to stop me. "We can get married wherever you want, Nat. As long as you and I are there, along with our friends and family, we can get married in the middle of a field for all that I care."

I pretend to consider his suggestion, murmuring, "There is that field by the Arboretum where I had a lovely chat with a couple of sheep... I wonder if the owner would let us rent it for a day..."

Edward barks a laugh, sending me into a fit of giggles.

The band eventually announces they are taking a break, promising to return shortly before turning the microphone over to my uncle. Harold stands centre stage, looking out at the crowd. He invites everyone to make their way to the dance floor for a special presentation. I glance at Edward, but he shrugs, as clueless as I am.

We gather with our friends and family, standing on the edge of the temporary floor. Gideon pushes Vivian's wheelchair to the front of the crowd, making sure she can see. I scan the sea of people, spying Sam from Craft Services holding hands with a woman who must be his wife. Nearby is the camera crew and sound team. Even Donald, the security guard, is enjoying the night. Mixed in with the cast and crew are their partners and close friends.

I look around, wondering where Will and Jill have disappeared, finally finding them off to the side of the stage. They are standing behind a couple of computers, watching my uncle for their cues.

"If I could have your attention, please," Harold speaks into the microphone. "As you all know, when I pitched the idea for this show to the executives, I had planned it as a mini-series.

Historical fiction is at the height of popularity, but the executives were skeptical about whether a show about a bunch of early scientists and philosophers would do well."

The crowd nods, smiling at the memory.

"Thanks to your incredible work, your passion and your creativity, the mini-series was a success. The executives ordered more episodes, which allowed us to come here to Oxford, to film in the very rooms where our historical figures lived and breathed. I have purposely kept the evening reviews of the daily takes limited to an extremely small group." Harold pauses, pointing to Andy and the other members of the camera crew.

"Before we came to Oxford, I would not have said it was possible. But somehow, something in the air has inspired you all into the performance of a lifetime. I could not be prouder of what we have accomplished here, and I look forward to sharing the end results with you all in a few weeks at a proper screening."

Harold is forced to stop as we break into applause. Mathilde, Kate, and I exchange knowing glances, all of us sure that the magic of Oxford played its own role in the filming.

When the applause dies down, Harold raises his microphone again. "However, a wrap party would not be the same without some reference to our hard work. Tonight, in a very *exclusive* showing, we've prepared a highlight reel for your viewing... our best moments together. Don't expect to see yourself reading your lines. We've got something different in store for you."

With that, Harold nods at Will and Jill, and the screen behind the band instruments goes to black. An old-fashioned movie countdown signals the start of the show.

The film starts with a speed-motion display of the crew setting up at the Botanic Garden; the team running around like ants as they lay out equipment and roll in the trailers. Soon, we see the cast arrive. The cameraman has caught Caleb marching around the garden paths, getting into character as Sir Christopher Wren. We see Gideon laughing with Sam near the Craft Services trailer. Vivian and Joe wave from inside the hair and make-up trailer. On and on it goes, making sure every single member of the cast, crew and even the extras are captured. Kate gasps when they show her straightening a portrait in the dining hall, and Mathilde laughs when another clip reveals her hidden away, reading in the Somerset library.

Before long, we see the back of my head, sitting at one of the picnic tables with Ilaria and Marcello. The Italian couple are mid-story, talking as much with their hands as their mouths. I find Ilaria in the crowd and she gives me a wink.

Just when I'm thinking I got off scot-free, I groan as I spot a familiar costume swish onto the screen. My cheeks flame as the film cycles through my best bloopers. There is the time I nearly dumped a tray of teacups onto Gideon, followed by a montage of my attempts to cross the room in my wide skirt. Edward nudges me and kisses my forehead, looking proudly at his future wife. As for me, I thank heavens I never dreamt of a career in film or television and laugh along with everyone else.

The screen goes black again, leaving us to think the film is over, but then flickers back to life, displaying a line of text.

"And now, for the real star of the show..."

Everyone looks around, wondering who it could possibly be. After all, we've seen everyone make an appearance.

The screen brightens further, unveiling a familiar scene. I'm there, in my costume and heavy make-up, holding an old-fashioned broom made of sticks. Standing in front of me is a certain black cat with white patches on his side.

"H!" I gasp, and I hear Mathilde, Kate, and Harry say the same.

The memory surfaces. It was the day H and Molly showed up, coaching my performance from the sideline. Although there was no cat mentioned in the script, H had darted in front of me, taunting me as he swished his tail.

The scene begins. I scowl at the cat and threaten him with my broom, my annoyance very much real. H dances out of the way, stopping just beyond my reach. The camera zooms in close, tightening in until H is sitting alone in the middle of the screen.

Right as it seems the film will end, H looks deep into the camera and gives an exaggerated wink, looking very satisfied with himself.

The cast and crew cheer and roar with laughter, several people calling out questions about when they got a budget for special effects. The video ends with a thank you to everyone, followed by a long list of credits. H flies up beside me in time to see his own name identified within the list.

"Do you think I'll win a BAFTA for my acting, Nat?" he asks, polishing his talons against his chest.

"I wouldn't be surprised in the least if you did, H." I sneakily press a quick kiss on his snout before he can stop me.

Shortly thereafter, the band returns. I check in with Will and Jill, asking whether they need any help. They chase me off, telling me to let loose and enjoy myself.

The night wears on, my friends and I dancing to Gloria Gaynor's *I Will Survive*, singing along at the top of our lungs. That song is always a party favourite, but tonight it takes on a special meaning. We throw our hands in the air and shake our heads, swinging our hips in time to the music.

When a slower song comes on, we pair off into our couples, spinning around on the dance floor. Kate and Bartie are lost in one another, while Mathilde and Trevor show all the signs of a budding love. Mine and Edward's parents are there, but I can't find Harry anywhere. Her husband is sitting alone at the table, so where could she be?

I worry, but then she twirls past me, dancing cheek to cheek with none other than Caleb Farrow himself. I guide Edward close to Mathilde and Kate, making sure they don't miss this once-in-a-lifetime vision of Harry dancing with her favourite celebrity. Mathilde pulls out her phone and snaps a picture of Harry's historical moment.

Before the song ends, I notice my grandfather has joined in, looking like a professional dancer with Molly in his arms. The pair spin and dip in perfect time to the music, looking like something off one of the dance reality shows. It's a shame only a handful of us can see them.

When the night draws to a close, Molly invites H to stay with her at Somerset, promising him she knows where the catering company will store the leftovers. After we say our goodbyes, Edward and I link our arms and begin making our way back home.

The moon hangs high in the sky, the full circle lighting the pavement better than any streetlight could do. Cars pass by, few and far between. My ring sparkles in the moonlight, where my hand rests on Edward's arm.

We walk in a comfortable silence, not needing to fill the space with words. Instead, we leave ourselves free to soak in the memories of the occasion. I don't know about Edward, but I don't want to forget a single moment of it.

Soon enough, we turn onto our street, our doorway lit by the overhead light. Edward takes the key from his pocket but stops before putting it into the lock. He pulls me into a close embrace.

"Did you have a good time, Nat?" he asks, gazing into my eyes.

"One of the best nights of my life, Edward," I reply, meaning every word.

Edward smiles, his gaze softening. He takes a hand and strokes my cheek.

"Let's see if we can't make it even better."

Chapter Nineteen

I wake up to find Edward looking at me, his head propped up on his hand.

"Good morning, future Mrs Natalie Thomas," he says with a smile.

"Good morning, my love," I reply, smiling. I blink the sleep from my eyes and then correct him. "You know I'm keeping my own name, right?"

He winks, reaching out a hand to brush my hair from my face. "A man can dream... But yes, do whatever makes you happy."

My alarm buzzes interrupting our conversation. I push back the covers and climb out of bed, reminding Edward, "Everyone is coming over this morning for brunch, so you'd better get a move on it. I need you to run out for muffins and croissants from the bakery in Jericho."

"And a double order of sausage rolls for H, I know," Edward grumbles as he sits up, but I can tell he doesn't mean it. While he showers, I wander around the upstairs bedrooms, looking over the drawings taped to the doors of each room.

I knew Dominic wouldn't be able to resist the challenge of decorating my new house. While I was spending my days at

Somerset with Uncle Harold, I gave Dominic my spare key and invited him to pop over anytime he needed a break from the canal boat they'd rented.

Dominic knows me well enough to read between the lines of my open invitation. With the upstairs bedrooms and baths still a blank canvas, he couldn't resist putting a few of his ideas down on paper. The result was a series of sketches, complete with recommendations for paint colours and furnishings.

I pause outside the back bedroom. It is the smallest of the lot since we took part of its square footage to add a master bath to the floor plan. I told Dominic I wanted to convert it into a small office, and he followed my instructions. However, he also produced a second sketch, which he tacked up underneath with no further comments.

In one version, shelves line the wall, with a built-in desk sitting in the middle. A comfortable armchair sits in front of the window, waiting for me to curl up with a good book. In the second version, the shelves and desk are replaced with a cot and changing table, and my armchair has become a wooden rocker.

"Cheeky bugger!" I whisper to myself as I peel the tape from the door. I move to toss the sketch away, but something stops me. Instead, I take it back into my bedroom and put it on the top shelf of my cupboard. "Someday!" I think wistfully, "but not anytime soon."

Edward steps out of the bathroom, sending a cloud of steam rolling into the hallway and putting a stop to my daydreaming. "Your turn, Nat. I made sure to leave you some hot water."

Half an hour later, I'm clean, dressed, and ready to greet our guests.

Kate arrives with Bartie, followed quickly by Mathilde and Trevor. We're no sooner seated in the front room than Harry rings the doorbell. My grandfather and H let themselves in through the garden door and walk through the house to join us.

Although this is the first time we've included Trevor in our group get together, he settles comfortably on the sofa next to Mathilde, Kate and Bartie. It is amazing how quickly he has acclimated to living with magic. A week ago, he was running, terrified by my fire-breathing wyvern. Now, he is giving H a high five. Once Mathilde convinced him magic is real, that was all it took. He shifted from fear to acceptance and launched into questions about how it all works.

Trevor wraps an arm around Mathilde's shoulders, and she shifts over, snuggling up against his side. I don't know how their relationship will turn out, but so far, so good. I hope it works out for them.

Edward takes charge of passing around plates and food while I show off my ring again. The women *ooh* and *aah* suitably while the men shift uncomfortably in their chairs. Marriage somehow always makes a single man sweat a little, no matter how new or unusual his relationship might be.

"I've barely begun planning the big event," I begin, addressing the group.

My grandfather coughs, interrupting me. "He only asked you last night, dear. I'm surprised you've had time to plan anything."

Harry holds up a hand to stop him. "Alfred, this is Nat we're talking about. The role of the groom might be new, but I'm sure Nat's been envisioning her wedding day for most of her life."

"Ahem," I say, as the rest of the group snickers. "As I was saying, I don't know when or where the wedding will be held, because that will depend on all of you. Edward and I would like you to be in our wedding party." I turn to the women. "Kate, Mathilde and Harry, you've already said yes to being bridesmaids."

"Matron of Honour," Harry clarifies, sitting up straight and patting her white pageboy cut.

"Of course," I agree, looking suitably chastised. I shift

sideways so I can better see my grandfather. "Grandfather, would you walk me down the aisle? Along with dad, that is."

My grandfather nods, too choked up to speak. I leap to my feet and rush over to give him a hug.

Edward steps in, giving us a moment to collect ourselves. "Bartie and Trevor, I wondered whether you'd stand beside me as groomsmen?"

Both men agree, looking chuffed to be asked. Edward reassures Bartie that the ceremony will be in Oxford, where he can use the magic to make himself visible.

Lost in our conversations, I almost forget about our last role. "H? Where are you, mate?" I hunt around the room, finally locating him curled in his cat bed, looking despondent.

"You didn't think we'd leave you out?" I ask.

H shrugs, sending a puff of black smoke from his nostrils.

"Your role is the most important one of all. Without your help, we can't complete the ceremony," I explain. H perks up, looking hopeful. "H, we would like you to be our ring bearer. What do you say?"

H flies up and turns somersaults in the air. "Ring bearer! I'd be 'onoured. Wait til Princess Fluffy sees me in a bowtie. She'll lose her loaf, for sure."

"I'll mark you down for a plus one," I promise, giving H a wink.

Not long after, we exhaust wedding talk and move onto other topics.

"It's strange, you know," Bartie says, looking around at our group. "Every other time we've gotten together like this, it has been to discuss our problems with the magic."

"That's true," Kate admits, frowning. "After spending so many months trying to figure out who was stealing the magic and then how to stop them, it seems like we should have more of a celebration."

"I, for one, am thrilled to have closed several open cases this past week," Trevor remarks, looking pleased. "If you all hadn't brought me into the group and told me about the existence of the magic, we would never have identified Beadle as our thief, arsonist, and murderer."

"Now that the magical border has been re-established, the wave of minor crimes should dry up," Bartie reassures Trevor. "We Eternals have always seen justice served quickly."

Trevor considers Bartie's remark, rubbing his chin. "I wonder... if I brought over some of our cold case files from the city, do you think you and the other Eternals could have a look? Maybe one of you might have an insight which would be helpful."

"I can't make any promises, but we'd be happy to try," Bartie agrees and my grandfather chimes in as well.

Trevor's comment reminds me of something I wanted to ask him. "Trevor, what will happen to Beadle? And Joyce, for that matter?"

"Joyce was granted bail and is staying with her parents while she awaits her trial. Beadle, however, is still locked away. He is shouting to anyone who will listen, telling them magic exists. Of course, no one believes him. I think his lawyer is planning to claim insanity, but it will be a tough battle. The staff at both the Ashmolean and the Torture Museum have provided statements attesting to his sanity."

Edward leans forward to grab another croissant and relaxes back into his chair. "I'm glad it is all over. I have several conference deadlines looming over me, and a new course to deliver next term. I could use some quiet to catch up on my day job."

Harry twists in her seat, glancing at me, Kate, and Mathilde. "You three are quiet. Why don't you look happier?"

Mathilde is the first one to reply. "I am happy, of course. We all are. Yet, I have to admit that despite all the stress and worry, the last few months have been some of the most exciting ones in my life."

Kate and I nod, encouraging her to continue.

"I know Nat and Kate love their jobs here as much I love mine. And I'm sure there is still much we can learn about the magic and how we can utilise it to help the university. But I can't help but be a little sad to think our lives will go back to... well... normal."

My grandfather rises from his perch on the window seat and moves to the front of the room. "Do all three of you feel this way?" He waits until we all nod our agreement.

"In that case, I've got a couple of Eternals who would like the chance to speak with you. Is it okay if I bring them over?"

Mystified, I tell him to go get them.

After my grandfather disappears, I raise my eyebrows and look at Bartie and H. "Do either of you know where he has gone?" Both shake their heads, looking equally baffled.

Within minutes, my grandfather is back. He appears on the other side of the room, in the open space near the dining room. Behind him stand two men, Warden John Wilkins and Sir Christopher Wren.

I struggle to keep my expression free of any sign of my inner turmoil. While I am grateful the men ended Hobbes's evil existence, I am still bristling from the way Wilkins treated me that day at Somerset. If he hadn't dismissed me and my friends, hadn't all but blamed us for Beadle and Hobbes' actions, would I have rushed off to the Botanic Garden on my own?

From my seat in one of our armchairs, I can see Mathilde and Kate out of the corner of my eye. They, too, are taking great care with their own responses to the men's sudden appearance.

Wren steps forward, preparing to address the group, but Wilkins reaches out a hand and stops him.

"No, I should go first," he murmurs to Wren. Sir Christopher gives him a questioning look, but eventually cedes the floor.

While Wilkins clears his throat and shifts uncomfortably, my grandfather returns to his place on the window seat. *Perhaps making his allegiance clear?* I wonder to myself.

Finally, Wilkins speaks. "Nearly four centuries ago, Wren and I stumbled across the existence of the magic of Oxford. Although we were good friends, at the time, I was Wren's advisor. It fell to me to make the final decisions of whom we should bring in on the secret. Having lived through the terrible war years, I feared what such knowledge might bring. More battles, invincible troops, ancient warriors. And so, I set forth strict rules — the magic would be limited to the very few, for the benefit of the many."

I hold my gaze steady, not daring to move my eyes from Wilkins. Where is he going with this speech?

He crosses his arms, almost defensively, but just as quickly uncrosses them. "In the beginning, Wren, I, and the others stayed close to Oxford. First our children, and then grandchildren, were born with the ability to interact with the Eternals. Who better to entrust with the responsibility of keeping the secret than our own bloodlines? We lived our lives and then returned as Eternals. Eventually, however, the passing of time weighed on us. We drifted further and further away from the colleges, exploring our new Eternal world."

Wren steps forward, taking his place beside Wilkins. "As Eternals, we guided the early prefects in creating the materials they would need to sustain the magic. Then we insisted they hide away our journals and papers in a safe place. They chose Barnard College, as you all now know. But there was one piece of information we kept solely to ourselves. It was never written and never passed on."

Mathilde, enraptured by the men's tale, leans forward and hazards a guess. "The secret of how to connect to the magic in the first place?"

"Indeed," Wilkins says, smiling at her with approval. Soon enough, his expression turns grim. "We thought we were so clever, hiding the real key away and ensuring the magic could never expand beyond the boundaries of the university. In doing so, we unknowingly opened ourselves up to another risk."

"The risk that someone might aim to steal the connection by stretching the borders far beyond their limits," Wren explains, taking over again. "If Beadle and Hobbes had known how to make a connection of their own, perhaps they would have left you all in peace. Wilkins, I, and our group of fellow philosophers should have foreseen this possibility and put in place protections against it."

Wilkins sighs heavily, his expression pained as he turns his gaze to me. "I owe you an apology, Miss Payne. I should never have treated you how I did, questioning all your actions. I had my back up, and it was easier to blame you three prefects than it was to admit my culpability. You paid a heavy price and sustained injuries because of my selfish actions, and for that, I will be eternally sorry." He lifts his hands up and then lets them fall.

Wilkins is so utterly downtrodden, I cannot hold on to my indignation. I release the breath I didn't realise I was holding in, letting it whoosh out in a rush. Edward leans over and pats my hand as I give Wilkins a small smile of forgiveness. None of us are free from mistakes, myself included.

Wren takes the lead again. "The world as Wilkins and I know it has not existed for hundreds of years. It has changed time and time again, in dramatic ways. Our restrictions, guidelines and protections are no longer fit for purpose. Strangely, in many ways, Hobbes was right. Oxford is no longer the centre of the academic world. Many make discoveries, in places far and wide."

Kate shifts, drawing our attention. "What are you trying to say, Sir Christopher?"

Wren glances at Wilkins and then at my grandfather, making a last check of their agreement. Neither of the other men intervenes, leaving it to Wren to answer Kate's question.

"Natalie, Kate, and Mathilde, you are the prefects. You may have been born of the right bloodline, but you have also shown you are immensely capable and worthy of your roles here at Oxford. You have borne up under incredibly difficult circumstances and stood strong in the face of unimaginable challenges."

Wren points at himself and Wilkins. "In our day, we valued the pursuit of knowledge above all else. The status quo was a starting point. Our gains came from being willing to push the boundaries and experiment with new ideas and theories. We laughed in the face of anyone who dared to suggest that things could only be done a certain way. Of all the prefects over the centuries, you three alone have exhibited this same willingness to try and fail, to break the rules to accomplish the unthinkable."

Wren opens his coat, rifling through an inner pocket to pull out two yellowed scraps of paper. He takes three steps forward and holds them out for me to take.

Spidery handwriting, almost illegible, fills the pages. Bewildered, I pass them to Mathilde. She stares down at the top sheet, her eyes narrowing as she reads the words.

"Wait!" she exclaims, her head snapping up, eyes bright with excitement. "I know what these are. They're the missing pages from your journal — the one we found in Barnard's secret chamber. But I thought Hobbes and Beadle had taken them."

Wren looks suitably impressed, turning around to make sure Wilkins has noticed Mathilde's quickness as well. "I tore out these pages and hid them separately, reclaiming them when I returned as an Eternal. They were never in the secret chamber. No prefect has seen them... until now."

Mathilde flips the page over, her mouth moving silently as she skims the paragraphs of text. She looks up, her mouth hanging open, and just as quickly looks back again at the pages.

"What is it, Mathilde? What do they say?" Kate asks, trying to read over Mathilde's shoulder.

Mathilde raises her head, her eyes wide. When she speaks, her voice is barely louder than a whisper. "These are the instructions for creating a new connection to the magic. The list of materials, the exact mixture of metals, how to position them in the room..." she trails off, suddenly overwhelmed by the momentousness of the information in her hands.

The hair on my arms stands up straight as my mind grapples with Mathilde's words. Kate is equally stunned, sitting speechless with her hand covering her mouth.

Wren smiles broadly for the first time since he appeared in my front room. Even Wilkins looks pleased.

Clasping his hands behind his back, Wren addresses the room. "Natalie, Mathilde, and Kate, to you three, we entrust the true key for connecting the magic to Oxford. Where will you take it next?"

The Oxford Key Mysteries continue in Post Mortem at Padua.

Post Mortem at Padua
OXFORD KEY MYSTERIES - BOOK FIVE

In Oxford's newest twin city, a case of mistaken identity puts a woman's life in jeopardy

The invitation to visit Oxford's twin city of Padua couldn't have come at a better time. Natalie, Kate, and Mathilde have spent weeks trying valiantly to expand Oxford's magic, only to have every attempt end in failure. A trip to the land of pasta, high fashion, gelato, and wine sounds almost too good to be true.

They pack their suitcases and jet off for Italy, bringing Harry and H, Nat's cheeky wyvern, along with them. But within minutes of landing, Harry falls prey to a series of mishaps.

As the danger grows, Nat wonders if perhaps Oxford isn't the only thing with an Italian twin. Could a case of mistaken identity explain the malevolent force which has Harry in its sights?

Nat and her friends follow the clues, uncovering a decades' old cold case with a modern day connection. Friends new and old offer a hand with interpreting the clues as the investigation spans generations.

With the clock ticking, can they identify who killed Harry's lookalike before Harry joins the ranks of the dead?

Find out in Post Mortem at Padua. Pre-order your copy now on Amazon or save it to your wish list to read in Kindle Unlimited.

The Eternal Investigator

AN OXFORD KEY MYSTERIES NOVELLA

May 1941 - Money is missing from the coffers of St Margaret College.

Bartholomew Kingston is on the cusp of figuring out who is siphoning funds from St Margaret College when his friend Clark reminds him of their evening plans. He sets his work aside and travels to London for a night out on the town.

When he returns to work he makes a startling discovery: he's dead. Even worse, Bartie is horrified to learn he is being blamed for the theft.

As Oxford's newest Eternal, Bartie has some new tricks up his sleeve. With the help of the other Eternals, can Bartie find the real culprit? Or will his name be tarnished forever?

The Eternal Investigator is available on Amazon. Order your copy now.

Acknowledgments

This book started with a phone call from my mother.

"Make me a character in your book," she said.

"Okay, do you want to be a good character or a bad character?"

"Bad. Obviously."

And so I spent the next two months crafting a story around an evil-intentioned young woman named after my own mother. Anyone who knows my mom will not be surprised by her request. She and I are united in our appreciation for the "bad guys" - always preferring the Evil Queen to the milquetoast heroines. There is something uniquely freeing in giving yourself permission to cheer for the wrong team, to put yourself in their shoes and see the world through their eyes.

Thanks to my mom for standing behind me and cheering me on.

Next, as always, my editorial team. My developmental editor (Inga Kruse) and my alpha reader (my dad) suffer through a drip-feed of chapters, getting them one at a time without knowing where the story is going. Nonetheless, they persevere with me, never hesitating to tell me when my writing has gone awry. Anne Radcliffe, my copy editor and grammar queen, took on a larger role with this book, coaching me through traditional story arcs and asking thought-provoking questions. I love that we can message each other, out of the blue, with some oddball writing remark and end up in a twenty minute discussion via messenger.

To Emilie Yane Lopes, my brilliant cover designer. I threw a bunch of photos at her and as always, she came through with another great cover.

To my readers and fans - after Arson at the Ash, I was sure this book would be the last in this series. I was burnt out and ready to move on to something new. But getting your emails and messages, and being able to see how much you love these characters, made me give them a second look. Thank you for propping me up, cheering me on, emailing notes about typos, leaving reviews, and patting my head while telling me I'm pretty.

To the indie author community - I cannot say enough thanks. From group promos to newsletter swaps, answering all my questions and organising giveaways, I have so enjoyed being part of this incredible community.

A shout-out for my "day job" clients who showed endless patience as I juggled deadlines and writing time. Thanks for being so understanding.

A big thanks to my mother-in-law, who endured ten days of quarantine in our house, playing never-ending rounds of board games with my kids, so I could write over the Christmas holidays.

Finally - thanks to my husband, kids, and cats. This topsy-turvy year is one we will never forget. I am so thankful for the flexibility my writing career has afforded me this year. Our daily lunches and neighbourhood walks have fuelled my writing time.

About the Author

Lynn Morrison lives in Oxford, England with her husband, two daughters and two cats. Originally from the US, she has also lived in Italy, France and the Netherlands. It's no surprise then that she loves to travel, with a never-ending wish list of destinations to visit. She is as passionate about reading as she is writing, and can almost always be found with a book in hand. You can find out more about her on her website LynnMorrisonWriter.com.

You can chat with her directly in her Facebook group - Lynn Morrison's Not a Book Club - where she talks about books, life and anything else that crosses her mind.

facebook.com/nomadmomdiary

twitter.com/nomadmomdiary

instagram.com/nomadmomdiary

bookbub.com/authors/lynn-morrison

goodreads.com/nomadmomdiary

Also by Lynn Morrison

<u>The Oxford Key Mysteries</u>

Murder at St Margaret

Burglary at Barnard

Arson at the Ashmolean

Sabotage at Somerset

The Eternal Investigator

Post Mortem at Padua (2022)

<u>Midlife in Raven (Paranormal Women's Fiction)</u>

Raven's Influence

Raven's Joy

Raven's Matriarch

Raven's Storm (2022)

<u>Stakes & Spells Mysteries</u>

Stakes & Spells

Spells & Fangs

Fangs & Cauldrons (2022)

<u>Nonfiction (published by Fairlight Books)</u>

How to be Published

How to Market Your Book

www.ingramcontent.com/pod-product-compliance
Lightning Source LLC
Chambersburg PA
CBHW061612190726
48288CB00007B/2287